CANNABIS CHRONICLES

DARIELL FLORES

authorHOUSE®

AuthorHouse™
1663 Liberty Drive
Bloomington, IN 47403
www.authorhouse.com
Phone: 1 (800) 839-8640

Published by AuthorHouse 06/04/2020

ISBN: 978-1-7283-6388-2 (sc)
ISBN: 978-1-7283-6389-9 (e)

Library of Congress Control Number: 2020910227

Print information available on the last page.

This book is printed on acid-free paper.

INTRODUCTION

I look like I haven't slept in days, but I think all I've done is sleep. I don't know what day it is or what year it is; it seems like none of that matters now. I don't even remember where I am. I'm surrounded by sleeping strangers, and they look worse off than I do. I don't remember how I got here. I don't remember who I was. All the things I've ever wanted or worked for—and the people I've cared about—have vanished in a sea of I don't remembers. I've worn the same clothes for a week, I haven't shaved in weeks, and it's been three days since my last shower. I'm a wreck.

The smoke was still in the air as I walked over almost a dozen sleeping bodies on the ground. I looked around and realized I was in Andre's garage. I stared at the people on the floor and tried to recognize any of them, but I couldn't.

They are all strangers. Partying with strangers and sleeping in strange places has become my life. The last time I spent the night at home also falls on the long list of I don't remembers. Sometimes I miss the memories, the recalling of the terrible and happy events in my life. To be completely honest, I don't have lots of good memories, and all the bad ones just urge me to forget even more.

I slipped into Andre's house to try to find a bathroom. I found Andre asleep in the bathtub with lines of white powder on the bathroom sink. *Did we do that? Did I do that? No, I wouldn't have. Would I? Even if I did, the sad thing is the experience—along with everything else in my life—would just be infused with all the other I don't remembers.*

My thoughts began to stress me out, so I left the bathroom and went back to the garage. In the middle of an unconscious pile were four joints, two blunts, and my favorite blue dolphin bowl. I grabbed the bowl along with everything else and left as fast as I could.

I know someone will notice their entire weed supply being gone, but that's the fun in partying with strangers. They barely remember you afterward.

When I walked outside, I realized the sun hadn't come up yet. I looked down at my phone, which was almost dead, to check the time. It was 6:05 on Wednesday morning. I knew Charlie and Josh would still be up, trying to find ways to smoke before the day was done.

Smoking at Charlie's place felt like the best thing to do, so I began to walk in that direction. Charlie's bedroom was like the number one place to smoke for potheads. It was like a beacon for marijuana; it was all but guaranteed that you'd get high at Charlie's place. All I'd ever done was hang around his place for a while, and eventually—one way or another— I'd get stoned.

As I walked toward Charlie's apartment, I realized I was in danger of being arrested. *I hate cops—even though I know it's their job to put away dopeheads like me. I can't help but loathe—better yet, fear—every officer I see.* I couldn't help but walk a little faster.

Charlie and Josh never got paranoid when they have weed, mainly because they always smoked indoors. When I finally reached Charlie's apartment complex, I realized that several people were awake, at their cars, probably leaving for work. I couldn't help but stare at the ground to avoid their suspicious glares. I hurried toward Charlie's apartment, trying as hard as I could to not look back at the people. I ran up the stairs of Charlie's building and hurried to his door.

My fist met his door repeatedly for a full fifteen minutes before I decided to just walk in. Since Charlie's mom was hardly home, I wasn't worried about being rude. As I walked in, I saw Josh facedown on the couch. I could tell they had been smoking because the aroma of burnt weed still lingered in the air. Charlie was a heavy sleeper, and I tried to wake up Josh first. I shook him lightly, but he jumped up like he had heard bullets being fired through the air.

"What the fuck, Timmy? What are you doing?" Josh looked disoriented as he stood up to stretch.

"I brought weed," I said as I showed him the blunts in my pocket.

He stared at it for at least a minute and then went into the bathroom to wash his face. This was his feeble attempt to wake the hell up. I couldn't help but find the humor at Josh's efforts to sober up. *I always think it's funny when people come down from their high; it makes the experience more like a journey or a dream.*

When he walked back into the room, he sat on the couch, cracked his neck, and then looked at me and grinned.

"Well, let's get high then," Josh busted into Charlie's room, where Charlie was asleep on his bed. He started shaking Charlie violently for almost a full minute before Charlie woke up and swore he was going to kill us both for waking him up. He didn't calm down until I showed him the contents of my pockets.

"Holy shit, Timmy! That's the rest of my fucking day," Charlie shouted as he opened the drawer of his desk.

The glow in their eyes was priceless; they were like little kids on Christmas morning.

Josh started to prepare the room, and Charlie frantically searched for a lighter. He found one, started up his Xbox, and opened his window. Josh hooked up his iPod to Charlie's stereo and played a playlist titled "High Songs."

Charlie began smoking one of the joints, and Josh started playing *Black Ops.*

Charlie passed the joint to me, and I carefully grabbed it with my middle and pointer fingers and then slowly brought the joint up to my mouth. I pressed my lips against the end of the joint and inhaled as much smoke as I could take. In the back of my head, I felt wrong, but I didn't care. Any feeling of regret or guilt was usually burned away with the weed when we smoked. I had no worries when I was high or getting high. It was if nothing mattered, like the world's problems didn't apply to me, and I was isolated from it all.

Josh looked at me as he sucked in smoke. "Aye, remember the first time Timmy got high?" He looked over at Charlie.

Charlie grinned. "That shit was hilarious."

Josh and Charlie started laughing hysterically.

I cracked a smile because in an entire world of I don't remembers, I did remember the first time I ever got high. It was the start of my glorious demise, and it had only happened a few weeks ago.

CHAPTER

I was never really a social person. I always thought people were either too stupid or too arrogant to be around. Either way, I did have friends, lots of them—or perhaps *friends* isn't the right word. I had lots of acquaintances: people I only said hi to or people who had a very good conversation with me once and then never spoke to me again. All in all, I was sort of popular. You wouldn't catch me dead at a party, but I was still well-known at my school. I didn't hang out with the kids who were popular, but they all knew who I was, and they all liked me to some extent.

I did have close friends though. I had Andrew. We had become friends only a year ago, in eighth grade, but at that time, we were practically joined at the hip.

Sitting in geometry class that Friday afternoon was like waiting to die; the seconds were slowing down with every tick of the clock. It was almost as if time was mocking me. I looked around the classroom and saw that half the kids were asleep, and the teacher didn't seem to mind one bit. It felt good to know I was practically the smartest kid in class. Had I been in any other class, that might have been impressive.

The bell was going to ring in almost thirty minutes, and I couldn't wait. The teacher stopped teaching fifteen minutes ago and gave us some assignments that could be done in ten minutes. But of course, this being the "stupid" class, most of us wouldn't even turn it in any way. I turned in all my assignments. I never deemed school work to be hard. Unlike my classmates, I did my work and got out. I never understood why my disfavor for these burnouts was so strong. I guess people don't like people who aren't as smart as they are.

When the bell finally rang, I bolted out of class. I knew the teacher would probably yell at me for running, but I didn't care. All I knew was that the day was finally over, and I could go do something crazy with Andrew—something that didn't make me want to blow my brains out. I ran through a crowded hallway, bumping into everyone in my path. It didn't bother me one bit because I was free. I could go and be an obnoxious teenage boy without any judgment.

Andrew drove a 1998 Honda Civic and always parked at a church about a block away from the school. Andrew and I developed a routine of driving his old car around town every Friday, flirting with girls we hardly knew. We would always get their numbers, but neither of us would ever call them. Andrew had a girlfriend, and I was way too shy to ask anyone out.

Andrew was waiting in his car with his girlfriend, Allison. They had been together for almost two months, and they seemed pretty happy to everyone but me. They fought a lot. Andrew would complain that she was too "bitchy" and always seemed to want to argue. Funny thing was, Allison would say the same thing about him. My response to Andrew was always that she was a girl, a stereotypically complicated girl. Of course, having no real knowledge in that area, I tried my best not to give advice.

As I headed toward Andrew's car, I saw Sophia. She was a girl I had grown up with, she and was every guy's fantasy of what a cute, nerdy schoolgirl should look like. Also, I had a huge crush on her for almost four years. She was enchanting, the most beautiful girl I'd ever seen. She had light brown skin, big, brown eyes, and long hair that was so dark brown, the sun sometimes failed to reveal it was brown and not black. Sophia had a very casual way of dressing, which made me appreciate her modesty. The best part was her smile. Every time I saw her, she would smile in place of saying hello, and it made my heart drop. However, I'm getting ahead of myself.

Andrew looked at me and then Sophia, and he grinned that big, stupid grin that I wanted to wipe off his face. I sneered back at him, and in an instant, I decided I'd walk with Sophia instead of riding with Andrew.

"Hey, where you going?" Andrew shouted with a dumbfounded look, although I'd done it to him so many times. I hurried to where Sophia and Grace were walking and slipped in between them.

"Hey, guys." My voice cracked a little, and I was smiling like an idiot.

"We're not guys, Timmy. Gosh!" Grace spat.

Grace and Sophia were inseparable. Grace was loud and adventurous, and Sophia was quiet and reserved.

"You know what I mean." I actively avoided confrontation with Grace, knowing Sophia was always on her side.

"Hi, Sophia," I mumbled under my breath, just loud enough for her to hear. It was almost embarrassing how I managed to stumble over my words, even though I talked to her every day.

She smiled the way she always did, softly and intimately, and whispered "Hi, Timmy."

"How was your day?" I asked, regaining my composure.

"Oh my God! Do you guys know Andre? That stupid kid who always smells funny and is like never in school," Grace interrupted.

"Didn't he get in trouble for throwing food at Officer Williams's car?" Sophia asked.

"The school's resource officer?" I asked.

"Yeah, Andre called me a bitch yesterday because I wouldn't let him cut in line at lunch," Grace complained.

"What an asshole."

Grace and Sophia continued to gossip about the idiots at our school while I continued to walk silently, waiting to finally reach Grace's street. Speaking of Andre made me remember meeting him. I thought he was a pretty cool guy, although he always smelled like smoke and had a false sense of achievement.

When we finally got to Grace's street, we said our goodbyes and continued walking. I always waited all day for moments where Sophia and I were alone—just so I could fail miserably at making a move. Half the time, walking her home was awkward; the other half, it was great.

"So, what's up?" I asked, flustered again. I was shaking. I was so nervous. *Is today going to be the day I finally ask her out?* The reality of it was that today was just like every other day.

"Nothing," she said, half-smiling at me.

We continued up the street in almost complete silence. I didn't know what to say, and she never had anything to say to me. I tried to come up with something to say, but nothing came to mind. Sophia was a mystery to me. I had known her for a long time, but I still didn't know her well enough to spark an interesting conversation.

It was pretty pathetic.

"Andre's dumb," was the only thing I could come up with.

She nodded her head in agreement but did not say a word.

"Did he really throw food at a cop car?" I asked.

"That's just what I heard. I think someone said it was a burrito," Sophia replied.

We laughed lightly, neither of us really looking at each other.

"Didn't he know cop cars have cameras?"

"I guess not," Sophia answered.

"It's still pretty ballsy though. I wish I could pull a prank like that."

"And get kicked out of school? Be my guest," Sophia said.

I laughed, and she smiled, which was much better than silence.

I wanted to ask her out. I wanted to finally muster up enough courage to do it, but the fear of rejection swallowed me like a flame. When I finally could find it in myself to ask her anything, it was always too late.

We arrived at her street, and I knew my time was short, so I tried to just get it over with.

"Hey, Sophia?" My voice was hushed and shaky.

"Yeah?" Her voice was a lot softer than mine, but it didn't sound so pitiful coming out of her mouth.

I pondered the idea that maybe she was preparing herself for the guilt that would come from hurting my feelings, and then I decided it was a bad idea. "Never mind. I'll see you tomorrow." I quickly turned and walked away. I was so embarrassed that I wanted to hide under a rock.

"Um, okay?" she said as I was leaving.

I turned to watch her leave, hoping she would turn back too, but she never had, and today was no different. I continued my journey home, wanting to kick myself in the head for being so stupid.

I saw a group of people walking toward me, and they could not have appeared at a worse time. Walking up the street was a group of guys I always identified as the Riley brothers: Greg and Calvin Riley and their posse. I had never spoken to them; I only knew them by name because they had a terrible reputation for being in high school longer than most of the teachers who taught there.

The brothers and a group of strangers made their way up the street, laughing, cracking jokes, smoking cigarettes, and constantly calling each other "gay." They didn't notice me, thank God, but they still managed to irritate me with their stupid comments to each other. I was probably just being bitter, but I couldn't help it.

When I finally made it to my street, I found Andrew and Allison waiting by his car.

"So, how'd it go?" Allison asked as I approached them.

"Awful! Let's leave." I jumped in the back seat of Andrew's car without saying another word.

"All right, good, 'cause your neighborhood is ghetto, and my doors don't lock," Andrew said as he started up the car.

We spent the rest of the day doing the same thing we always did. We drove around with no real destination, eating like we would never eat again, people-watching, and singing along to every bad pop song that came on the radio. It was fun, or at least it was kind of fun. I couldn't help but notice I was always the third wheel. Not that they made me feel that way; they hardly even noticed.

Andrew dropped Allison off first, leaving me in the car so they could say goodbye for fifteen minutes. I was going to Charlie's house. Charlie was a kid I met in middle school, and even though I was a grade above him, we were both about the same age. We met in detention in sixth grade when I got caught helping somebody cheat. After that, we became close friends until one of us disappeared for whatever reason. We wouldn't see each other for long periods, but we would always reconnect somehow. Charlie moved to an apartment not far from my own after he and his mom were evicted from their house. There was a rumor surrounding his older brother and his dad—something about a drug bust—but I never asked, and Charlie never talked about it.

Andrew didn't approve of Charlie. No one approved of Charlie.

"So, now I have to take you to the trap house," Andrew joked as he started his car. Andrew liked to joke about the fact Charlie was one of the biggest stoners I'd ever met. I never smoked with him, and he never really asked me to, but when the time came for him to smoke, he would awkwardly ask me to leave.

"So, you think he could get me some molly?" Andrew asked with a smirk on his face.

"Charlie is not a drug dealer," I mumbled, leaning my head on the window.

"Stop lying. Yes, he is. He walks around with a smoke cloud, dude."

"Just because he smokes doesn't mean he deals drugs," I said.

"All right, maybe, but it's only a matter of time," Andrew retorted. As he was changing the radio station, he looked at me and asked, "Would you ever do it?"

"Deal drugs?"

"Smoke weed," he said halfway turned so he could see the road and me.

"Um, actually no because I think someone brought it up at lunch one time, and Sophia said she didn't like that kind of thing."

Andrew turned to face me all the way, holding the steering wheel straight. "Out of all the reasons not to do drugs, that's yours?"

"Any reason is a good reason, right?" I replied.

Andrew smiled and let out a long, sarcastic sigh. "We need to get you a girlfriend, dude."

When we arrived at Charlie's apartment, Andrew made his final jokes about Charlie and then left. I walked up to Charlie's door, and Charlie's mom swung open the door.

"Hi, Timmy," said Charlie's beautiful mother. "He's in his room go right in." She stepped aside to let me in.

I heard voices in his room before I walked in. I knew it probably meant Charlie was getting ready to smoke—which meant he was getting ready to kick me out—but I decided to go in anyway.

"Aye! What's up, Timmy?" Charlie yelled as I entered his room. Charlie was there with Josh and some other guy I hardly knew. Josh always hung around Charlie's place. I didn't know him very well; he was a big guy and wore a mean look on his face most of the time. He was kind of intimidating.

"Hey," I greeted Charlie, trying not to acknowledge the other people in his room.

"How you been, bro?" Charlie sounded a bit anxious. He and I had always had an awkward relationship, especially if we hadn't seen each other in a while.

"Pretty good, I guess." I looked over at the kid on the edge of Charlie's bed. I half-smiled and waved for some reason.

He leisurely nodded his head.

"What about you? How have you been?" I was a bit nervous. The kid looked so out of it. He was there, but it looked like his mind had wandered off the well-worn path. He kept his eyes glued to the TV; his eyes looked so bloodshot that it was as if someone had stabbed them with a fork. That kid was stoned.

I laughed a little, and when he figured out what I had figured out, he laughed too, quietly into his hands.

"Oh, yeah. That's Cole. He's high as a kite," Charlie said with a goofy smile.

"Yeah, he looks high," I said as I looked back at Cole. He seemed to find everything funny. *Wow*, I thought. *He doesn't give a shit about anything.*

"Yeah, I don't know how much he smoked, but we keep having to check if he's alive," Josh added.

"Yeah, dude, all we've been doing is fucking bitches and getting high. Same old shit," Charlie shouted.

"The only bitch that's been in this room is you Charlie," Josh countered.

"Shut the fuck up," Charlie yelled as he and Cole erupted in a pit of laughter.

That was the reason I liked hanging out with Charlie. He didn't make me feel left out—unlike Andrew and Allison, even though I knew they didn't mean to. I wasn't a stoner, but Charlie still made me feel like a part of the group. He also didn't try to pressure me into smoking with him—as long as I didn't try to pressure him to quit. Truth was I didn't care that he smoked.

Cole continued to laugh at every unfunny comment. I didn't know if his mood was infectious or if his state of mind could even be considered a mood. *Is he really happy—or is it just the result of doing drugs? If looking stupid, feeling tired, and finding everything funny is what happens when you smoke, how could it be so bad?*

I couldn't help but be curious about what Cole was feeling. He looked so content. He reminded me of the Riley brothers; they all looked so happy living their clearly miserable lives. I mean they had to be miserable. They were outcasts, they had no chance of making it to college or even finishing high school, they had to be poor, because they dressed like they were, but they still managed to not be depressed. Maybe that's what drugs do—they pull you out of reality so much that you fail to notice how much life sucks. Or maybe ignorance is bliss; I couldn't help but crave their ignorance.

"Yo, what you staring at?" Cole spoke slowly and sounded like someone had dropped a weight on his chest.

"Nothing," I replied.

"Yeah, why you staring, Timmy? You want his cock or something, you fucking faggot!" Charlie shouted loud enough to wake up the whole town.

"Jeez, Charlie, relax," Josh remarked.

"Hey! Fuck you, man."

"And you wonder why you don't have any friends?" Josh retaliated.

"I have no friends because fuck new friends. No new friends!" Charlie screamed and laughed menacingly.

"You don't have any old ones either." Josh was witty, which was a surprise.

Charlie, on the other hand, was the most explicit, cynical, and immature person I'd ever known. I'd never really found people who still made sex and fart jokes funny, but when Charlie made those jokes, you couldn't deny the truth. They were kind of funny.

They continued to crack on Cole about how high he was, and then I noticed it was getting late. I lived alone with my mom, but she was always at work or church. I was hoping she wouldn't notice I hadn't been home, but if she had, I knew she would be calling me soon—screaming. I often made a habit of staying out late. That was why my mother was always insisting that I was out doing drugs. Sometimes I think she would just call to reassert her dominance, which was annoying.

As I was getting comfortable, Josh grabbed a little bag from the top of Charlie's desk. It was a small brown piece of plastic that looked like it came from a grocery bag. Josh took out a cigar from his pocket and used his thumbnails to gently split it down the middle. He moved toward the trash can to remove the dark black tobacco that was inside the cigar. He ripped open the small baggie. I couldn't see what he pulled out, but it reeked.

"What's that?" I asked, genuinely curious.

"Oh, it has many names," Josh answered with a devilish grin on his face. "Some call it bud, some call it tree, oh the beautiful mistress Mary Jane that robs us of our senses and relieves us from stress. This, my friend, is marijuana."

I was a little surprised at how poetic he sounded, but of course, only weed could make poets out of assholes. I should've known it was weed. I was a little embarrassed about how much I didn't know about weed. I watched a lot of movies about it, but it wasn't the same. Charlie had a sympathetic look on his face, which meant he was getting ready to kick me out.

"Yeah, bro, we're about to smoke, so you might have to go." Charlie sounded like he felt sorry for me, like he knew I didn't want to leave.

As I stood up, a flash of a million thoughts ran through my head. A mixture of excitement and curiosity began to consume me as I began to debate with myself on whether I should stay and try it.

Why shouldn't I smoke? I have nothing to lose. I'm not doing anything— besides, I don't want to go home. What about Andrew? He doesn't like drugs. So what? I don't do stuff based on what he likes—besides, he doesn't have to know. What about Sophia? She doesn't care. Why would she? She doesn't have to know either. Is it worth keeping it hidden from them?

I didn't know if I was just tired of doing the same old thing all the time or if it was just because I, didn't want to go home, but I wanted to try it. I wanted to see what it felt like. I wanted the experience.

"You know what? Let me try it."

Charlie's face lit up after I said those seven simple words.

2
CHAPTER

I f you ever asked anyone who tried weed for the first time, they could probably sum it up in three words: really fucking weird. The weird feeling is always what comes first—maybe because you're in a state of mind you've never experienced before. Either way, it was strange. It was like being awake in a dream.

When I said I'd do it, Charlie was more than happy. He was ecstatic. He had a gleam in his eye I will never forget. They all looked a little excited, and I was too.

While Josh rolled the blunt, Charlie couldn't stop talking like it was going to be the best day of my life. "Dude, you're about to be so stoned. You're going to be giggling and shit. You're going to think everything is funny."

Josh seemed to be the only one indifferent to my decision.

"Dude, this is going to be awesome!" Charlie's excitement disrupted my thoughts.

I felt like a little kid whose parents told him they were going to Disney World—not that I knew what that felt like. I didn't know what it'd do to me. I was just praying it wouldn't make me do something stupid. Even though the effects of marijuana are commonly known, I was completely oblivious to how it would make me feel. Still, it was nothing compared to finding out for yourself. However, the thought of freaking out made me anxious. "I'm not going to go crazy, right? Like, am I going to hallucinate or something?" I felt kind of silly asking questions like that.

"Nah, dude, you're just going to be like super chill. Like Cole."

I glanced over at Cole.

"Look at him," Charlie said. "He doesn't give a fuck about anything right now."

Cole just nodded his head in agreement.

"Does it hurt?" I didn't want to keep asking stupid questions, but I had to know. I didn't know what it would do to me, and I didn't know what I would do on it.

"Honestly, it'll probably burn your lungs a little bit since it's your first time. Probably going to sting like hell, but relax. That's kind of the point, right?" Josh seemed more reasonable than I thought he was. It was easy to peg him as a big, dumb brute, but he was smarter than Charlie and Cole, which wasn't that impressive.

"Don't worry, man. You'll be super chill in a minute," Charlie said with a grin.

The anticipation was killing me. I had to do it—or I'd explode.

When Josh finally finished rolling, Charlie plugged in his phone into his stereo and started playing music.

"All right. Let Timmy get the first hit since he's a rookie," Charlie said as he took the blunt from Josh and handed it to me.

I clumsily grasped it with my pointer and index fingers and just stared at it while everyone else stared at me.

"Do it, you pussy!" Charlie yelled.

I took a deep breath, brought the blunt up to my lips, sucked in the smoke, and blew it out almost immediately.

"You're doing it wrong, bro. You've got to inhale it and suck in as much smoke as you can," Charlie said.

I tried it again and sucked in more smoke and kept it in my mouth longer. When I blew it out, I still felt nothing.

"I don't think you're getting it. You have to like swallow it. Like, it should be burning your lungs and throat right now," Josh said as he knocked on his chest as if to demonstrate where I should be feeling the pain.

"Yeah, bro, just inhale. Take a big-ass hit," Charlie added. He still looked excited, but I knew he probably would rather be smoking himself than teaching me how to smoke.

I tried again, this time sucking in as much smoke as I possibly could. Just as Josh said, I swallowed the smoke. I inhaled until I couldn't take in any more, and just as Josh mentioned, it burned.

I spat out the smoke, and then I proceeded to a series of uncontrollable coughs while Josh and Charlie laughed at me.

"There it is. That's how you do it. Now pass it here, chief." Josh reached for the blunt.

I handed it to him and continued to cough.

Charlie kept giggling, and Cole concentrated on the TV, which was still off. I still didn't feel anything, and I was starting to wonder if someone could be immune to its effects. I didn't have to wait long for the blunt to come back to me.

"All right, just take another hit, bro. Hold it in your lungs and try not to let it out so easily." Charlie handed me the blunt.

I grabbed it and quickly sucked in as much smoke as my lungs could handle, which wasn't much. It didn't take long for me to start coughing and choking again. It felt like someone was lighting my lungs on fire; it was also hard to breathe.

"You're a fucking rookie!" Charlie couldn't stop laughing. It was like he was already high, but I knew that couldn't be true.

I started to pass the blunt to Josh, but he refused. "Nah, man. Just keep hitting it."

I looked at Charlie who approved Josh's decision, and then I hit it again. I could hardly take any more smoke before I was gasping for air. I tried to hand it to someone else, but no one would accept it. They just watched me struggle to smoke it.

"You'll get used to it," Josh said as I handed him the blunt.

"You feel anything yet?" Charlie asked. That was when it began. Everything began to fall into slow and utter focus. Everything was coming at me—but not moving at all. It was weird and confusing. I looked over to Charlie's lamp on top of his desk, and it was shining brighter than it had before. *This is it. I am stoned.* My eyes felt heavy and glossy, and a smile crept onto my face, which was followed by inexplicable laughter.

I could feel everything—everything intangible that I knew existed but couldn't touch—the atmosphere, the music, the light, the emotion. I could feel it all, and it tickled me in every way. I was in a paradox, a matrix. I was standing on the thin line between dreams and reality, and it hit me like a train. Time slowed down and almost stopped completely. I became lost in the smoke that surrounded me.

"He's fucking stoned!" was the last thing I remembered hearing. I could still hear everything, but I could not pay attention to any of it. I was sheltered from everything. I was distant from the world. None of my fears or insecurities could get to me here. I was too high off the ground. They couldn't reach me up there. The voices in my head became silent, the world became silent, and for once in my life, all I had to do was enjoy the moment. The moment went by like a blur.

When I woke up in Charlie's living room, I felt like someone had dropped a bus on me. My head didn't hurt, I didn't feel nauseous, but I felt so tired. I felt sleepy, lazy, like someone had just woken me up in the middle of the night. I couldn't bring myself to sleep anymore, but I didn't have the energy to get up. There was crust in my eyes and food stains on my shirt, which weren't there before—even though I didn't remember eating. My muscles were sore from sleeping on the floor instead of the couch that was a foot away from me. I felt like I had slept for five years.

I was exhausted. I still felt a little high, but sobriety was creeping around the corner and was ready to drag me back to reality. I was a little disappointed; the thing I could remember from the night before was how it felt and how good it felt compared to how I felt when I woke up. I was already starting to miss it.

As I tried to sit up and clear my head, I reached for my phone to ask Andrew to come get me. It was noon already, but lucky for me, it was a Saturday. Just as I was texting Andrew, I heard the toilet flushing.

Josh stepped out of the bathroom as he zipped up his pants. "What up, rookie? How you feeling?" Josh seemed a lot less intimidating than he did before.

"I still feel funny," I answered.

"Give it thirty minutes, and you'll be fine. How was it though? It's always the best for first-timers. If only that were true for sex." Josh stepped into the kitchen to pour himself a glass of water.

"If I had any of that, I wouldn't need to smoke."

"Yeah, but even sex is better high, kid. Speaking of which, who's this Sophia chick? Is she like your girlfriend?" Josh asked.

"What?"

"Last night, you kept talking about some girl and saying you're all in love and shit. Nothing shut you up until Charlie fed you some old pasta he had in the fridge."

"Wait," I said before Josh could continue. "I ate old pasta? I don't even like pasta."

"Oh, yeah, when you're high, you'll eat anything. Don't sweat it though. Chicks dig a guy who can eat anything," Josh added with a wink.

"I think I should go." I stood up against my body's wishes and headed for the door.

"Go ahead. You'll be back."

"What?" I turned to face him as I reached the door.

"Let me guess … you're in love with a girl who friend-zoned you, and now you have to watch as she throws herself at every other guy when really you're the best one for her. So, instead of the love story, you're hoping you get to watch her plow her way through high school. Is that why you're here, kid?"

"What? No. Sophia isn't like that—and stop calling me kid. You're like a year older than me," I fired back.

"Two years older, freshman. You just peg me as someone sad about shit. I like figuring people out, especially when they take a step in the wrong direction."

"Smoking once is a step in the wrong direction?" I asked.

"Anything involving Charlie or Cole is a step in the wrong direction—and believe me when I say that hardly anyone only smokes one time," Josh replied.

"So, if you think it's a gateway drug, why are you here?"

"I think it's a game of Russian roulette. You don't know if it'll fuck your life up until after you've tried it. After it's too late. The weed itself may not be dangerous, but wait until you meet the people you have to meet to get it. It's a great big wonderful world of drugs out there, and it's filled with the worst kinds of people, which kind of makes you wonder what that says about us." Josh took a break to take a swig from his cup.

"I wanted the high," I whispered to myself but loud enough for Josh to hear it.

"With higher highs come lower lows," Josh replied. "Remember that."

3

CHAPTER

I didn't have to wait long for Andrew to pick me up. We usually spent the weekends together eating lunch and driving around. It was a tradition we had where we would gather up as much money as we could and find new places to eat. The truth was that we hardly ever had any money, so we always ended up going to any fast-food place with a value menu.

Andrew and I both had money, and we decided to eat at a Chinese buffet near the mall. Still feeling the aftereffects, I was craving Chinese food. I was practically gnawing at my fingers as Andrew filled up his tank. I knew Andrew would be curious about my appearance, but who hasn't had slack days? I knew he was wondering why I stayed at Charlie's that night since I usually never stay over there for more than an hour.

When Andrew finished pumping gas, he opened his trunk and started to throw out some of the trash that was in there. I got out of the passenger seat to go help him. I didn't want Andrew to notice me even more, but I was too late. I looked like a bum. I grabbed the last crumpled-up can of Monster from his trunk, and he gave me a weird look.

"Are you okay?" he asked as he scratched the top of his head.

"Yeah. I'm fine. Why?" I tried not to look him the eye.

"You look like shit, man. I don't know if you need a shower or a hose."

"I went to sleep late," I answered, wiping my eyes.

He gave me another curious look before jumping in the driver's seat. "Are you going to change today?" Andrew never cared about what I wore mainly because I always wore the same sweater and jeans. I didn't know how to explain how I looked. I felt dirty, and I wanted nothing more than to go home and shower.

"Probably if you take me home. Why?" I asked as Andrew started his car.

"Allison and Jackie want to hit up the movies tonight. Do you want to? I can take you home after we eat, but you have to dress nice."

"Why?" I asked.

"It's a secret," Andrew laughed and turned up his radio, promptly ending the conversation.

To be honest, I didn't always like going to the movies with Andrew and Allison. I pretended to love it, although I secretly envied what Andrew and Allison had. I never knew what it was like to have someone like you enough to call them yours. Jackie would always make it worse; she was talkative and hardly ever spoke to me. It was almost like Jackie was Andrew's second date instead of the girl Andrew invited so I wouldn't feel alone. I appreciated his gesture, but nothing could ever not make me feel alone, especially Jackie.

I never understood why Jackie and Allison hung out with us in the first place. Neither of us was very funny, cool, or attractive. Jackie and Allison were both stunning. Jackie had long, curly blonde hair and bright blue eyes; she could have been the poster girl for the Aryan race. Her best feature, if you didn't account for her figure, was her smile. One thing everyone loved about Jackie was how often she smiled. It warmed your heart when you saw it; it could brighten the darkest of days. It was a smile that demanded a smile in return. Jackie was outgoing and loved to speak louder than everyone else. She was also very flirtatious and very touchy, but no one minded the touchy part. She was ditsy but smart, and you could never really tell if she acted stupid on purpose. She would use hair color as an excuse for every senseless act and sometimes laughed at things that weren't even funny. She also liked to gossip. Andrew once made a joke that if reality shows were a person, they'd call her Jackie.

Allison, on the other hand, was a bit more relaxed. She had light green eyes that would sometimes change color. Allison also had a pretty smile, although it wasn't as jaunty as Jackie's. She was a bit more bashful without being shy. She carried herself with a quiet confidence—as if she knew she didn't have to be as bubbly as Jackie to attract attention. Allison, like Jackie, had a vigorous figure. Unlike Jackie, however, it was the result of years of athletics. Allison was a volleyball player, but she loved to try her hand in every sport. She was cool and collected and very sarcastic. She never took anything too seriously, but she was sometimes cynical about things.

Andrew was a little taller than me and looked goofy. His dirty blond hair covered his eyes most of the time, and he had a build that could only be described as almost muscular. Even though he was an honor student, Andrew always had a dopey expression on his face. Andrew was far more charismatic than I was, and he also played baseball. He was very talented and very athletic. Andrew was also very conservative, which must have been admirable. He was someone you knew would go off to college, find a wife, get a decent job, and live in a two-story house. That's the American dream, right?

Me, on the other hand, well, I was just me.

When we arrived at the Chinese buffet, we waited behind a family of twelve to be seated. The entire restaurant was packed, but we didn't want to eat anywhere else. Andrew was still interrogating me, but I couldn't give him a straight answer.

"You look like a donkey's ass, bro. That's ass times two. What did you do last night—and why won't you tell me?"

The people around us began to give us strange looks.

"Calm yourself. We're in a restaurant," I hissed.

"All right, all right, just tell me. Come on. I tell you everything. We're bros, remember?"

I felt guilty, but I knew Andrew wouldn't take the truth lightly. He was never very tolerable, and I'd seen the way he looked at kids like Andre or Charlie.

"Just forget it. I feel like shit." I felt fine, but feeling sick was the only way I could disguise the truth.

"All right. I'll stop, but what about Sophia? What happened with her, man? Did you ask her out?"

My so-called relationship with Sophia wasn't something I wanted to discuss either—even though I was infamous for talking about her all the time. "What do you want to know?" Usually I would jump at the opportunity to discuss the potential love of my life, but for once, Sophia was the last thing on my mind.

"I want to know why she isn't coming to the movies with us instead of Jackie, but hold on, they're about seat us."

A nice Asian woman led us to a small table right by the exit. We sat down, ordered our drinks, and then stood up to get our food. I loved having a variety of foods, but I always got the same thing. After filling up my plate with fried rice, sesame chicken, lo mein, two egg rolls, and a chicken wing, I sat down in front of Andrew. He had also filled his plate beyond its capacity.

Andrew started stuffing his face, but I ate my food slowly. I thought I was hungry, but I was still full from all the pasta.

"All right. Spill it," Andrew said as he wiped his face. "What's on your mind?"

I was never good about talking about myself, but Andrew was the best at getting me to talk.

"I don't know, man. I've just been kind of depressed lately. I don't know why. I don't." I stared at my food and avoided Andrew's worried looks.

"Is it about Sophia?" Andrew asked.

"I don't know. Can we drop it." I started to pick at my food with my fork like a little kid.

"Aw, come on, dude. Talk to me," I looked up and saw an earnest and honest face. I hated feeling remorse when just a few hours earlier, I couldn't have cared less who knew I smoked weed. It felt that good, but Andrew wouldn't understand. He was too stubborn.

As the feeling of regret disintegrated into one of anxiety, I suddenly wanted to smoke again. Josh was right; the feeling was too great to only be felt once. How could you go to a place to be relieved of stress only to wake up back in your stressful life? I didn't know why I was stressed, sad, or anxious, but I was.

"Timmy, you know there are other girls out there, right? Sophia seems great, but she isn't the queen of England," Andrew said, snapping me out of my daze.

"What?" I asked.

"I think she's great, dude, I do, but come on, you're all over her. Like, I get she's smart and good-looking, but she isn't the only one. She's a dime in a dozen, dude."

I felt completely defensive about a girl who didn't like me. "She's different. She's not a dime in a dozen. Fuck you, okay? I don't want to talk about this," I replied.

"I'm not trying to insult your girl, dude. It's just that you get so worked up over a girl who doesn't even know you like her—and doesn't like you—when there are so many other girls who would love you, dude. Come on. You're a catch, Timmy."

"No," I interrupted. "You're a catch. I'm a nobody."

"Aw, come on, man. Don't say that," Andrew said, finally putting his fork down.

"She's just," I sighed and mumbled, "she's just the best part of my day, all right? I don't do anything or have anything to look forward to except for her. Whenever I can see her again, even if it's just for a minute, I don't know what I want from her. I like it when she's around. When I get ready for school, the only thing that keeps me from locking myself in my room in a poor attempt to sleep my life away is the off chance I could see her smile at me."

Andrew took a deep breath and said, "That's nice and all, but that's dangerously depressing."

"You mean it's pathetic," I said.

"No, that's not what I mean. It's just that you barely know her, dude. After like four years, you still barely know her. It's like you're putting a stranger on a pedestal."

"Can we drop it?"

Andrew was right, but knowing he was right wasn't exactly comforting. I didn't like anyone else, and even if I did, I wouldn't know what to do about it. I had always liked girls from a distance, longing for the day I could be that close to someone.

We continued to eat in complete silence. I hated to think about how lonely I was, but that was all I could think about. I wasn't anything special. I wasn't athletic, smart, or outgoing; everybody just tolerated me. No wonder Sophia didn't like me.

After we finished eating, Andrew drove me home. The awkward silence continued, and I wanted to apologize to Andrew, but I couldn't think of a reason to. I wished the awkwardness would just pass—and we could continue to be goofy with one another—but that wasn't happening. When we arrived at my apartments, Andrew gave me a somber look that made my stomach turn.

"Look, dude, like I said, I like her—I mean your face lights up when you bring her up—but don't you think you're losing yourself to this?" he asked.

I glared at him, opened the door, and stepped out of the car. "No, I don't," I said.

I stormed into my empty home and listened to Andrew's old car drive away. He would return as soon as he got dressed and picked up Allison and Jackie. My mom always left the house spotless whenever she was going to be gone overnight. She was a very devout Christian and sometimes spent Friday nights praying at the church until the sun came up. On those nights, she would leave me some money for food and a note, which I found in the dining room, which was also the living room. She left a twenty-dollar bill and a note: "I'll be back in the morning, please sleep at home. I love you very much."

I stopped attending church a few years back. It was not because I believed in God any less; it was just that church was boring, and my mother stopped forcing me to go. I loved how strong her faith was, although I sometimes hated how she would put God before everyone—even me. I sometimes envied the omnipotent being that had more of my mother's love than I did, but her faith was still inspiring. She could get through any crisis knowing God would somehow pull her out if it. I, like many kids who grew up in die-hard Christian homes, had my doubts. I had a lot of doubts, but my mother never did. Not once.

I hopped in the shower after an hour of doing nothing. Andrew texted me to say that he would be picking up Allison soon, but Jackie was still getting ready. I figured I still had thirty minutes, which was more than enough time. I didn't know why Andrew asked us to dress up, but for once, I was happy about my appearance. I was going to wear a black collared shirt with a solid purple tie, black denim jeans, and black Nike sneakers. I also had a silver watch, which didn't work—I stole it from Charlie—and dog tags with the Batman symbol on them. After getting dressed, I sprayed myself with cheap cologne and waited on my couch with the TV off.

I watched from the window when Andrew's car finally pulled up. Allison stepped out first in a sleek dark purple dress and black heels that made her an inch taller than Andrew. Jackie emerged from the back seat in a light blue sweater and a tight black skirt. I couldn't but stare. They looked so good, but Andrew wore the same orange polo shirt and khaki pants as he wore to lunch.

I opened the door for them and was greeted by one of Jackie's famously tight hugs.

"Hey," she said with a flirty smile.

"What's up?" I responded coolly.

"Uh, oh, you're looking sexy in that purple tie."

I blushed despite myself. Jackie had a way of making everyone feel a little bit better about themselves.

"Thanks. You're looking pretty sexy yourself. That skirt looks tight though," I replied.

"You like it? I bought it because it makes my butt look big." She giggled and playfully slapped me on the shoulder. "I'm just kidding."

"No, you're not," I said.

Andrew and Allison walked through the door.

"What up, playa?" Allison said with a flip of her brown hair.

"Chilling same shit, playa," I responded.

Andrew stood at the center of my living room, and we all looked at him dumbfounded. We were all probably wondering the same thing. Why did he ask us to dress up? What's the occasion?

Jackie was the first to speak. "So, why am I uncomfortable right now? What gives?"

Andrew paused for effect before answering. "Well, you guys know baseball season is coming, and we had tryouts." Andrew paused, but we remained silent. Andrew hardly shut up about baseball, but it somehow slipped my mind that he had tryouts.

"I made the varsity team, and my coach said I have real potential. He's thinking about having me start at shortstop. We have a scrimmage in two weeks, and if I do good, the position is mine." I had never seen him so happy.

"Oh my God. That's awesome." Jackie leaped up, hugged Andrew, and wrapped her arms around his neck.

Allison looked at me, smiled, and rolled her eyes, and then we both joined Jackie in a group hug.

After joking and laughing and talking about how proud we were of Andrew, we finally left for the movie. We were already late, but I don't think any of us would have cared if we missed it. We were all too happy.

Jackie and I were flirting in the back seat, and Allison and Andrew were talking upfront. The music was playing way too loud, and everyone was talking all at once. Allison and I cracked jokes. Jackie was practically screaming. Andrew sang obnoxiously to any song that played on the radio, and Jackie and Allison giggled at Andrew horrific singing voice.

I rested my head on Jackie's lap and sang with Andrew.

Jackie just looked down at me, smiled, mouthed the words to the song, and rocked her head from side to side. As Jackie ran her fingers through my hair, I shut my eyes.

I enjoyed moments like that. I could pretend for five seconds that Jackie and I were dating—and that this was a real double date—but it wasn't. Jackie had no real interest in me; she was only being friendly. I wanted to be as happy as they were, and I was for a brief moment, but I could never fail to see the truth. I was a fifth wheel.

After the movie ended, we decided to get a midnight snack. We stopped at the closest Burger King. Allison and I stayed in the car while Andrew and Jackie went to buy food. I was still struggling to keep my smoking experience a secret. I felt like I had to tell someone, but it couldn't be Andrew. Allison was far more laid back than Andrew—and far more understanding.

"Hey, Allison," I said leaning forward.

"What's up?" She looked so tranquil, almost like she had smoked weed, which I knew couldn't be true. I didn't want to go right out and say I smoked weed. I was too afraid she'd tell Andrew.

"Do you know a lot of kids who smoke weed?" I asked.

"Like, in my classes?"

"Yeah, like do you know any honor students who smoke weed?"

Allison raised her eyebrow at me and then said, "Not really. They're all super nerdy and like never leave their houses unless it's for extra credit. Why?"

"Just curious," I said and sat back in my seat.

Allison pulled out her phone and started texting, not paying any attention to me.

"Have you ever smoked weed?" I whispered.

"No. Have you?" Allison replied still not looking the slightest bit interested.

"Yeah," I said hoping she wasn't listening.

She finished texting and set her phone down. "So, wait, you've done it? When? Last night?"

"Um, maybe." I felt guilty.

"You did, didn't you? Is that why you spent the night at Charlie's?" She started looking a bit more interested.

"How did you know about that?"

"Andrew told me you stayed there last night."

I looked out the window to see if Andrew and Jackie had gotten their food yet. They were still waiting by the counter, and once I was sure they were occupied, I turned to Allison and said, "You can't tell Andrew."

"What was it like?" she asked.

"What?"

"What did it *feel* like?" She turned to face me.

"Did you hear what I said?" I could see Andrew and Jackie getting their food, which meant it wouldn't be long before they made their way back.

"Yeah, I know. Don't tell Andrew. You can't tell Andrew. You can only tell him what he wants to hear." Allison looked away and took a deep, frustrated breath. "Drink one freaking beer at a party, and he flips out," she added.

"You go to parties?" I asked—even though I should have asked her what was wrong.

Andrew and Jackie were walking to the car and were dangerously close.

Allison whispered, "I won't tell Andrew."

It was a quiet ride home. It was late, and we all were tired.

Allison was giving Andrew the cold shoulder, and Jackie and I pretended not to notice. The only one of us who was remotely awake was Andrew. After dropping off Jackie and spending nearly an hour in front of Allison's house trying to figure out what was wrong, Andrew hopped in the car and rested his head against the steering wheel.

I was already in the passenger seat with my head against the window.

"Everything all right?" I mumbled without looking at him.

"Yeah, I think so. I never know with this girl, man." Andrew started the car and began the route to my apartment. We drove with the radio off for a little while, which was strange. I could tell Andrew was upset about something, but I was too sleepy to wonder what it was.

As my eyes were starting to close, Andrew said, "Did you smoke with Charlie last night?"

"Who said that?" The best part of being tired was that it was hard to look surprised.

"No one said anything, but be honest. Did you?" He tried to look at me while keeping his eyes on the road.

"No, I didn't. Come on, man. You know me." I rubbed my eyes and struggled to sound casual.

"Yeah, I know, but you go there every day—and you never smoked once?"

"No, I haven't. Would it be that big of a deal if I had?" I readjusted myself and took off my seat belt, suddenly feeling claustrophobic.

"Yes, dude. It's a huge deal," Andrew exclaimed.

"Relax, man. I didn't do anything. I'm just saying if I did, who cares? Everyone does it." I yawned, stretched, and unconsciously avoided eye contact with Andrew.

"Drugs ruin lives, okay? They're illegal for a reason—"

I said, "Save it for your FCA meeting, dude."

Andrew clenched his jaw and held the steering wheel tighter, and I immediately regretted saying that to him.

When we arrived in the parking lot, I wanted to apologize, but Andrew spoke before I could.

"You know, I had a cousin named Alice. She was my best friend, and she was like the older sister I never had. She used to read to me, she used to babysit me, and when the kids at school would be dicks to me, she let me cry on her shoulder. When high school started, she was the most popular girl in school, so of course, she would party. The first few times her parents caught her with weed, which I guess wasn't such a huge deal, until she started getting caught with prescription medication. You name it, she's done it—and it never stopped. She would come home late, and she would get caught with drugs, liquor, boys.

"Do you know how hard it was to hear that the girl who helped raise you was some kind of slut. Her parents tried everything, but she kept running away, and when she came back, she would always look worse. Eventually, they sent her to rehab, but even that didn't work. It might have made it worse because when she came back, that was when the real drugs started for her.

"All I could do was watch, dude. She would babysit me and smoke weed in the bathroom. I even heard her snort something once. Allison just doesn't get it. I don't want to watch the same thing happen to her—or you." Andrew's eyes began to water, but he was far too proud to let me witness him cry.

I got out of the car without saying anything. I didn't know what I could say until I finally thought of a question. "What happened to her? Like, where is she now?" I looked at the ground.

"She died, Timmy. She's dead."

4
CHAPTER

I knocked on the door for almost thirty minutes before I finally gave up and walked home. I came over the next day, and there was still no answer. As days passed, it seemed like Charlie and his mother had vanished. Instead, I hung out with Andrew. Luckily, he had forgotten about our talk—or at least was pretending it didn't happen. Allison had kept her word and had not told Andrew or anyone else about my first time smoking. Everything was back to normal. Almost.

It was hot that Tuesday afternoon, and I found myself walking Sophia home in silence.

Grace was gossiping about the girls at school and gushing over a guy she thought was cute, but my thoughts kept going back to Andrew's cousin. I tried to picture what she'd looked like. I imagined she'd be pretty, just like all the girls who surrounded Andrew. What bothered me the most was that Andrew didn't tell me how she died. Something like that could happen to anyone, even Sophia. I hated the idea, but my imagination got the best of me. I began to picture Sophia ten or maybe even twenty years older, struggling to get by. It was easy to picture a drug addict as a skinny, wide-eyed mess, but no matter how vivid my imagination was, I could not see Sophia that way. Even if she was an addict ten years from now, I'd probably still think she was beautiful. She'd probably still take my breath away, and I'd want to help her. I knew, however, that I didn't have to worry about that. Sophia was a lot smarter than anyone else I knew, especially me, and if anything, she was going find me one day all washed up and addicted to cocaine or whatever had these people looking so dreadful. Would she help me? Would she even care? And if she did, would I deserve it?

Grace turned on her street and waved goodbye. Sophia and I walked home in silence. My mind raced, and for a while, I forgot that she was even there. I stared at the ground or straight ahead, not even realizing Sophia had been looking at me most of the time.

She was waiting for me to say something and was probably thinking it was weird that I'd escort her home just so I could ignore her. She tapped me on the shoulder and said, "Hey."

I turned to her, and she looked up at me with those big brown eyes. I loved the way the sun reflected off her eyes; it was almost like they were made of glass or crystal. I never really liked looking people in the eye and always kept my head down to avoid it, but Sophia's eyes were hypnotizing. Every time she'd look at me, my eyes would lock on hers, drawing me in like a magnet.

"Hey," I answered, shoving my hands into my pockets.

She smiled, and my heart dropped. "So, you're like really quiet. Is everything okay?"

I cracked a smile and replied, "Yeah, of course. Why wouldn't it be?"

"I don't know you just look like something is bothering you."

"No, it was just a long day, I guess."

Sophia shrugged her shoulders and just looked ahead. She was never the type of girl who would try to play therapist. I knew most girls jumped at the opportunity to listen to your problems just so they could give advice, but Sophia wasn't like that. If she asked you what was wrong and your answer was nothing, she'd just assume nothing was wrong. Either that or she didn't care what was wrong.

"Hey, do you remember Richie Daniels?" I asked.

"Richie Daniels? From middle school?"

Richie Daniels was the son of our vice principal in middle school. Although his dad was the nicest vice-principal any kid could hope for, Richie was a notorious troublemaker. He wouldn't get into fights, skip school, or get into any actual trouble most of the time, but he would curse at the teachers. Richie got caught buying weed from an older kid while we were at recess, and his father sent him to a private school. After he left, rumors spread around school saying that he was arrested and went to juvie, which couldn't be true because the baggie of the so-called weed that he bought was oregano.

"Wasn't he that kid who smoked weed at school?" Sophia asked.

"I don't think he smoked it. I think he bought it, and I heard it wasn't even weed. It was oregano."

"What an idiot," Sophia sighed and rolled her eyes.

"Would you ever do it?" I asked.

"Would I ever do what? Buy oregano?" Sophia joked.

"No. I mean, like, would you ever smoke weed?"

"Um, no," she stated firmly.

"I mean it's not the worst drug in the world, right?" I mumbled. I was nervous. Andrew and Sophia had the same disgusted reaction to the idea of smoking weed.

"It's still a drug, Timmy."

"Well, I mean, it's like the safest drug though," I said.

"And you would know this how?" she asked.

"I mean, I wouldn't know, I guess."

We stopped at a stop sign and looked both ways even though we knew we weren't going to be able to cross anytime soon. I was nervous, but Sophia didn't notice because she never noticed anything. It was admirable how focused she was. No matter what she was doing, she directed all her attention toward it—even if it was just crossing the street.

We jogged across the road once we had the chance, and Sophia finally said, "Why do you ask?"

"I don't know. Wouldn't you want to try something crazy and adventurous?"

She thought for a moment and said, "Maybe not that crazy."

"I mean, not everyone who smokes weed turns out to be a hard-core drug user."

"True," she said as she nodded her head. "And not every drunk driver crashes, but it still doesn't seem like a good idea."

She was right. She was *always* right. There was never an argument with Sophia because she would always win. You couldn't talk her into believing anything other than what she believed.

I took a deep breath as we were about to reach her street. She probably wanted me to say something about how I felt, but I knew it was pointless. I would get the same subtle rejection, which would shatter me, without her using words. I knew it bothered her sometimes. I could see it in her face that she didn't like to hurt people's feelings, but I also knew she wasn't afraid to. Sophia would probably just feel bad about hurting my feeling and get over it by the time she got home.

When we got to her street, she turned to me. Just before I could embarrass myself again, I heard a voice calling from behind me. It was the voice of a guy who loved to do the embarrassing for me.

"Aw … ya look so cute together!" It was Amiel. He came toward us in his designer clothes and a Superman book bag with just one notebook in it. Amiel walked with big, confident strides and wore a sleazy smile as if he were about to sell me a used car.

"What up, brah?" he shouted as he slapped both his hands down on my shoulders. He turned to Sophia and ogled her in a way that made me uncomfortable. I couldn't say anything because he was doing it on purpose.

"Hi, Sophia. You look pretty today. Doesn't she look pretty, man?" He turned to me and waited for an answer.

I hated being put on the spot like that, but I still managed to mumble, "Yes, she always does."

"I'm sorry. I couldn't hear you. What?"

I glared at him, knowing damn well he had heard me.

Amiel just laughed, and Sophia started to step away from us.

"Bye, Timmy," she almost whispered.

I waved with an awkward smile, and Amiel stared at me with a goofy grin raising both his eyebrows up and down.

Once I was sure she was too far to hear us, I shoved Amiel off of me. "Why'd you do that?"

"Do what? Man, I was helping you." He chuckled and pulled a cigarette out of his back pocket. He pulled out a match and used the bottom of his shoe to spark it. Amiel was an old friend. I had known him all through middle school, but we didn't hang out much. When we did, it was always interesting. Amiel was only two years older than me, but he liked to think he was twenty years older. Amiel was a smart-ass who didn't do well in school. He was charismatic, but he had a quick-trigger temper. He was overly complicated yet remarkably simple. I never really understood why he hung around me so much since a guy like him could make friends with anyone.

"Seriously, though, you need to get some ass." He intentionally blew a cloud of smoke in my face as I glared at him.

I rolled my eyes and continued walking down the street.

"Oh, come on." Amiel caught up to me. "Let me hook you up, bro. I'm telling you one girl, one time, and it'll be simple. All you got do is maybe dress a little better and say everything I tell you to say."

"I don't think it is that simple," I said, doing my best not to look at him. "Look, I don't want to talk about."

"Then what do you want to talk about, man? What's on your mind? Let me help you." Amiel tended to sound like he was mocking me even when I knew he was being genuine.

We walked past a few houses and started walk toward the harsher part of town. I was so used to the change of scenery and how the houses transformed as you walked down the sidewalk. They would start with nice lawns, American flags, and driveways, and then they would transition to front yards that were just dirt and dead leaves, rusty metal fences, and Confederate flags. The final stage—where Amiel and Charlie lived—was be nothing but crumbling apartment complexes for people raising families of five in one-bedroom apartments. I didn't particularly like where lived, being just on the border between the haves and the have-nots, but most of the time, I hardly noticed how we were living—and neither did anyone else. Home is home, I guess.

When we were a few minutes away from my home, Amiel started to bother me again. He smoked his cigarette to its butt and was already fiddling with another one. "So, what's on your mind?"

"I smoked weed the other day," I said.

Amiel was a lot easier to talk to than Andrew. Andrew was the kind of person who was okay with what you had to say as long as it was something he wanted to hear. Amiel, however, was indifferent to everything.

"Oh, yeah? Well, why did you that?" As usual, I was stumped by his question.

"I mean, I don't know. Why not? Weed isn't that big a deal, right?" I answered.

"If it's not a big deal, why is it on your mind?" Amiel fiddled with his cigarette some more before finally lighting it, and by then, we were right in front of my street.

I turned to and him and asked, "You didn't feel guilty your first time smoking?"

"Nope," he said as a puff of smoke left his nostrils. "By the time I started smoking, all my friends had been doing it for two years."

"How old were you?"

"Twelve."

"Oh, shit." I stared down my street and did not want to take another step.

Amiel noticed how reluctant I was to go home and offered to hang out at his house. I accepted, and we continued walking. My book bag was heavy, my shoulders ached, and the back of my shirt was drenched in sweat.

Amiel swung his book bag around on his finger. He lived on the second story of a really old house. He shared the house with a few other people and shared his room with his older brother who was hardly ever home. His house mirrored some apartments that looked more like rundown motels than actual places to live, but you couldn't glance over there and not see life. Whether it was children running around in the daytime or the parents drinking at night, there was always someone outside.

Amiel went inside to say hi to his mother, and I waited outside. He returned with a can of soda and a basketball. "Catch!" He tossed me the can of soda, and I fumbled it to the ground. Amiel laughed and shook his head at my lack of coordination, and then he started dribbling the ball and shooting it at the hoop in his driveway.

He stopped to catch his breath and said, "Why do you feel guilty?"

"I don't know. My friends aren't as understanding as yours are," I replied.

"Shit, 'cause all your friend are lame-ass white kids, man, some FCA-ass niggas, man." He continued to dribble the ball as he spoke. "You think they'll ever understand?"

I shook my head. He was right. They never would, but that didn't make me feel any better.

"Look, bruh, all I'm saying is your so-called friends live in their perfect little worlds where the worst thing that could happen is not getting an A on their math quiz. I'm telling you, you start to look or act differently from what they're used to, and they'll look at you different, they'll treat you different, and even place you in a different spot."

"Andrew lost cousin to drugs though. Maybe it's not so perfect on that side," I replied.

Amiel rolled his eyes and said, "Come here."

I followed him to the edge of his driveway, and he pointed at an old man who was crouched under a. "You see that guy right there? Ever since I moved here, which was like what three years ago, he has sat in that same spot and asked people for change. I made the mistake of giving this nigga twenty dollars, thinking he would use it for food, but I went back twenty minutes later, and he asked me for more money. Think about where he came from and what he must have seen, dawg. Your friend lost his cousin, while this man lost his life—and there are niggas like this crawling all over this place, man."

"So, what are you saying?" I asked.

"I'm saying that he could be somebody's dad, bro. Look at him. He can barely walk! Those are the addicts we get. Those white-bread assholes can't call you out on shit they don't know about, but they will 'cause they always do."

"Man, ain't you half white!" Josh shouted from a block away.

"Half Puerto Rican, you wetback bitch."

"Damn, I feel like your conversation was about racism, and you're being super racist right now." Josh approached Amiel, slapped him five, and only acknowledged me with a nod.

"The conversation was about weed," I said.

Josh smiled and replied, "Weed can't be racist. Everyone loves weed—white, black, yellow, gray."

"Timmy says he feels guilty about smoking weed," Amiel added.

"Why? Shit. You don't like smoking weed? Don't smoke weed. It's as simple as that."

"It's 'cause of his girlfriend," Amiel said.

"She's not my girlfriend," I growled.

"Ah, see? I knew it. You have 'friend-zoned' written all over you. Is she slutty?"

"Nah," Amiel answered before I could. "She's smart and shit and like hella nerdy. She don't talk to nobody either. I ain't never seen that girl with a boyfriend … never heard of her with a boyfriend."

Josh nodded his head as if he approved of Sophia without even knowing her name.

"Seems like the perfect candidate. What's the problem?" Josh started to juggle with a lighter and his house keys.

"He don't have no game. That's his problem," Amiel said.

"Well, shit, Timmy. You'll figure it out. It's trial and error."

"And mostly error!"

Amiel and Josh continued to go back and forth, dissecting my nonexistent love life without letting me get a word in edgewise. I couldn't help but admit that on some level, they were right about me and about why I liked Sophia, but I didn't like the idea that someone, especially someone like Josh, knew more about me than I knew about myself.

"All right, enough," I exclaimed, finally stopping their conversation.

"Whatever, man," Josh said. "What are ya gonna do about it?"

"I might be going to this girl's house later," Amiel answered.

"What about you, Timothy?" Josh asked.

I shrugged. I found it a bit weird that Josh called me Timothy. Not even my mother called me that.

Josh was strange—or at least strange to me. My first impression of him was a cool, popular athlete who was super confident and very relaxed. I was starting to realize that Josh wasn't any of those things. He was unambiguous, wore an angry look on his face everywhere he went, and was surprisingly smart, but he was terribly pessimistic. "There's weed at Charlie's place. You want to come?" he asked.

I didn't know if I fully trusted Josh, but I jumped at the opportunity to go smoke some more, completely disregarding the guilty feelings I had about a minute before that.

We said goodbye to Amiel and started walking to Charlie's place. As we left, we walked past the old man Amiel pointed out. He was withered, his eyes were glazed, and his teeth were bright yellow. He wore a black shirt and jean shorts, and I didn't have to stand too close to him to catch his smell. He was disgusting, but I wasn't disgusted. I felt sorry for him. I honestly didn't know which was a worse fate: to die young like Alice or to grow into someone who survives solely on the pity of others.

"You heard what happened to Charlie?" Josh said. "Someone gave him some pills. He freaked out had to spend a week in the hospital."

"Seriously?"

"Yeah, man. Shit, he better be careful—or he might end up like that old man," Josh added with a wink.

5

CHAPTER

Since Charlie's mother was gone, we decided to just walk in. We found Charlie playing video games in his living room with a bag full of half-eaten burgers and about four joints already rolled right next to him. I, still feeling high, was very excited to see food and was even more excited to see the weed. I had already felt as though I would fall asleep, but I was excited to smoke more.

Charlie looked over at us with bloodshot eyes, and I realized we had all gathered to smoke weed when we were all already high. Charlie seemed a lot paler than I remembered, and he also seemed exhausted. His hair was a mangled mess, and he had enormous bags under his eyes. He must have gone through an ordeal at the hospital.

"What's up, bitches?" Charlie yelled. Although he seemed sickly and pale, his graphic mannerisms seemed intact.

"What happened to you?" Even though Josh had told me the story, I wanted to hear it from Charlie.

"TJ fucked me up. That's what happened. I swear, when I see that fucker again, I'm going to beat his ass. Watch!" I could see the anger in his eyes. I wasn't exactly sure if Charlie would carry out his promise, but either way, I felt sorry. I was also I little bit confused. If Charlie was the one who took the pills, why was he angry with TJ? "Why did you even take those pills?" I asked.

"I was fucked up! He shouldn't have given me them if I was drunk, dawg! I swear I'm going to beat the shit out of him." Charlie stood up and began to pace around his living room.

"TJ is a grown man, bro, and he is on some crack or something. I would just leave it alone," Josh said.

"I don't care how old that motherfucker is. I'm going to rip him a new one!" Charlie pulled out a cigarette from his left pocket, brought it to his mouth, he lit it, and began to furiously shadowbox the air. For someone who was a huge stoner; he was pretty fast.

Josh ignored him, grabbed one of the joints, and began to smoke it.

Charlie sat down and continued to smoke his cigarette.

I looked around at Charlie's cluttered apartment. There was a file cabinet in the middle of his small kitchen along with various canoeing, paintball, and camping equipment that perhaps gave evidence to a previous middle-class life. I knew Charlie had lived a middle-class life because I was there. He had a lovely home right by a pond near the high school. His father owned a small business that did very well, but when he was imprisoned, it all went to waste. They spent months on the road, or so I was told, and they often struggled to find available jobs and food.

When Charlie's mother finally obtained work, she rented a small apartment in a crappy neighborhood. A part of me always felt sympathy toward Charlie, considering that out of all the people I knew, including myself, he had lived the toughest life.

Charlie began to finish one of the burgers on the table, and I was reminded of how hungry I was. I looked over at Charlie with begging, bloodshot eyes. He glanced at me, threw me a burger, and then threw one to Josh. I devoured the cold hamburger, barely allowing myself to chew, sat down, grabbed one of the joints, and asked Charlie for a lighter.

I was hardly awake, but I still felt the need to smoke. I lit the joint, leaned back in the couch, and focused on the paused video game. Everything suddenly became even more cloudy and dark. My eyelids felt exceptionally heavy, and I struggled to keep them open. I continued to smoke, but it felt like I was stepping deeper and deeper into a void. I was being sucked into an enormous black hole, and I was only allowed glimpses of actual reality. I fought sleep with all my might, but it was much stronger than I was. In an instant, a warm, dreamy darkness swept over me, and I fell into a profound and intense slumber.

I had forgotten it was a school night.

The next morning, I found myself in the same place where I had fallen asleep. I looked up, and it seemed like the TV and game console had stayed on all night. My eyes still felt heavy, and I still felt sleepy. I stood up and looked around the apartment for anything with the time on it.

When I reached into my pocket for my iPod, it wasn't there. I slowly walked toward Charlie's bedroom and found Charlie on his bed. I shook him lightly and whispered, "Hey, Charlie. Wake up." I continued to shake him. "Charlie, wake up!"

He began to make minor movements, proving that my methods of waking him barely had any effect on him. I then yelled with all my might right into his ear, "Wake up!"

Charlie leaped up furiously and shoved me off his bed. "What the fuck do you want!" His face went red with fury.

I had to admit I was afraid of Charlie's wrath, but I knew he would calm down. "What time is it?"

"I don't fucking know." He was still angry at me for waking me up, but I didn't have time to waste on apologizing. He grabbed his phone from his desk and threw it to me. I caught it just as it was about to hit me in the face. It was nine forty-five. I was an hour and fifteen minutes late to school, and to make matters worse, I hadn't gone home the night before—and my book bag was missing. My phone was also missing, and I had almost no recollection of the night before.

"I've got to go to school!" I stood up as if I had some idea about what to do next.

"What time is it?" Charlie asked calmly.

"It's nine forty-five!" I showed him his phone.

"Damn, we are late."

I had almost forgotten that Charlie even went to school. "Yeah, you lost my book bag and my iPod, and I didn't even go home. My mom is going to kill me!" I had no idea what to do, but I had to get school somehow.

"Calm your tits, bro. You didn't even bring your bookbag when you came here. Your iPod is on the floor by the couch, and you passed out last night. It isn't my fucking fault you missed school. Besides, who gives a damn if you missed one day."

I was angry, but I had to admit he had a point. I hadn't missed a day of school that year, so nobody would question why I was absent. I could tell my mother I fell asleep there while watching a movie, and if I didn't bring my bookbag, it must still be at Amiel's place. I could just ask him to bring it to school tomorrow. Perhaps I did overreact, but I still felt the impulse to run to school as fast as I could with some terrible excuse as to why I was late. I felt like I was committing a crime.

"I guess you're right," I said as I sat down, feeling a little bit less worried. I relaxed, even more, when I realized I wasn't going to school. I didn't have to deal with moronic adolescents or the disappointment of seeing Sophia. I then recalled the promise I had made to Amiel yesterday. I had no idea how I would carry out that promise, but missing school was probably a good start. I felt a little bit angry with myself for even making such a promise. Sophia had been a big part of my life for a long time, and even if we weren't together, we were at least close friends. It was unfair of me to just ignore her after all these years. On the other hand, Amiel was right that she hardly showed any affection to me—even as friends—and except her compassion yesterday, she never showed me that she cared about me at all.

Maybe Amiel did have a point. If she didn't care for me, why should I care for her? I decided I would keep my promise—not for Amiel but myself. I had to lose this strange dependency on her, and ignoring her was an excellent way to do it. I felt like a gaping hole had just opened in my chest. I would miss her tremendously, but I had no choice. I sat there and wondered how I could get rid of the deep agony I was feeling.

Charlie looked at me and asked, "Yo, you want to get stoned?"

That should do it. I happily agreed to smoke with Charlie. He pulled out a joint from under his bed and stuck it in his mouth. He opened his window, shut his door, stuck a towel under it, and pointed a little white fan toward his window.

My eyes were still heavy, and I still felt awfully tired, but I still wanted to get high.

Charlie had no clue who Sophia was and wouldn't bring her up.

Being high might not allow me to forget her, but it would at least make me feel better about the situation.

Charlie lit the joint, sat next to me, and looked at me with apologetic eyes. "I'm sorry I made you miss school, man. I should have sent you home before you passed out."

I was a bit taken aback. "No, you're fine, man. It was my fault," I answered.

"I feel bad. I feel like I'm turning you into a stoner, bro." He passed me the joint.

"Don't feel bad, man." I inhaled as much smoke as possible and then passed it back to Charlie.

We smoked in silence for what seemed like hours. Anything we talked about seemed insignificant.

I was stoned after the first one but discovered that he had two more already rolled and a bag and some joint papers to roll more. I, feeling the unexpected urge to eat, asked Charlie for food.

He said, "I've got some money. We can walk to the Chinese store."

I nodded in agreement, and we slowly made our way out of his apartment. Walking in the sweltering heat in a sweater with my eyes barely open presented a challenge. I quickly eliminated the obstacle of walking in a sweater by tossing mine onto his stairs.

Charlie took off his shirt to reveal a very scrawny and almost skeletal body. Right below his rib cage, his abdomen seemed more a product of malnourishment than actual physical fitness.

We walked for fifteen minutes, slowly making our way to the end of the street. Charlie didn't say much, and neither did I. We were both probably worried about police asking us why we weren't in school. I didn't know if Charlie was afraid of the police, but I knew I was. I had never dealt with cops before. I had always been afraid of the police—even before I started smoking weed. I always felt like it was in their power to arrest me for no reason other than looking suspicious. I was more worried since I was breaking the law, and they had every reason to antagonize me.

At the Chinese restaurant, Charlie walked up to the counter to order, and I snuck into their filthy bathroom. It was appalling. There were stains on the wall, and the smell was repulsive. I looked into the mirror and saw a scruffy teenage boy with bloodshot eyes looking back. I laughed a little and smiled at the fact that I could barely lift my eyelids enough to look at my reflection.

I found Charlie sitting in one of the two booths the restaurant provided. I could tell the restaurant was mostly for takeout and not for someone to sit down and eat. Who would want to have dinner in a dump? I sat across Charlie and rested my forehead against the wall.

"You look stoned," Charlie said.

"Only a little," I replied.

"Man, I can't believe I got you smoking weed. That's crazy. You were all like I'm never smoking weed *ever.*"

"We *all* said we were never smoking weed."

"Not me. I always knew I'd be a stoner. Ever since I was twelve, I knew. Now I'm a bad influence and shit."

I was a bit taken aback by his statement. "How are you a bad influence?" I asked.

"I got you smoking weed. I don't know, but that incident with TJ got me thinking about my life and shit. Maybe I should quit smoking."

I was taken aback now. "Why?"

"I don't know. I think I need to get my life together and shit. You know, I don't want to end up like my dad or my brother."

I had almost forgotten about Charlie's brother. I knew he and his father were both incarcerated, but I had no idea why. I never knew Charlie's dad too well, but his brother was probably the toughest kid I knew. I kind of knew he would end up in jail; actually, we all kind of knew. "Why is your brother locked up?"

Charlie's face transitioned from one of deep thought to one of resentment and pain. "'Cause he gave somebody what they deserved. This one dude tried to run up on his girlfriend, right, so my brother beat his ass. Then the same guy saw my brother's girlfriend at this bar, and he fucking raped her, dawg! Real shit, he raped her, so my brother went and found his ass and popped a cap in that motherfucker!"

I was shocked by the brutality of his words. Charlie was still so angry about it as, and I could only imagine his brother was too. I didn't know what to say. I was never very good at dealing with angry people.

"Aw, fuck it! That bitch was a ho anyway."

Since I didn't know how to respond to his morbid tale, I asked about his father.

His reply, although short, was not exactly a step up from his brother's story. "My mom finally called the cops on his drunk ass," he grumbled.

I didn't need further explanation.

When the food finally came, we carried the two bags back to Charlie's apartment.

I thought I heard Charlie mumbling under his breath as we walked, but I was not sure. I didn't like hearing about his violent family, and I sort of wish I hadn't asked. When we arrived at Charlie's place, we remained silent. We didn't even dig through the bags of food. We walked directly into his room, leaving the bags of food in his living room, and he lit up another joint and sat down on his bed.

"Now I'm depressed, dawg." He sighed.

"Why?"

"Cause, I'm a freaking stoner, bro. I smoke too damn much, and that's why I got into that shit with TJ."

"I thought you were drunk?"

"Same shit. I need to be more like you or Josh, you know. You guys are smart, and you have futures and shit."

I once again found myself at a loss for words. Josh had plans, but I didn't. I had no clue what to do with myself after high school. I considered joining the military, but that was cliché. Everybody who didn't make good enough grades in high school thinks the military is just a way to make quick money. They think they have their lives figured out because they decided they'd sacrifice their lives—not for their country but the perks. To be completely honest, joining up did seem like the best option for someone like me without options.

I still found it bizarre and a little bit irritating that people as stupid and as insignificant as the Riley brothers could just sign up—and all their problems would be answered. *Is life ever that simple? I wish I could see the people who failed miserably in high school and decided to join up five years after their service was up. I would probably laugh at how many of them were still failures.*

In my head, all these thoughts of all these outcasts quickly came to mind, and each one of them failed at leading a socially acceptable life. I wasn't exactly much different from any of the kids I thought of. If I kept my grades at least somewhere in the middle that, maybe I could get into some small college—and then get a job, marry Sophia, and have kids. Sophia was the only thing I had ever been determined to obtain. I never even thought about pursuing any other goals. *I've got to get my shit together.*

"Timmy, you know you're my friend, right?" he asked, interrupting my thoughts.

"Yeah?"

"Then be honest with me. Why do you even hang out with me? Like if I'm such a bad influence and such a fucking stoner, why are you still my friend?"

If I only had a dollar for every time I didn't know what to say. I shrugged.

"You're fucking stoned," he said before puffing on his joint.

We relaxed in silence for nearly an hour. We smoked and listened to Charlie's phone playing music through his speaker. I enjoyed the sound. If we weren't stoned, I'd probably be bored out of my mind, but I wasn't. We did absolutely nothing, hardly making any sudden movements, but I still felt as though I was enjoying myself.

An uncontrollable smile soon crept across my face as I leaned back onto Charlie's bed and attempted to stay awake. Then the giggles started up, and not soon after, the hunger did too. I slowly attempted to stand, but I could feel gravity pushing me back onto his mattress like a bully at the playground. Everything around me was moving so leisurely that I began to feel as if I was floating on thin air. I didn't feel the mattress under me, and my eyes were failing in desperate attempts to stay open. I could hear my laughter as echoes in an empty hallway, and the music was drifting in and out of my conscious mind.

Charlie's eyelids were open just enough to reveal dark, almost scarlet red eyes. I realized Charlie hadn't moved in a while and began to get worried. When I finally managed to stand, I put my hands on Charlie's shoulders and was about to shake him.

He yelled, "What the fuck are you doing?"

"I thought you died, bro," I said just before laughing frantically. I stumbled across his room until I reached his door, unlocked his doorknob, and pulled as hard as I could, nearly slamming the door against his wall.

In the living room, his mother and a strange man were eating Chinese food. We stared at each other for a while. I was dazed, and I did not what to do. Charlie's mom had never seen me stoned before.

Charlie yanked the back of my shirt, pulled my back into his room, slammed the door, and shoved me onto the bed. "Yo, you're going to get me in fucking in trouble."

I didn't answer. I didn't even respond to the fact that I had just been manhandled by a stoner. I wasn't exactly the most athletic person around, or the most aggressive, but I could at least handle someone as skinny as Charlie.

Charlie walked out of his room and slammed the door behind him.

I stared at his ceiling and began to think everything over; everything that happened in the past two weeks for some reason began to change everything dramatically. *I'm not a stoner. I don't skip school. I don't just randomly decide to ignore the woman I love. What is going on with me?*

I was thinking things over, in the same way, I always did.

My life isn't lost, right? This was only my fourth time getting high. I can't have a problem. No matter how hard I pondered the guilt, I couldn't feel any of it. *This is great, and I know it. This is me enjoying being bored. This is me having fun just staring at a ceiling. I love Sophia, but she doesn't care about me—not even remotely. She wouldn't even notice if I ignored her; half the time, she hardly notices I'm there.*

I started to remember the first time I noticed how amazing she was. We had a class together in the sixth grade, but I was very strange and had crushes on everyone. It wasn't until the eighth grade when I felt like I saw her for the first time. I was very close friends with a kid named Drake—a stoner who is in AP classes—and I would go into his class to bug him.

In middle school, they wouldn't allow us to sit with other classes, but I would always do my best to sneak a seat at Drake's table. One day, I sat next to Morgan, a bitchy redhead who said she was too good for me in the seventh grade, and Sophia, but I hardly noticed her.

The students at the table cracked immature jokes and asked who would get paid more: a porn star or a stripper. I didn't even notice the girl who would steal all my effort and attention for the next four years. A kid asked if Morgan would be a stripper or a porn star. They asked me because, for some reason, they thought I was the most knowledgeable in this area.

Morgan asked, "What about Sophia? Which one of us do you think would end up a stripper, and which one of us would end up a porn star?"

Of course, being only thirteen years old, I answered, "Um, Morgan, you have bigger boobs, so you would probably end up a porn star, and Sophia would end up a stripper."

After a couple of immature giggles, Sophia turned to me and asked me a question I never answered but one I would never forget: "Which would you rather see?"

I told her I'd tell her another time, but I never did. It may seem like juvenile words to everyone else, but to me, it was the sweetest poetry I'd ever heard. I should have told her the truth because she clutched my heart and held onto it for four years—whether she intended to or not. There wasn't a thing I wouldn't do for her, and even now—when I claimed I'd ignore her—I wanted to see her.

Even when I was stoned, she still managed to slip into my barely functioning brain. I could see her so clearly in my head: her long, black hair, big brown eyes, and almost pale skin. I remembered the way she'd sneak up from behind and tickle my side. I would leap fifty feet in the air because it made her laugh, and I would give anything just to make her laugh.

With all this in mind, it depressed me that she did not feel the same way. How could she? She was all kinds of wonderful, and I was just another unimportant high school kid who might be earning the title of druggie rather than outcast. I couldn't help but love her. I couldn't help it. She was my drug before weed, and even at that very moment, I couldn't get off. I was addicted.

I could feel that warm darkness sweeping over me, but I didn't want to stop feeling the way I felt. I fought sleep with everything I had, and I would win this time. Even if I did sleep, she would visit me in my dreams.

I started to doubt my sanity. Was I obsessed? Was Sophia that great—or was I fantasizing to escape the unforgiving truth, that she was just a regular person, and I didn't have anything else to look forward to than her admitting she cared, which she never would because she never did. I idolized her almost as a god, yet the only thing it ever did for me was make me seem like a stalker. Was I a stalker? I used to bolt out of class just so I could catch a glimpse of her face. I would sprint to wherever she's walking and wait however long it took just to walk beside her. I was one step behind when following her home. It had to stop. Of course she's great, but it can't be meant to be—not after four years. She was bad for my health, and I knew it. She drove me insane, and she didn't even try to. I meant nothing to her, and I would always mean nothing to her, so why should I care?

I did care though, and that was the problem. How can you love a person so much who doesn't love you back? I was hardly sane, and what I used to believe was maintaining my sanity was destroying it. Was that what drove me to marijuana? It seemed unfair to blame her, but it did seem like a logical conclusion. Maybe she did. Either way, she wouldn't felt guilty, and neither would I because I'd be high as a kite and I'd stay high for however long it took to forget her.

It might've been me just being melodramatic, but I decided I'd excommunicate her from my thoughts. She would not be allowed to enter the boundaries of my imagination, and I would force myself to walk in the other direction wherever she may be. I would remain sane because she would no longer take my sanity away from me. She was nothing to me— just as I was nothing to her.

Josh seemingly leaped out of nowhere and landed on my stomach.

"What the fuck, yo?" I asked as I sat up. I glanced out of Charlie's window and realized the light that once shone brightly into his darkroom had diminished to a faint blue glow. "What time is it?"

Josh smiled. "It's six o'clock."

"What?" I screamed.

"Yeah, man, you passed out staring at the ceiling and shit. You kept talking to yourself too. It was pretty hilarious."

I couldn't have fallen asleep. "I wasn't sleeping," I said.

"Yeah, sure, you weren't," Josh said sarcastically. "Who's Sophia?"

"What?" I suddenly realized that my high wasn't there anymore. I must have dozed off thinking about Sophia.

"In your sleep, you kept saying, *Sophia.* Who is she? Is she that girl you're obsessed with?"

"I'm not obsessed," I answered irritably.

"Hey, man, it's cool. I know what you're going through. You're crazy for a chick who doesn't feel the same. Man, everyone goes through that."

I glared at him. "What do you mean?" I asked.

"I mean everyone wants what they can't have; it's just human nature. You know, the reason you probably like her is because you can't have her. You put her on this pedestal when in reality, she's just another girl. You treat her like an idol when maybe she wants to be treated like a person. I bet you if you dated her, you wouldn't think it was all it's cracked up to be because you thought it would be ecstasy." He sat down on Charlie's computer chair. "I think she drives you crazy, and that's okay. There is always someone or something that will make us question our sanity—whether it's a girl or some event in our lives that we thought would never happen to us. We will always doubt our sanity because life is fucked up. Maybe you should just do something else—join a club or something or play sports. There is more to life than girls. Not much more, but there is."

He was right, but I had already decided I wouldn't speak to her anymore. That conversation was pointless. "I already told you I'm not speaking with her—so it doesn't matter." I slumped down and rubbed my eyes.

"All right. Whatever, man. What did you and Charlie do today?"

"Nothing. We just talked and smoked and shit." I didn't want to talk to Josh. I didn't want to talk to anyone. For once in my life, I wanted to go home.

"What did you guys talk about?"

"Nothing ... about his dad and his brother." I stood up to stretch and realized that my book bag was on top of his desk. "How'd that get here?"

"I brought it. Did he tell you how they got arrested?"

I gave him a strange look. "Yeah, his brother shot someone who raped his girlfriend," I answered.

"Really? That's what he told you?" he asked.

"Yeah. Why? What happened?" I once again regretted the question.

"I'll tell you, but don't breathe a word of it to anybody, especially Charlie."

I nodded my head.

"His brother was dating this chick, and this guy was flirting with her and shit at school. He walked up and beat the fuck out of him. Lucky for him, the fucker hit back, and it was during school, so the best he got was a couple days of suspension. Well, it turned out the guy she was flirting with was fucking her. It had been going on for a while, and nobody fucking knew. They had been dating for like a year. The dude who got his ass kicked wasn't just seeing her though; he was seeing a lot of people. Well, the girl ended up with herpes or some kind of STD, and his brother caught it. When he found out it was with that dude, he beat his ass again—and he beat his girlfriend pretty bad too."

I was astonished at the end of his tale. "I thought Charlie's brother shot that guy. What happened to that? And Charlie told me she was raped."

"Well, I wasn't done, and I guess that's true, but not really. You see, when his brother found him, the kid was so scared that he stole his dad's revolver to defend himself. The dumb-ass kid never held a gun before and didn't even know how to take off the safety. They fought for it, and Charlie's brother won. He took off the safety, and he shot his ass in the shoulder. He wasn't a murderer … if that's what you were thinking."

Indeed, I was.

"Anyway, he threw the gun down and beat his ex, and now he's in jail," Josh spoke with such indifference.

"That's crazy. How do you know all this?" I asked in amazement.

"That's the story his brother told my brother, and that's story Charlie told me. And you want to know why it was so crazy."

"Why?" I asked.

He looked at me with the same indifference and said, "Because it never happened."

"What?" I was beyond confused.

"Charlie didn't know that his brother was a cokehead and a compulsive liar. The story his brother told him was a lie that I guess Charlie believed. His parents didn't have the heart to tell him the truth, and neither do I. A bunch of people tried to tell him the truth, but he didn't believe them. He kept the story his brother told him. They were both kind of crazy, I guess, and the story always changes. I guess you and I heard different lies. It's all a sham. Everything has something that makes them crazy."

"What happened?"

Josh still was not deterred. "What do you mean? His brother was a cokehead, and he got caught with a shit-ton of coke or enough to arrest him for it."

I was shocked. "That's insane. How does he even stay sane?" I asked.

Josh turned his attention toward Charlie, who was still talking to his mom, and looked back at me. "He doesn't."

6

CHAPTER

"Why did he lie to us? Does he not know?" I whispered as Charlie exited the room once again to use the bathroom. "I think he does, but he doesn't want to believe it. Do you have a brother?" he asked, keeping a lookout for Charlie.

"Yeah, so?" I said.

"Would you want to believe it if your brother was a coke addict?"

I thought about it for a moment and then answered, "I mean, I guess I wouldn't, but I wouldn't have a choice. It's the truth."

Josh stood up and sat next to me on Charlie's bed. "The truth can be whatever we want it to be." He put my book bag down next to me.

"No. The truth is the truth—no matter what we believe," I refuted.

"Is it? What about religion huh? What about all those people who believe in Buddha, Allah, or Jesus Christ—or people who believe in things like aliens or Bigfoot? No matter how many people declare the big bang theory is a fact, it's still just a theory—just like everything else—but do we have the right to judge anyone for what they think it's true? No, we don't. The truth to us is whatever we believe is true."

I found everything he said to be idiotic. "But that's religion and science. Of course, we can believe whatever we want because we don't know. The truth is fact. I can choose to believe that rain is coming from a very well-hydrated dragon pissing off a cloud, but that doesn't make it true," I countered.

"Look, that's not what I meant. I probably should have worded it differently. All I'm trying to say is we only accept what we want to believe. For example, you can't accept the stone-cold fact that the chick you like doesn't like you. So, you hold on to the belief that she may one day turn around and love you, which may very much be true, but as of right now, it's not, but no matter what, you can't accept it. Charlie can't accept that the person who's been defending him all his life is addicted to cocaine, and he chose to believe his lie."

I scowled at him and stood up. "Stop bringing her up, you son of a bitch." I picked up my book bag and headed for the door.

"Look, I'm sorry. I was just trying to make a comparison. Just don't be too quick, my friend. You don't know all that he's been through," Josh said.

I stopped at the door. "I'm his friend too, asshole. I know what he's been through, and aren't you the one who said everyone had a sob story? That no one has sympathy for anyone because everyone's life is sad and fucked up. Well, why is Charlie an exception? He should just accept the fact that his brother is a drug addict instead of concocting some lie. And stop bringing her up. Damn it. I get she doesn't like me, but fuck off. I barely know you—so stop acting like you know everything about my life when you don't know shit."

I didn't know where that sudden burst of rage came from, but I was upset. I understood hearing about Sophia from Andrew, Amiel, or even Charlie, but as far as I knew, Josh was still a stranger. Hearing about Sophia was stressful enough. "Tell Charlie I had to leave!" I slammed the door before he had a chance to retaliate.

For someone as big as Josh, he was pretty calm. If I yelled at Charlie like that, he'd probably swear a hundred times and then punch me in the face. I was still angry. I didn't like hearing about Charlie's problems when I still had some of my own. I was concealing a smoking habit from my best friend and still found it appropriate to confide in his girlfriend. The thought of Sophia still hung over me like a ghost stalking me wherever I went.

I walked down the stairs and saw Cole and two girls I had never seen before. One of them was short with dirty blonde hair and dark brown eyes. I couldn't get over how short she was. She looked as though she was barely fourteen. She turned to me and waved weirdly. I had never seen her before, yet she waved like we'd known each other forever. I didn't know what it was about her, or the other girl, but I could already tell they were loud. Something in their faces just screamed loud person.

I didn't want to deal with Cole. I didn't want to deal with anybody. I wanted to go home. I wanted to curl up in bed and not think about anything for a hundred years. I knew I wouldn't though. If I went home, my mom would interrogate me for an hour—and then I would stare at my bedroom ceiling until three o'clock in the morning and think about everybody's problems, including my own.

I knew if I stuck around, we'd be getting stoned, but I didn't want to talk to Josh or Charlie. I didn't want to talk to anyone, but if I did, then I'd be high and that super amazing feeling that makes all my problems fade away would return—and then everything would be okay. I wouldn't have to feel like shit, and I would avoid all my mom's inevitable nagging.

Cole stopped me in my tracks as my right foot took the final step. My left foot rested on the last step.

"Bro, you got to hit this joint, dude."

By the look in his eyes, I could tell he was stoned. He passed me the lit joint, and it didn't take more than a millisecond before I was pulling clouds of marijuana smoke into my lungs. Cole laughed in awe of how long I held my breath.

As I exhaled, everything around me started to creep into focus. I thought about Sophia. I hated how much I wanted her. What I hated, even more, was that I had to ignore her and know some other guy would swoop in and take her breath away. He would be able to do something I never could, and perhaps it'd be for the best for her, but it would drive me insane. I would hate that guy, and to be honest, I would hate her too. I would hate her for loving him and not me. I would hate her for not noticing me. I would hate her for never telling me yes or no. I would hate myself for never asking.

I looked to the ground, suddenly saddened by the realization that the only thing I ever worked for didn't like me. I had nothing else to do. I had no other goals to pursue, and I had no other dreams to chase. As sad as that was, I managed to crack a smile because I knew nothing would matter after I hit the joint a couple more times. I would be in a different world—one where there was no Sophia, no Andrew, and no guilt or sadness. I'd be so baked, and the only thing I would be worried about was food.

I took a couple more hits from the joint before Josh and Charlie emerged from the apartment. I took my final pull from the joint as it reached the point where it was burning the tip of my fingers. I quickly tossed what was left of the joint on to the ground and crushed it with my heel.

"What's up, Cole?" Charlie asked as he stepped off the stairs.

Josh was ignoring me, but I didn't care. I wanted him to ignore me; anything was better than hearing him nag.

"Dawg, you got more weed?" Cole asked.

"Yeah," he responded.

"Well, spark it up then," Cole replied.

Charlie pulled out a blunt and started smoking.

Josh started to smoke a blunt of his own, and the rest of the group began to gather in a circle. The two girls hadn't said much since I'd stepped outside. I didn't even know any of their names, but one of the girls seemed eager to introduce herself.

"Oh, and by the way," said Charlie, "that's Chelsey and Veronica."

The two girls waved, and I nodded my head. I felt it was rude not to introduce myself, but they didn't seem to notice.

When the blunt reached me, I began to realize how stoned I already was. I didn't even know how my throat had survived so long. My chest burned like crazy, and sucking in more smoke felt close to impossible, yet I managed to handle the pain. As I exhaled, I closely examined the smoke that had recently entered my lungs. I stared, hoping to see some proof that it was the weed lifting all my problems away.

"Yo, I'm about to have some more people over. We're about to have a party!" Charlie said.

We continued to smoke the blunt as people arrived at Charlie's improvised party. I couldn't tell where they were coming from, and I didn't recognize most of the people who showed up beside the Riley brothers and their posse, Andre, Amiel, and two other girls. The one who caught my attention was Gina Smits. She was about a year younger but an inch taller than me. Her blonde hair almost reached her lower back, and her eyes were enormous. She looked like an anime character. She was very pale and had a very innocent look. She was cute in the same way as a little girl at a playground. She didn't look like she belonged there, but that was the reason nobody noticed her. Gina stood in the back while everybody mingled. She looked sweet, and for some reason, I wanted to know more about her.

I wanted to know everything about her, and being stoned gave me an enormous burst of confidence.

She caught me staring and returned my gaze with a flattering smile. I couldn't keep my eyes off her; she seemed to be drawing me to her. I finally decided to walk up and say hi. We knew each other enough to have a decent conversation, but I was trying to do better than decent.

"Hey, what's a pretty girl like you doing on this side of town?" I tried to sound smooth.

"I only live around the corner." She giggled, which was a good sign, but it didn't matter what sign she gave me because I was too high to worry about rejection. "You look like you should live in a castle."

She smiled and looked at the ground. "Do you remember me?" she asked.

I gave her a questioning look.

She said, "I was in your history class last semester."

I didn't remember, but it seemed rude to tell her that. "Of course, I remember. How could I forget?" Just as I prepared my next line, somebody walked up behind her and tickled her side. She jerked her body in the opposite direction and quickly attacked the stranger with a hug.

The stranger, who wasn't a stranger at all, was a boy named Abel. He had played basketball for the school—until he quit and dropped out of high school. He had been my friend a couple years ago, and he said, "Hey, Timmy. You met my girlfriend, Gina?"

Son of a bitch, I thought as I smiled and nodded.

"Yeah, we had a class together," she said.

I nodded and then, without another word, walked back over to where Josh and Charlie were smoking. I felt so stupid. Of course, she had a boyfriend; a girl like that never stays single for long.

I noticed that Charlie and Chelsey had been holding each other very close. Charlie seemed to be having an intimate moment, but she didn't seem too interested in him. She looked angry, and she held her gaze away from his face. She looked like she was glaring at the trees.

Josh didn't seem fazed by all the people. He sat on the steps and smoked as if none of them existed. I couldn't tell if he was still upset about what I'd said, but I was too afraid of hearing another rant to ask him.

"Aye, Timmy. I didn't know you smoked bud." Andre smiled a sarcastic smile—as if he'd always knew that this was what I'd become.

"Yeah, I kind of just started," I replied.

"Dawg, you need to come smoke with me. Like, I got some good shit. You need to hit me up when you need bud. I got you, and I'll hook you up."

I nodded as a response. I stood there watching everybody interact with each other. They all looked as though they were in a worse position than I was, yet they all looked like being that way didn't faze them at all. They were all so careless, and truthfully speaking, they all sounded so stupid.

I began to observe Charlie a lot more because something seemed strange. As close as he was to his so-called girlfriend, he couldn't keep his eyes off of Gina.

I started to observe Gina more closely, and she was the same way. Every time Charlie had the opportunity to look at her, he would, but it would only be for a moment. He would glance at her whenever he thought no one was paying attention with an expression I couldn't read. I'd never seen anybody look at someone the way he looked at her. She would look back the same way, and each time, one of them looked away. It was almost as if they longed for each other. In my confusion, I decided to ask the one person who would know anything about Charlie that I didn't already know.

Josh remained at the bottom of the steps of Charlie's apartment. I sat down right by him and realized we were the only ones sitting down. "Can I ask you something?" I said.

"What's up?"

"What's the deal with Gina and Charlie? They keep looking at each other. Did they date?"

He kept his gaze on the empty sky and let out a sigh. "They kind of did have a thing together, but I don't know. I guess it's something only Charlie can answer."

"Why do you say that?" I asked.

"I still think they like each other, but there are just certain things that prevent them from being able to put a label on whatever they had." He kept looking up without even blinking.

"How come he has never mentioned her before?"

"He's a complicated guy … in a complex situation." He finally turned his attention from the sky and toward me.

"Why can't they just go out?"

"Well, from what I understand, they're both with different people they don't even like, and I think her parents won't allow it. Something like that." I looked back over to where Charlie and Gina were standing and watched as they continued to exchange looks.

I was determined to uncover this strange love story between them, and the only person who could give me any real information was Charlie. I decided I would save that conversation for another night.

I began the short journey home, hardly saying bye to anybody who acknowledged me leaving. Walking down the road was more frightening than I had imagined. It was like the world had been amplified, the night was darker, the street was scarier, and I was far more paranoid. I felt more tired than afraid, and I was walking slowly.

Arriving home was almost as scary as walking there. I was late, and my mom had long ago gone to bed. I snuck into my room through my window as quietly as I could. Once I stepped into my boring, dull, white room, I flopped on my bed and entered a sleep-like death—not at all concerned about the questions I would have to answer tomorrow.

✄

I was nervous about going to school the next day. Luckily for me, the day went by quickly. It was as if nothing had happened. Many people were still oblivious to my new smoking habit, mainly because they were oblivious to my existence altogether. As sad as it sounds, I preferred it that way. No one would badger me about where I'd been.

I hadn't seen Andrew or Sophia all day, which came as a relief. As I walked home after school, when I would usually be searching for Sophia or Andrew, I discovered a familiar face walking down the street by herself. It was Gina from the party. She was dressed in a light pink top and blue jeans. She looked amazing, yet she walked with her headphones in and her head down. It was as if she were afraid of being noticed.

I quickly caught up to where she was walking and lightly tapped her on the shoulder. "Hey," I said.

She smiled big and responded, "Oh, hey. I know you. What's up?"

I couldn't help but smile. She looked so happy to see me, yet we were strangers. "Oh, nothing. Just walking home. Are you walking by yourself?"

"Yeah, all my friends kind of left me. I'm a loser." She giggled and checked the time on her phone before putting it back in her pocket.

"Well, I'll walk with you. I think we're heading the same way," I said with the same smile on my face.

"Oh, it's okay. You don't have to. That's sweet though." She giggled again.

Part of me wanted to believe she was flirting, but in the back of my mind, I knew she was just being nice.

"No. It's cool. I want to," I said.

She giggled once more. "Sure, I don't mind the company." She kept smiling at me. She wore that smile like an accessory.

"So, how was the rest of the party?" I asked out of genuine curiosity.

"It was okay, I guess. We didn't do anything … just hung out and got fucked up." She giggled again.

I chuckled along with her. "I wouldn't have guessed it. You don't seem like the type."

"I wasn't, but then my boyfriend got me into it, and now it's like all we do." She checked her phone again, probably waiting for a text.

"I'm kind of the same way. Charlie got me smoking weed, and now it's like all I do."

"It's great, isn't it?"

"What is?"

"Being high," she responded as she checked her phone again.

"Yeah, it sure is," I replied.

She kept her eyes locked on mine for a few seconds before she giggled again and turned away. "You seem chill. We should talk more."

I nodded my head and shoved my hands in the pockets of my gray hoodie. I then realized why I had wanted to speak with her in the first place. I said, "So, how long have you known Charlie?"

She almost flinched at his name, but she kept her happy expression. "I knew him since like middle school. He was one of the first people I met when I moved here." She tried her best to look as though the subject didn't bother her, but I could read her like a book.

"Do you usually party with him?" I asked.

"No, he, like, never talks to me. Yesterday was, like, the first time I saw him in months." She tried her best to conceal her sadness, but even I, a stranger, could see through her smile. I feared that I had touched on a very personal subject. I wanted to lighten the mood, but I continued to bring him up. "Why don't you come hang out with us? All we do is smoke; you might enjoy it." I smiled, but she remained distant. It felt like something was troubling her, and there was nothing I could do to change that.

"I don't know, I mean, I want to, but my mom never lets me leave the house, and she kind of hates Charlie." Her ability to disguise her emotions started to fade.

"That must suck," I said.

"Yeah, more than you know, but anyway, what about you? How long have you known Charlie?"

"As long as I remember, I guess," I responded.

"Well, tell him I said he should talk to me more and that he sucks." She laughed after she spoke.

I found it odd that she looked so sweet and innocent and spoke like she was completely different. I could understand why Charlie would be so attracted to her, due in part to the fact that I was partially attracted to her. If I was any good with girls, I'd try to steal her away from Abel, but I wasn't good with girls—and I couldn't compete with Charlie and Abel.

It turned out she lived right down the road from me.

"So, I guess I'll see you later?" I asked in a soft voice.

"You should give me your number so we can text." She pulled out her phone for the last time. *Did she ask for my number?* I thought as I pulled out my phone. "Um, sure. I mean, you live right across the street. I can just come to see you," I said.

"Then come see me. I'm sure my mom wouldn't mind." She leaned in and hugged me before she turned and walked down her street.

As I approached my own home, I noticed Andrew's Civic parked in front of my building. I didn't know what to expect from Andrew, but I couldn't keep avoiding him. Otherwise, he would think something was up. He was sitting on the hood of his car with a tennis ball in his hand. He didn't look troubled; he didn't have any sort of facial expression, which made him very hard to read. I approached him the same way a scared child would approach his father.

"What's up?" I asked.

"Where the hell have you been, man? You, like, dropped off the face of the earth." He continued to toss the ball in the air as he spoke.

"I've been sick." That had to be the most cliché response for why someone didn't come to school, yet it was the only one people would accept. He didn't read much into it, but it did seem as though a lot had happened while I was away.

Andrew and Allison had gotten into another monumental argument. Allison went to a party and apparently got terribly drunk and said some pretty mean things to Andrew. He showed me the texts, and although the things she was saying were terrible, she didn't seem drunk at all. Perhaps she was just angry with him. Everything I read was mean, but it looked like she was completely coherent.

He continued to vent about his relationship and all of his problems, but I was barely paying attention to any of it. It wasn't that hard to drown him out without making it seem like I was. I would nod in agreement when he talked badly about her. I would try my best not to look away from him, and when I would, he would ask me a question to see if I was listening. I wasn't listening; everything he was saying evaporated in my brain.

My mind wandered through the memories I had of the past few days. I wondered if I should have that much on my mind in the first place. I kept thinking about Gina and Charlie; what about them intrigued me so much? I also thought about the party, how weird it was, and how many people I didn't know. For some reason, they knew me. I also thought about Sophia. I hadn't seen her in days, and half the time, I hadn't even thought of her. I began to wonder if she thought about me.

A sad, lonely feeling began to crawl through my veins, and I wanted nothing more than to just erase it. I knew I should be way more concerned with the fact that I missed two days of school. My mother hadn't seen me in two days, but amid everything, those things didn't seem to matter.

"You know what I mean?" he said.

"Yeah," I responded, not having the slightest idea what he was talking about.

"Anyways, are you okay? You seem out of it," he asked, finally changing the subject.

"I'm good … just still kind of sick." I tried to imitate a sniffle, but I was a terrible actor.

Andrew asked if I wanted to go with him to the store, but I said no. As much as I didn't want to go home, I knew I had to see my mother at some point.

When I walked into my apartment, my mother was cooking something that smelled amazing. I slowly walked into the kitchen, and she finally realized I was home. She gave me an indifferent look as I stared at her. She grabbed a plate from the cabinet and placed it on the counter. "You hungry?" she asked.

I nodded and let out a breath of relief. She served me a cup of orange juice and a plate of chicken, white rice, and beans. She handed me the plate, grabbed her coffee cup and a blueberry muffin, and then moved next to me. It was weird. My mother usually would be yelling at me, lecturing me about how I should go to school, but she was as calm as could be.

I tried not to make eye contact with her as I ate, but I could feel her eyes on me. She sipped her coffee slowly, keeping her gaze on me. I tried with everything I had not to look back. Having her be so tranquil was a lot more frightening than having her yell at me. I knew I was due for a lecture. I could feel it coming. It was almost like I was a bird who could sense a coming storm. I knew I was going to feel her wrath the second I stepped through the door, and the anticipation was killing me.

After I had finished eating, I slowly maneuvered myself around her to drop my plate in the sink. As I turned around to take a break in my room, she quickly stepped in front of me and glared at me with eyes of controlled fury. "So, do you want to tell me where you were? And be honest."

I knew it was coming. I didn't want to have that conversation with my mother, but it was a simple question. I didn't see any point in lying—mainly because she was going to yell either way—and I said, "I was at Charlie's house."

CHAPTER 7

My mother lectured me for almost an hour about how I should tell her when I was going to stay at a friend's house, that I should call her and let her know where I am, and that missing school was unacceptable. I was accustomed to drowning out my mother when she spoke. Everything she said was almost irrelevant; I knew I couldn't miss school. I knew I should call her. She didn't have to tell me things that I was already fully aware of. It was as pointless as trying to teach a high school kid how to count.

After my mother finished laying into me, I sat on my bed and stared at the ceiling. My mom never said I wasn't allowed to leave. She didn't take my phone, and she didn't try to do anything to punish me. Even if she had, I wouldn't have listened. I never really used my phone, and if she said I couldn't leave the house, I would've just hopped out my window.

As I continued to stare at the ceiling, I heard a light knock on my window. I turned and saw Charlie standing outside my window with a small baggie of weed and a bottle of Everclear. "What's up, man?" he asked as he crawled through my window. He set the bottle down and motioned me toward the door. I locked the door as he set the weed down on my desk.

"So, how was your party?" I asked as I sat down on my bed.

"Dude, you should've stayed. It was fucking awesome. We all got fucked up. I was drunk and high. I got head!"

"You got head?"

"Girlfriend," he replied.

"Speaking of girlfriends, how did you meet yours?"

"She lives like right under me," he responded.

"So, how did you guys start talking?" I didn't want to bombard Charlie with a lot of questions, but I wanted to ease my way into a conversation about Gina. I didn't know Gina very well, but she seemed like a much better choice than whoever Charlie was dating. If what Josh said was true, Charlie preferred Gina as well.

"I don't fucking know, dude. Quit asking questions and take a shot!" He tried to hand me the bottle, but I didn't want to drink, especially with my mom right outside my door.

"Okay … I have one more question," I said.

"What?" he replied irritably.

"Who's Gina?"

Everything went silent.

Charlie stared and then took a long sip from his bottle. "Why do you ask?" he said, keeping his gaze on the wall.

"She was at your party," I said. "She was there with Abel, but she kept looking at you."

He finally turned toward me with a grin on his face, and if I didn't know any better, I would have thought he was blushing. "Was she really?" he asked in the softest voice I had ever heard from Charlie.

"Yeah, you two kept staring at each other. What's up with that?"

"Why do you want to know?" he asked as he continued to sip his bottle.

"I'm curious."

He squinted his eyes as if he were questioning my response, let out a gentle sigh, and set his bottle down back on my desk. "It's kind of a long story," he said.

"I've got time." I wanted to hear his story, but I didn't understand why. It had to be more than pure curiosity.

"Well, I guess I should tell you, huh?" It seemed like Charlie was conflicted. It felt like part of him wanted to tell me his story—but another part wanted to keep it a secret. I wanted to know why he was keeping it a secret in the first place, He confided in me with almost everything else, yet when it came to some girl, he hesitated. "Well, we were in the same class in middle school. I think it was like sixth grade. I don't know … she was pretty hot, and I liked her. Why the fuck do you want to know so badly?"

"Just tell me, dude. What the hell are you hiding?" I replied.

"I'm not hiding anything! I don't like you all up in my business," he shouted again.

"Oh, come on. You've told me worse things. Why can't you tell me about some girl you dated?"

"We never dated, you asshole. We just talked. We used to walk home the same way since we both lived so close to the middle school. When we started talking, I would walk her home every day, and we would split up by some big-ass oak tree in front of her street. I don't know. We wanted to date and everything, but her parents said she was too young for a boyfriend.

"It makes sense, I guess, so we kept flirting and talking. Her parents never let her out the house—they were strict—and she wasn't even allowed to have a phone until she turned fourteen. I hardly ever had a chance to see her. I guess the only real way we talked was in school, but when summer came, I didn't see her at all. When school started up again, it was like nothing changed. It was harder to hang out since we didn't have the same class anymore, but I would run to that big-ass oak tree and wait for her. She would talk to me for as long as she could, which wasn't long at all.

"We kept doing that until she turned fourteen. When she got her cellphone, we would be up all night texting each other. We would talk for so long just about bullshit. I guess we stopped talking to each other. Almost overnight, we lost touch—and then I heard she was dating some dude named Abe. That pissed me off. Her parents told me that I couldn't date their daughter because she was too young, but they let that fucker date her? I guess it hit me that I still liked her. I started texting her again, and it was just like before. We flirted and shit, and then she told me how much she still liked me and how she was going to break up with Abel, but it was a fucking lie. She never broke up with Abel. I walked over there one day to try to talk to her. Before I was even close to her door, her mom stepped out and saw me with a cigarette in my mouth.

"She started yelling, and I got mad—and I started yelling too. We cursed each other out, and that's when she said I wasn't allowed anywhere near Gina. Gina got in trouble too. Her mom looked through our messages and was fucking furious. She took her phone and said she wasn't allowed to talk to me anymore. I haven't seen her since."

After concluding his lengthy tale, he took another swig of the Everclear. Charlie still liked Gina; that was clear as day. Whether or not Gina liked him in return was still up for debate.

"So, you guys don't talk anymore? Like at all?" I asked.

"Not really. The last time we texted was months ago, but she's still with Abel—that motherfucker." He continued to drink, trying to drown his sorrows.

"Yeah, but you're with that other girl—and you still like Gina. Maybe she still likes you." I didn't know why, but I wanted them to be together. I wanted to help them. If I couldn't have a love life, maybe helping someone else's would satisfy me a little.

I pondered how I could help Charlie win his girl back, feeling a little sad in the process. It was always the guy who can't get a girl who plays matchmaker. I wanted to have a love story, I wanted to meet someone by a big-ass oak tree, I wanted to have her parents hate me, and I wanted to be wanted. Despite my feelings, I wanted to help.

"Who the hell said I still liked her!" He giggled hysterically, and I realized the alcohol had finally hit him.

"It's pretty obvious. Look, we can work around her parents—and we can kick Abel out of the picture," I said.

"How?" he asked as he took the final sip from the bottle.

"Do you still have her number?" I asked.

"Hell yeah!" He pulled his phone out of his pocket and slung it at me. I dodged it just before it hit my face. It banged against the wall but remained intact. I picked up his phone and began scrolling through his contacts. Charlie didn't save many numbers on his phone. Except for a few family members and Gina, he had no one else saved on his phone.

I took the liberty to text Gina myself since Charlie was too intoxicated to even stand it anymore. He spread out on my bed and babbled about the time he smoked weed in California. Paying no mind to his nonsense, I texted Gina: "Hey."

As I patiently waited for a response, he continued to ramble about anything that crossed his mind; it was hard to follow any of what he was saying. His words were slurred, and he was speaking too fast for me to comprehend. When his phone buzzed—before I could open the message—Charlie snatched it out of my hand.

I sat quietly as he texted furiously with an enormous grin on his face. I couldn't help but smile a little. In all the years I'd known Charlie, I had never seen him so happy. I knew he was drunk. Half the reason he looked so happy was the thinning of his blood, but I knew Charlie, and I knew when his smile was genuine.

As I watched my drunk friend texting his crush, I heard a buzz from my cell phone, which was depressingly odd because no one ever seemed to text me. I thought it'd be Andrew, but as it turned out it was his less uptight counterpart.

Allison: Hey, can we talk?

It was a little out of the ordinary that Allison wanted to talk to me—of all people—but then again, if I could talk to her about my secret smoking habit, she should be able to talk to me about anything.

Me: Sure, what's up?

Charlie kept laughing and talking, mostly to himself as I sat there and thought about Allison. I had a hunch she wanted to talk about Andrew. I knew their situation wasn't great, especially after hearing Andrew rant about it. Charlie kept talking to me about how the conversation was going, but I wasn't listening in the slightest.

Allison: Have you talked to Andrew lately?

Me: Yeah, why?

Allison: I don't know if I want to date him anymore.

Me: Oh.

I didn't know what else to say. Andrew was my friend. I didn't want to see him hurt, but I was also baffled that she would share that with me.

Allison: I know he's a good guy and all, but he's so damn controlling—and honestly he's judgmental. Did he tell you about the party?

Me: Yeah, he said you got drunk.

Allison: I didn't get drunk … that is such bullshit. I had a few beers, but that's it—and I even told him about it. I could've lied to him, but I decided to tell the truth. He could have at least appreciated that.

Me: Yeah, you have a point, but why did he say you were drunk if you only had a few beers?

Allison: Cuz he's stupid.

Me: I can't argue with that. LOL.

Allison: I'm serious, Timmy. What do I do?

Me: What do you want to do?

Allison: I don't know. That's why I'm asking you.

Me: I can't tell you what to do.

Allison: What do you think I should do?

Me: Well, I'm not gonna tell you to break up with my best friend, but I'm also not going to tell you to stay if you don't want to.

Allison: Okay. And?

Me: It's up to you.

Allison: I don't want to break up with him.

Me: Then don't.

Allison: But I can't stand all this fighting.

"Dude, she said she wants to hang out with me today," Charlie said as I continued to stare at my phone.

"Then do it," I responded without looking up.

"Dude, she said she's with Abel right now." He stood up and paced around the room as if he were planning some master plan for world domination. He had a devious look in his eyes.

"If we get someone to distract Abel while I go over there, maybe she and I can hang out," he said.

I was too focused on Allison's texts to notice anything Charlie was saying; his words were just noise at the moment.

Me: Can I ask you something?

Allison: Sure.

Me: Why are you asking me about this?

Allison: What do you mean?

Me: You've never asked me for advice before. Why now?

Allison: Well, I mean, you probably know him better than I do, and I don't know. Ugh. That's such a weird question. I mean, you're my friend, and friends give advice.

I never knew Allison considered me as her friend since she was dating my best friend. I always thought of her as just that, but come to think of it, she was always there when I was with Andrew. We even met each other around the same time, and she would do everything Andrew and I would do. She hung out with me as many times as Andrew did. That could mean she knew me just as well as he did. She was just as much a friend to me as Andrew was, but I never saw it that way. She considered me close enough to ask for advice, and I barely saw her as a friend.

"Dude, here's the plan. You distract Abel, right? Go hang out with him and keep him away from her house—and then she and I can chill."

Allison: We are friends, right?

Me: Yeah.

She didn't respond after that.

"Okay all you have to do is hit him up for weed, and he'll roll with you to get it."

That sentence caught my attention. Everything he had been saying had been completely ignored until the word *weed* broke through the static that blocked out his words.

"I want you to go get weed from Abel so I can hang out with Gina," he said as if his idea was completely bizarre.

"So, you want me to go distract the boyfriend while you fool around with his girlfriend?" I asked with a dumbfounded expression.

"Who said we were going to fool around?" He began to giggle like a schoolgirl.

"What? How would I even get weed from him? I don't any money," I responded, hoping Charlie would realize I didn't want to do it.

"I have money. Just get it for me from him. It's foolproof." He had the hopeful look of a five-year-old who thinks he can make a rocket ship out of a cardboard box.

"Yeah—until you get caught. I thought Abel was your friend."

"Yeah, he's cool and all, but Gina is better— and besides, you're the one who told me I should go after her."

I suppose I didn't realize that Charlie could just as easily have an affair with her as actually date her. A relationship would be tough, but cheating is easy, especially if you have your buddy Timmy to help you do it.

He reached his hand out to me, gave me a serious look, and said, "You shake my hand now, and you're agreeing not to tell anybody and also not to fucking judge me." He put a lot of emphasis on the last part.

I guess I had no right to judge him since most of it was my idea. I didn't want to help Charlie cheat, but I couldn't find a reason not to. I decided I would go along with his deluded plan since it couldn't be very long before Abel knew. It would last two weeks—tops.

"Fine," I said, rolling my eyes as I shook his hand. I wasn't sure if it was the right thing to do, but at the end of the day, I was hanging out with the kid. Charlie gave me Abel's number, and I texted him. I asked him for weed, and he told me to meet him at the corner of his street in twenty minutes. It was a little bit weird. I only talked to Abel in school, and he dropped out a year ago. It was worse than going to talk to a stranger; with a stranger, at least you don't have to feel the guilt of not remembering any previous interactions.

Charlie was filled glee as he texted Gina while I reread some of Allison's texts. As sad as it sounds, it was nice to have a girl text me for once—even if that girl was completely off-limits. Either way, I knew she didn't deserve the way Andrew was treating her. What made me feel guilty was not exactly getting both sides of the story. When Andrew was telling me about her, I deliberately ignored him, but when it was Allison texting me, the situation seemed dire.

I guess girls have the gift of making things more dramatic—or perhaps it was just the fact that Allison was a pretty girl and Andrew wasn't. I didn't listen to Andrew's side, and although Allison was my friend, it wouldn't be fair if I didn't give Andrew the benefit of the doubt. It was the very least I could offer him. That's all I had to offer him. I was becoming involved in two relationships that weren't mine. I should have minded my own business.

8

CHAPTER

A bel took me into a part of the town I had never seen before. It was a dark and terrible place; the structures were crumbling, and the people looked as worn down as their homes. Old men and women were begging for money on the corners. Their withered bodies slowly deteriorated as the bugs and maggots assumed they were already dead.

I kept a straight face the entire way, trying my best not to let Abel know I was frightened.

Abel wasn't scared; he looked like he was taking a stroll through a park.

When we were about a block away from Andre's house, my phone buzzed in my pocket.

Allison: Hey, you still there?

I didn't want to text her back—I wanted to deal with one issue at a time—but I suppose the technological era makes that quite impossible. It isn't fair that some people have to deal with actual real-life problems and then have to go online to deal with whatever bullshit drama their classmates can concoct. I was on my phone, and Allison never asked me for help before, but it didn't make it any less true.

Me: Yeah.

"We 'bout to smoke in his backyard, that straight?" Abel pulled out the culprit of the horrific aroma that revolved around him. He stuck it in his mouth and offered me one from the box.

I shook my head no.

He shrugged and stuck the box of cigarettes back in his pocket.

Allison: I'm sorry for getting you involved in this. I was thinking about what you said earlier, and you were right. I never asked you for advice before and never really talked to just you.

Me: I mean, we are friends.

As we approached his house, Andre busted out his front door with a cigarette in his mouth and a big green cup of purple Kool-Aid. "What the fuck is up, man?" he shouted.

I nodded my head at him and smiled. There had always been something about Andre that made me want to be quiet. It wasn't because I wanted to hear what he was saying; it was quite the opposite. I figured out the less I talked to him, the less he would talk to me. "We about to smoke some weed or what?" He punched my shoulder and offered me some of his drink with the goofiest grin I'd ever seen.

I said no.

Allison: Yeah, but you're like his best friend, and I feel bad.

Me: For what?

Allison: For getting in the way of that.

Andre let me into his house and out to a metallic shed that looked like it was made during the Great Depression. I glanced inside, expecting cobwebs and dirt; instead, I saw a TV and three beanbag chairs. He had posters on the wall of some of the hottest girls I had ever seen. To be honest, I was impressed. The walls had been painted purple, and the darkness was illuminated by the bright, kinetic colors that leaked out of the television screen.

"This is cool." I stuck my head into observe even more. He had posters of busty girls in bikinis, he had black lights, and there was a wooden box on top of a glass coffee table in the middle of everything.

"You like that shit? I did it myself. This is about to be the fucking chill spot." He looked upon his work proudly.

We walked in and sat on the beanbag chairs. As soon as we were all settled, Andre reached for the wooden box. In it was a sandwich bag filled almost halfway with light green and slightly purple weed, two empty Swisher Sweets packets, and a bright blue glass sculpture. "You ever smoke out of a bowl?"

He opened the sandwich bag, grabbed a small piece from the large pile, ripped the bud into little pieces, and packed it into the bowl. "Here—hit this shit."

I studied it for a moment before he passed me his lighter.

"Just hold the carb, light the bud, and pull out smoke."

I assumed Andre meant the hole on the bowl, and I put my thumb over it and followed Andre's instructions. I inhaled nothing but marijuana smoke for almost ten seconds. When I started coughing, I passed it back to Andre and pulled out my phone.

Me: You're not. You're both my friends, and I'm not the type who picks sides.

Allison: You might not have a choice.

Once Andre had the bowl again, he began bragging about the weed he had. The scent was strong, and the aroma hit you as soon as the bag was open, but with all the smoke in the air, it was kind of hard to tell where the scent was coming from. Andre passed the bowl to Abel and took a big swig of his Kool-Aid.

Me: What do you mean?

The bowl had reached me once again; the weed inside was black and a little bit gray. I lit the bowl and pulled with all my might. I pulled so hard the ash shot to the back of my throat. I almost swallowed it. I spit it out as fast as I could and started coughing hysterically.

Andre and Abel did nothing but laugh. The taste was horrible. It tasted like I had just swallowed an ashtray.

"Shit. I could've told you it was cashed, bruh," Abel said in between laughs.

"Then why didn't you, asshole?" I said.

Before Abel could respond, I heard my phone buzz again.

Allison: You're his best friend; if we break up. we won't talk … not for a while at least.

I hated that. In high school, the two people in the relationship weren't the only people involved with the relationship. It could never just be the two people. Everybody had to have an opinion, everybody had to put their two cents in, and everybody was right. No wonder most high school relationships didn't last. It's like the two had to date each other—along with all their friends.

Me: That's not true—we'll still be friends.

"Yo, you know what I want to try?" Andre practically shouted. "A freaking gas mask. Dude, them things will get you so stoned, bro. It's not even funny."

I thought it strange how Andre knew the effects of a gas mask without having tried it himself.

Abel didn't seem too interested in either of us. He seemed pretty distant. It was not the type of distance you get from being high; it was the distance you get from the world when you're in pain.

I wasn't the only one who noticed.

"Abel! What's up, man? Why are you so quiet? Timmy is always quiet—I'll excuse him—but something seems wrong with you."

I sneered at Andre, but he paid me no attention.

Abel continued to stare at the floor.

Andre shouted, "Hey! Wake up, man. What's wrong with you?"

Abel finally snapped out of his daze and said, "Huh?"

"Y'all are blowing my high, man. Why are you so quiet?" He took another big sip from his cup, burped, and let the stench of his breath flow through the entire shed.

"Ain't nothing wrong with me, dawg." Abel took a huge pull from the bowl before passing it to me. I grabbed the bowl, set it on the table, and started to realize how high I was. The entire room was clouded; it was a miracle any of us could see, let alone breathe.

My eyelids began to feel unbearably heavy, and the sudden urge to laugh was slowly creeping up on me. My phone buzzed again, but I didn't bother to pick it up. I was too high to care. I felt like relaxing, and worrying about other people's problems wasn't exactly helping. Instead, I sat on my beanbag chair and stared at the roof of the shed as if it were a telescope that could see into the farthest galaxies of the universe. At that moment, it might as well have been a telescope. It was sort of beautiful—in a weird and probably terrible way. The smoke in the air floated around the shed in swirls so peacefully, and the light in the television, acting as some sort of strobe light, flashed a million different lights instantaneously.

At that moment, Andre decided to silence his TV and play music on his phone.

I felt my phone buzz again, but I decided to ignore it. Instead, I drowned out the rest of the world with Andre's loud rap music. It wasn't great, but it was something. I couldn't complain, and I thought it would be rude to insult a man's music selection. Andre was rapping along, Abel was nodding his head, and I couldn't help but join them. There wasn't anything in the song I could relate to. I didn't sell dope, didn't have stacks of money, and didn't have a ton of girls. The only thing I could say I had in common with whoever wrote the song was that we both spent most of our time smoking weed.

Andre was still rapping, and Abel started concentrating on the bowl.

I wanted to know how long we had been here. It felt like years, but when I checked the time, it had only been twenty minutes. I no longer wanted to be there—even though Charlie probably wanted more time. It felt like Andre and Abel were dragging it out. My chest hurt, my head was in the clouds, and all my worries had taken refuge in the emptiness of my mind. Why stay any longer? Honestly, I felt like lying in bed and going to sleep. I didn't want to walk with Abel, but I had to. I had to make sure he wouldn't catch on to what Charlie was doing. Then again, how could he? He looked so dumbfounded, but he was completely oblivious to what I was doing there. It was kind of cruel. I barely knew the kid, but he didn't seem like a bad guy.

My phone buzzed again, and I checked to make sure it wasn't Charlie. Allison and Charlie had texted me, and to make matters worse, Andrew had texted me as well. I was stoned, but I read all the text messages.

Allison: Thanks, Timmy. You're sweet—even though I know you're lying.

Charlie: Aye, bruh, come to the crib and bring the weed.

Andrew: Hey, dude, we need to talk.

I didn't want to reply to any of them, but Charlie's text indicated that I no longer had to be here.

"Hey, I'm about to be out," I announced as I gradually rose from my beanbag chair.

"I'll walk with you, dawg." Abel stood up as well.

Andre grabbed his bowl and handed it to me. "You want this bowl, man?" He dug in his pocket, gave me a little piece of bud wrapped in a sandwich bag, and stretched out his hand for the money.

Just like that, we said bye and were on our way.

The walk back was awful, but I didn't expect anything else. Everything, including myself, moved in such a horrid slow motion, and the trek back to Charlie's house seemed endless.

Abel didn't seem to mind. He was pretty quiet too, which made things kind of awkward.

"So, what is up with you? Why are you so quiet?" I wasn't wondering what was bothering him so much, but I wanted the silence to end.

"I don't know, man. I don't give a fuck anymore," he responded.

"About what?" I asked.

"People, man. You can't trust no-fucking-body, dawg, for real." Before I could ask him anything, he said, "Man, I went to Charlie's party the other day for a little bit. I know you were there, but this is what happened when you left." He stopped to light a cigarette. "Anyways, I was chilling right, and you know how I was with my girl, right?"

I nodded.

"Well, I was smoking in Charlie's house, and she was outside, right? Well, I'm chilling. I go outside, and I swear that fucker Amiel was flirting with Gina. I mean, I don't know for sure, but they was doing something alone. Man, I'm going to beat the fuck out him of him, man. I thought me and him was cool too, man." He concluded his story with a sigh and a puff of his cigarette.

It was a little ironic since Abel already had trust issues. I didn't know what kind of relationship he had with Charlie, but I knew he probably wouldn't take too kindly to him hitting on Gina. I knew Amiel was probably just trying to get lucky. I knew Amiel well enough to understand that he'd aim for any girl, taken or not. He was ruthless, which was why he was so successful.

"Gina doesn't seem like the type to cheat though," I said, trying to soothe him.

"Oh, I know she doesn't cheat. I trust her. It's everybody else I don't trust," he said.

We continued to walk in silence, and we barely said goodbye to each other when we split up. I tried to hurry to Charlie's house, but I was too high and too lazy to walk faster.

Just before I made it to Charlie's street, Andrew's car pulled up in front of me. He looked very upset.

"Shit," I said right before Andrew stepped out of his car.

"Hey, man. What are you doing?" he asked.

"Just walking to Charlie's place. What's up?" I sounded sober, but I knew that my eyes told him a different story.

He stared at me for a moment, didn't say a word, and didn't move a muscle. He squinted his eyes, clenched his jaw, and said, "Me and Allison broke up, but you're probably too high to care." He left without saying anything else and without a response from me. I had nothing to say. I watched as he sped off in a fit.

She did it? She broke up with him? If she didn't want to, why did she talk to me about it? Why pretend to be conflicted when you had already made your decision? The only real explanation was that the decision wasn't hers, but why would Andrew break it off with Allison? I felt less high and more confusion.

Josh walked up the street after leaving Charlie's place. "What's up, stoner boy?" His expression was indifferent.

"Nothing. I think my best friend hates me though." I chuckled to make it sound like I didn't care, but I did.

"He found out you got high?"

He knew the answer—so I had no clue why he asked—but I decided to respond to him anyway. "He saw me high. Just now." My high was vanishing almost as quickly as it came.

"Yeah, you looked pretty baked. See, that's why I like you, Timmy. You're not very good at hiding your emotions. If you're sad, you look sad. If you're happy, you look happy, and if you smoked, whether you smoked a lot or a little, you look high as fuck."

"Is that a good thing?" I asked.

"You tell me," he replied. "You know, Timmy, the best way to not look high for some people is to not be high."

"This coming from a guy who gets high all the time," I said.

"Hey, I know when to quit, and I know what I'm doing. The real question is if you do." He gave me a look I had never seen before. It was somewhere between empathy and indifference. This was a guy who cared enough to try to analyze my life, but he didn't care enough to worry about it.

"No, not really, but does anybody? How can you say you know what you're doing if you smoke all the time?" I asked.

"Like I said, I know when to quit. I'm only a stoner when I want to be. That is the difference between me and all the addicts. I like addicts though. I like their dream."

"What dream?"

"Hollywood," he said. "They all want Hollywood."

I gave him a questioning look.

"Haven't you ever noticed that Hollywood stars and people like us often die the same way? You know, overdose, suicides, it's all the same. Why? To us, those stars are immortal; to us, those stars have it all. They have what we only dream of. They have the American dream. Hollywood is heaven for people like you and me, but isn't it strange that even those guys have something missing—something they need to fill. Oh, but when they do it, it's cool. It's funny. So, why can't we do it? The people who have it all do the same drugs that I do. And I want a taste of immortality. I want a taste of what they have. A taste of Hollywood. A taste of heaven. If you can't live to be a star, why not die like one?" He looked down the scar on his palm; it reached from his wrist up to his middle finger. "The world can be a nasty place. Life is going to hit hard, and worrying about your friend judging you isn't going to soften the blow." He lifted his hand and showed me the scar. "Hollywood isn't worth it." He turned to walk away.

I stopped him and said, "Hey, wait. How'd you get the scar? I never noticed it before." I had to know how he had gotten that scar, mainly because I had to know something about Josh. He had so many opinions about my life when I knew nothing of his.

"Another time, Timmy. Another time." Josh turned and walked away.

I stood there pondering my life and his. I was questioning my existence along with everyone else's. I was so stoned; it was easy to get lost in my head. It was so easy to drown out the world.

The reality is that the world and everyone in it was just a bunch of noise. It was noise that clouded your thoughts and opinions—just so you can try to agree with theirs. It's a loud collaboration of sob stories. It's a collection of satire, irony, and bad jokes. The noise is meant to distract you; it's meant to blur the line between reality and fantasy. It makes you think the drama that surrounds you matters. As I was staring down Charlie's street, the weed finally silenced the world. I began to realize what this whole endeavor was coming to. I began to realize that I was losing myself. I realized that Josh was right. I was chasing Hollywood. I suppose I had to be high to understand what he meant, but I understood. I was too busy chasing love and fantasies to see that my life might be falling apart. The strange thing was that I didn't care. I was analyzing my life the same way Josh was—with complete and utter indifference. I realized Charlie and Gina would never work. Andrew and Allison weren't working, and Sophia and I would never happen. I stood there and didn't care. I suppose I should've been happy to finally be released from all the stress, but it wasn't happiness. It was numbness.

I finally snapped out my daze when I realized I probably looked weird just standing on the corner of the road. I walked across the street as soon as the coast was clear.

My phone buzzed, but I decided to ignore it and just walk across. I had enough bullshit for one day.

Once I arrived at Charlie's apartment complex, he was outside smoking a cigarette. He wore an enormous and annoying grin, along with a tank top that was drenched in sweat.

"Did you have fun?" I asked sarcastically.

He responded with a mischievous grin and a shrug of the shoulders. "Yeah, I guess." He continued to smoke his cigarette and looked completely satisfied, and I stood there feeling less high and guiltier. I looked at my friend with a sense of disgust that was buried under all the fears I had of becoming like him. I had lost my best friend—what was next?

Charlie suffered losses far heavier than my own, and just when you think people become better from their trials, here Charlie was. I guess that's what was to become of all us who were willing to go down the same road as Charlie.

"I think I should stop smoking," I said as the thought arrived in my head.

Charlie responded with such unbearable indifference, "Me too, Timmy. Me too."

9
CHAPTER

Charlie and I hung out on his steps for about fifteen minutes before we decided to go back to his room. He didn't tell me much about what he did with Gina, and I didn't want to know. As I sat down on Charlie's computer chair, I decided to pull out my phone. Allison had texted me.

Allison: We broke up.

I sighed and put down the phone. When I realized the bowl was still in my pocket, I pulled it out to inspect it. It was small and glossy, and it had the texture of a clay plate, like the ones we'd make in art class. I was a bright blue with a single poorly drawn dolphin. I liked it because it was something I could smoke out of—and it was all mine.

"Yo, where'd you get that?" Charlie asked as he pulled out a Swisher Sweet packet from his pocket.

"Andre gave it to me," I replied.

"Keep that shit close. You never know when you're going to need something to smoke out of." Charlie continued to break down the cigar. I took the weed that Andre gave me and put it on Charlie's desk. I realized I had been smoking all day. I was exhausted and wanted rest. "Hey, man. I'm going to head out." I stood up to leave.

"All right, man. Hit me up tomorrow so we can do this shit again."

I walked out without another word. I didn't know how late it was, but since I knew I was going to sleep as soon as I went home, I was already starting to dread school. Andrew was pissed, and Allison was doing her duties as a female and confusing the hell out of me. Nevertheless, I knew I couldn't miss another day.

When I got home. my mother was sipping her coffee and reading a book on the couch. She looked up at me as I walked in the door and then returned her gaze to her book. "Do you have homework?"

"I didn't go to school, Mom," I responded.

"Well, you better have homework tomorrow," she said as she continued to read her book.

"Yes, ma'am." I chuckled before entering my room.

"Hey," she said as she looked up at me. "I love you."

I looked back with the warmest smile I could imitate. "I love you too, Mom."

I stepped into my room and locked the door behind me. I didn't want my epic slumber to be interrupted. I stared at the ceiling, and my exhaustion drew me nearer and nearer to unconsciousness. I was dreading the day ahead.

I woke up feeling the same way I did the first night I smoked. I wanted to roll over to sleep more, but the noise coming from my mother banging on the door prevented that from happening. I made a valiant effort to get up and get ready for school. I was tired and was running late. Instead of taking the time to carry out my entire morning routine, I threw on a new shirt, grabbed my bookbag, and walked out the door.

I hated walking to school because it was a mile away—and it took me twenty minutes to arrive at a place I don't want to be. The walk often gave me quiet time to think and listen to music, but the three textbooks in my bookbag made it almost impossible to make it to school without breaking a sweat.

It was a pretty standard morning. The sun was barely visible among all the clouds, and a cool breeze whistled through the air, making for a cool spring morning. On my journey to school, I saw a figure in the distance. The person was wearing a gray tank top, but it was hard to tell from far away. It looked like Charlie. As I approached, he started to look more and more like Charlie. He threw his hands up in the air and shouted my name, and I realized it was Charlie. I returned his gesture by throwing up the peace sign and continued walking.

"What's up, man?" he shouted when he finally reached me.

"Going to school. Where are you going?" I asked once I realized he was walking in the opposite direction of the school.

"I'm going to get fucked up! Hit me up after school," he said as he walked past me in a hurry to get to wherever he was going.

I turned and continued my journey to school. I wasn't in a hurry, but I could hear the first bell ring from distance, and I started walking faster. I was just about to reach the rec center when I noticed Allison sitting in her car. She drove a blue Dodge Avenger; she hardly used it since Andrew always drove her to school. She was staring at her steering wheel, and she wasn't moving. It looked like she was crying.

I walked up and knocked on the window. I knew I was late to school, but if I was going to be late, I might as well be late as fuck. I walked up to the car and knocked lightly on the windshield. She finally looked up and saw me. She unlocked the door and motioned for me to come inside. I opened the door and sat down in the passenger seat.

"Yeah, I know. Mondays suck," I said.

Her cheeks were bright red and wet from all the tears, and her eyes were glossy enough to make me think she was stoned.

"It's Tuesday, Timmy," she responded.

"Damn, really?" I kept an awkward smile, and my eyes on hers, even though she wouldn't look at me.

"I don't want to go school," she whispered. "I don't want to talk about it either." She finally turned and looked me in the eye. I knew it was about Andrew, but I didn't see the point of making her feel worse by explaining what happened.

"Fuck school!" she said.

"You can always skip, you know. What's one day?" I didn't exactly know what to say to make her feel better, but she looked devastated. Also, convincing someone that school isn't going to be excruciating is a lot harder than telling them to just go home.

"But I never skipped before," she responded between sniffles.

"Well, there's a first for everything," I said as I shrugged my shoulders.

"Will you come with me?" she asked.

"What?"

"Will you skip school with me?" She looked me dead in the eye, and it felt like she was trying to see into my soul. She also had a different look in her eyes. She looked unsure of herself. It was as if she was judging whether she could confide in me. I honestly didn't want to go to school, so agreeing to it didn't feel like a problem.

"You don't have to," she said.

"No, it's okay. I'll come. Like I said, I hate Mondays."

She cracked a smile at my joke, but it quickly faded. She took a deep breath and turned the keys to start the car. She slowly turned onto the street, and we drove in silence for almost ten minutes. She concentrated on the road and just drove. I didn't know if she had a destination, but I thought it better not to question anything. She focused so hard on the road. It was as if the simple act of driving the vehicle was helping her calm down.

I wasn't doing anything to make her feel better either, but I didn't know what to do.

"I don't know where we're going," she finally said with a little laugh.

I smiled and laughed along with her.

"I never skipped school before," she said between sniffles.

"Where do you want to go?" I asked as I rolled down the window.

"I don't know. I couldn't go to school. I didn't plan this out." She stopped to look at me again. It was just a glance, but time slowed down enough for me to notice how beautiful she looked under that mask of sadness. Her eyes still sparkled from the tears that she would not allow to fall onto her cheek. It was funny how—even in the shadow of a gloomy situation—her presence welcomed mine. It always would. Being around her made me want to be around her, and hearing her voice made me empathize with her. I didn't know why she and Andrew broke up, and I also didn't know how he managed to hurt her so badly.

"My mom should be at work by now ... if you just want to go there," she said.

"Sure, whatever you want," I responded softly.

She half-smiled and continued to stare at the road.

We drove the rest of the way in almost complete silence. A part of me felt a little bit guilty for skipping school again, especially after that long, agonizing lecture about how important school was. I knew there wasn't a way to escape another lecture, but being around Allison made it easy to bite the bullet.

Once we arrived in her neighborhood, she began to slow down, keeping a sharp eye out for her mother. We pulled up quietly to her street, but we didn't even get close to her house until Allison was sure her mother wasn't home.

We pulled into the driveway, and Allison stopped the car and took another deep breath. She wasn't crying or sniffling anymore, but she still managed to look depressed.

"I've never had a guy over here before," she said as she opened her door.

"Well, I guess we're breaking all the rules today, huh?"

She smiled as she stepped out of the car.

I got out and followed her to the front door. She juggled her car keys before finding the right key to open her door. Once she did, she let me into her home—and I was jumped by a very small dog.

"Who's this?" I asked as I knelt to pet the adorable puppy.

"That's John Lennon."

I stopped and gave her a questioning look. "John Lennon?" I asked.

She shrugged and responded, "My mom likes the Beatles." She set her keys down on the kitchen counter and walked into what was probably her bedroom. I walked into her living room, sat on the couch, and stared at an enormous TV that almost took up the entire wall. I didn't even need to see it on to be amazed by it.

As I admired her TV, Allison stepped out of her room wearing short boy shorts and a light green tank top. Her body was perfect. I didn't know if I was starting to feel for her, but looking at her now, it seemed like the best idea.

"What do you want to watch?" she asked.

"Whatever you do, I guess," I responded.

She looked at me with another questioning look.

I had no idea how to talk to her. She needed me at that very moment, but that was almost the last thing in my mind. The first thing was that she was vulnerable.

"What happened?" I asked, finally addressing the situation.

She looked at her TV like the answer to my question would be on there. I could read her like a magazine; she wanted to tell me something, but she was troubled by the decision to trust me.

"I didn't fit right into his plan anymore," she said.

I tried to look into her eyes, but every time I did, she would look away.

"What do you mean?" I knew she wanted to talk about it; otherwise, why was I there? It was strange. I assumed Allison had her own friends and her own people to tell everything. Why was she sharing a best friend with her ex?

"I don't know. I guess he wanted someone perfect. I wasn't that. He decided to leave. I told him I wanted to work it out, but he left. He said he never wanted to see me again." She looked like she was ready to cry again.

"I don't get it. He used to adore you," I said to make her feel a little bit better.

"Well, I guess I changed," she replied.

"What did you do?" I asked.

"It's not what I did—and that's what hurts the most. He left me alone, and it wasn't my fault." She started to tear up again.

I didn't know what to say to her. I stood up and sat by her side.

She wiped the tears away, looked at me, and took a deep breath. "How's your day going?"

"It's fine, I guess," I mumbled.

She said, "What did the weed feel like?"

I wasn't too sure how I was supposed to describe it, especially to someone who had never smoked before.

"I don't know. It was really weird. Time like slows down, and you just feel like happy and giggly," I responded.

"I bet that'd be nice, for even a little while, to just feel good," she said.

"Yeah, it's pretty great."

We sat in silence for an awkward moment, both trying to find things to discuss other than Andrew.

"Can I ask you something?" she said.

"Go ahead."

"Why do you like Sophia so much?"

I paused for a moment before I responded. If Andrew or Amiel had asked, I'd present them with a long list of reasons why I was head over heels for her. Since it was Allison who asked, and although the list was easy to remember, I had a strange feeling that repeating it wouldn't be answering her question. "I don't know. I guess I do," I replied timidly.

"Do you even really know her?" she asked.

It hit me like a rock. It finally hit me. I didn't know her—not even a little. I was clueless about her, and she was clueless about me. I suddenly felt a little embarrassed. I felt like a foolish child chasing fantasies. "No." It was all I could say after chasing the same girl for years.

"Why is it so easy for some of us to fall in love?" She returned her sad gaze to the ground.

"Maybe we are just wired that way," I said.

"So, you're saying that some of us were just born stupid? Great insight, Timmy."

"No, maybe some of us just feel more than everybody else does. That kind of makes us special in a way, I guess," I replied.

"Is being special worth feeling the pain?" she retorted.

"I guess that's up to you," I answered.

She looked away from me. "I used to think we all felt the same pain. Why is everybody else so numb to it now?"

"Maybe they are just used to it. Maybe they just hurt so much that they can't feel it anymore."

"So, wouldn't it be better if we joined the rest of the world and just stopped caring?"

"Maybe we will. Maybe, one day, it just stops, we say fuck love, fuck people, and just do our best to stay alive," I responded.

"Maybe?" she said. "You seem so unsure."

"I am unsure," I said.

"How come, guys, like you get tossed to the curb?" she asked.

I shrugged my shoulders. "You wouldn't want to date a scrawny guy who smokes weed?"

"No, but if he's nice enough to randomly skip school with you, then it wouldn't be so bad." She smiled shyly, stood up, and walked into her kitchen. She started to pull out pots and pans from under her kitchen sink and set them lightly on the stove. "You hungry?"

I thought for a moment and realized I'd missed breakfast. I still felt a little full from the day before, but there was no way in hell I was missing the opportunity to have a beautiful girl cook for me. "Sure, you know how to cook?"

"Duh, I used to babysit my nephews all the time." She pulled a carton of eggs, butter, milk, a packet of cheese, and a couple strips of bacon out of the fridge.

"I didn't know you had nephews," I said.

"Yeah, they live with my sister in Florida. They visit during the summer, and I would be forced to take care of them. It used to be annoying having to watch a bunch of kids, but then I got good at it, and I even started liking it. I like it when they visit now; they make me feel grown." She poured milk into the blender, chopped up bananas, and dropped them into the blender with strawberries, sugar, and ice cubes.

"You know how to make smoothies too?" I was impressed; it looked like she was about to treat me to a feast.

"I can do a lot of stuff. My mom used to bring me to her job at a juice bar, and when they were slow, she would let me help her make some of the smoothies." She looked content as she cooked; it was easy to see she wasn't lying. It looked as though making a little breakfast made her feel better.

"How come I didn't know you could do all this before?"

"You never asked." She smiled at me, and it was such a pleasant smile that it almost fooled me. I was almost tricked by her brilliant and well-rehearsed performance. It was her eyes that gave her away. I could see the pain in her eyes, but she hid it well. I was empathizing with her because I knew she was masking her tears with a smile. That's how she dealt with things. She didn't do drugs, and she didn't drink; she forced a smile onto her face to keep from looking broken. She bit the bullet until the wounds eventually healed. She didn't hide behind the effects of marijuana; she hid behind a beautiful smile. That's when I realized I wasn't there to give her advice, to tell her what to do, or to fix any problem. I was just there to tell her one thing: "You're going to be all right, Allison."

She stopped and looked up and said, "How do you know?"

"I do."

She did not smile or frown; she nodded.

Once she was done cooking, she led me into the living room and set the plates on the coffee table. She poured the smoothies into blue plastic cups with a straw and a little umbrella.

"Wow, fancy," I commented.

"I told you I know how to do stuff." She took a sip of her drink and flipped through the channels.

Just as I was about to dig into my food, my phone buzzed. I decided to ignore it.

Once Allison got tired of flipping through channels, she turned off the TV. She started eating her food, and I joined her. Just as I was about to dig in, my phone buzzed. It was Charlie. I decided that Charlie could wait. It didn't take much to read the text, but if it was anything about weed, I knew it would encourage me to leave her alone and go smoke. I put down my phone and started eating Allison's delicious breakfast. "This is really good," I mumbled as I chewed.

"Yeah, I know." She gave me a confident smile.

We started talking about how much the cartoons had changed since we were younger. We talked for hours about almost nothing; it was hard to keep up with the conversation since the subject was always changing. I started to notice stuff about Allison I hadn't noticed before. She was so much more than just another pretty face. It was like she had no idea who she was. Everything she told me about herself that was impressive and amazing, she shrugged off as if everybody could do the things she could do. She knew how to play the piano, she knew how to cook, she knew how to dance, and she was a certified lifeguard, and what blew my mind was that this wonderful girl, who could do so many things, was still insecure. She wondered about herself and whether she was good enough, but I couldn't understand who she was trying to impress. She wondered about me too. It was difficult to answer questions about myself when the only thing I knew how to do was smoke.

When it was my turn to uncover my roots, it became a conversation about the effects of weed. I told her how many times I have smoked with Charlie.

"So, why do you smoke so much now?" she asked.

"I don't know. I do."

"Yeah, but I feel like there's more to it, you know. It's easy to say that you do something because it feels good, but that isn't the reason you do it all the time. Like, people can drink and not be alcoholics. Is it that good of a high?"

"I can't even describe it. Before I hit the blunt, the problems I thought were such a big deal weren't even problems anymore. When I'm high, that's all there is, and it's like the rest of the world can't get to me. Of course, I know how bad everything is getting and how bad I'm getting, but when

I'm high, I feel all right." I was proud to conjure up a well-thought-out answer as opposed to not being able to respond.

"I want to try it," she said.

I suddenly had a rush of déjà vu. "Why?" I asked.

"Because I want to feel all right."

10

CHAPTER

I had Allison drop me off at Charlie's house when it was time for her mom to come home. She came home almost thirty minutes before school let out, but the radio predicted heavy traffic. By the time we reached Charlie's apartments, kids were being let out of school. As she pulled into a parking space, I noticed Josh sitting on the stairs. Allison and I exchanged goodbyes, and I stepped out of her car. I almost didn't notice Cole walking up the stairs. Allison pulled away, and Cole gave me a sinister look.

"Damn. She bad. That your girl?" Cole said with an evil smile slapped across his face.

"Nah," I responded.

He nodded and watched her drive away. "You need to bring her around here more. Save a little for the team." He started chuckling at his joke. I looked at him a little disgusted but shrugged it off.

We walked up the stairs together, and Josh greeted us with a nod.

Charlie was eating a hamburger on his couch and laughing at some ridiculous cartoon. "Timmy, what the fuck is up? How was school?" He leaped up and walked to his room.

"I didn't go," I said as I followed him to his room.

"Fucking asshole, I knew it. Why didn't you come through?" He continued laughing. His eyes were glazed and bloodshot, his words were slurred, and his puny filter, which kept him from going too far, seemed to be gone.

"I was at my friend's house." I sat nervously on Charlie's bed.

"He was at a bitch's house," Cole interrupted obnoxiously.

"Oh, shit. Timmy's getting ass!" Charlie started rolling on the floor and laughing hysterically.

"I thought for the longest you were going to be gay!" Charlie said.

Cole and Charlie seemed to be in the same state of mind. Josh and I were the only ones not laughing.

"Nah, for real though," Charlie said. "Did you pipe?"

"Pipe?" I asked.

"Did you fuck?" Cole interpreted.

The rooms got quiet just long enough for me to answer, "No."

Charlie and Cole burst out laughing again.

Josh still hadn't even chuckled. He shrugged, pulled out a cigarillo from his pocket, and started breaking it in half with his nails.

"How do you go over to the bitch's house for a full school day and not pipe?" asked Cole.

"No, hold on. Answer me this. Are you a virgin?" Charlie looked me in the eye.

I didn't give them a response, but they didn't need me to. He waited for me to answer his question, and when I didn't, he started laughing again.

"She broke up with my best friend," I said.

"That's perfect. That's when you're supposed to swoop in and ..." Charlie put his hands out in front of him and started humping the air as he laughed like an idiot.

"I didn't want to do that to her." For a second, it sounded like I was making excuses about why Allison and I had never done it.

"Bullshit. You're going to tell me that you hung around that sexy-ass girl for all that time and didn't once think about fucking," Cole said.

I paused for a moment and realized that he was right, but who could blame me? She was gorgeous, and sex was what I thought about more than anything. I mean, I was a guy after all. "Well, yeah, but she wouldn't do that," I retorted.

"You know what your problem is?" Charlie paused for effect. "You have no game!"

They exploded with laughter again. Even Josh couldn't help but laugh. I felt humiliated.

"Yo, I'm about to go to the corner store to get us some forties," Charlie announced.

"I'm going to go with you. I need a cig. You want to wait for the blunt?" Cole stood up.

"I got more. You good," Josh said.

Charlie and Cole shrugged and walked out of the room.

Josh finished up the blunt, turned to me, and said, "Don't sweat it, kid. We were all virgins once."

"Allison wouldn't do that though; she's a good person," I responded.

He lit a blunt and blew out a smoke ring. After hitting it one more time, he passed it to me. "So, sex makes someone a bad person? If that's true, the whole world is fucked up."

"The world is fucked up," I replied.

"Touché."

I hit the blunt, slowly pulling the smoke in. As I released the smoke, I could feel the relief of my worries melting away.

"I'll tell you what. I saw that girl, and she's better than all the hos those two dumbasses fuck with." I passed the blunt back to Josh, and he hit it twice before returning it to me.

"Yeah, but how do I even get to that point? We'd have to go out, and it'd be awkward," I said between coughs.

"You make shit so difficult. Do you think sex is that complicated? People meet the person once and fuck that same night. Then, after no relationship—nothing—just on to the next one." Josh pulled out his phone and started texting.

"Yeah, but Allison isn't like that." I wanted to defend Allison. I didn't know what kind of girls Charlie and Josh were exposed to, but I knew Allison wasn't like that.

"She will be—one day—they always are." Josh took another pull from the blunt like a Mafia member would pull smoke from a Cuban cigar.

"Great, so every guy who smokes is a stoner, and every girl who has sex is a ho. For a second, I thought you were smart. You're just a pessimist."

Josh chuckled and passed the blunt back to me. "I'm not a pessimist. I'm a realist. If you smoked as much as I do, you would be too."

I sighed just before inhaling a massive amount of smoke and erupting into a series of uncontrollable coughs.

"Easy there, you dope fiend," Josh said sarcastically. "Look, all I'm saying is if you smoke weed, you do it more than once, the same with sex. You can maybe make an argument with the weed, but with sex, that's always true. And a girl who has sex isn't always a ho, you know. We have those parts for a reason."

Josh had a point, but to be completely honest, I hated when Josh had a point. I returned the blunt to Josh.

"Look, man. I've been there before, believe me. You think that shit on TV and in movies is real, but not out here. Not anywhere really. A relationship isn't anything but a pain in the ass, and in the end, you have to decide what's worth sacrificing: your heart or hers." Josh took a long pull from the blunt.

I thought he would have been coughing hysterically from the amount of smoke he inhaled, but he was giving me an emotionless look.

Before I could reply, Charlie and Cole came walking through the door.

"Damn, that shit smells good," Charlie said as he reached for the blunt. He hit it twice before passing it to Cole.

"Yo, Timmy. Call Abel." Charlie sat down on his bed and made himself comfortable.

"For what?" I asked. I didn't want to call Abel.

"You know why, motherfucker. Call him!" he yelled.

I sighed, pulled out my phone, and dialed Abel's number. I waited as the phone rang and rang until Abel picked up.

"Yo," he said.

"Yo, it's Timmy. What are you doing?" I asked, not knowing anything else to say.

"Shit. Chilling. What's good with you?" he replied.

I paused for a second, not knowing what to say. I wasn't exactly used to deceiving people.

"Yo, just ask if he wants to go to Andre's or something," Charlie said.

"Yo, you want to go hit up Andre?" I asked.

"Shit, yeah. I guess meet me at the same spot." Abel hung up the phone.

"Yeah!" Charlie yelled. "I'm about to get ass."

I looked away and shook my head.

Josh did the same and gave me the rest of the blunt. "Here ... take this. He's going to want to match you."

"Match?" I gave Josh a questioning look.

"That means he's going to want to smoke your weed too—not just his. Damn, this kid doesn't know anything." Cole chuckled to himself.

I stood up, left the room, and started walking toward the end of the street.

As I left Charlie's apartment complex, I began to notice how worn down his place was. There was sort of a dark presence, a sort of sadness about it. The people I saw there were the same every time, and they were always doing the same thing. They all sat right in front of their homes smoking cigarettes or drinking beer. They all looked out at the world around them with weary eyes. Life had taken a toll on these people, and for a second, I thought it was a product of being a minority. I realized they were all different colors, shapes, and nationalities. Some were black, some were white, and some were Latino, but they all were suffering losses. As I walked past them, they all nodded at me, greeting me in a way, but it seemed to be something more than that. They all looked at me with the same indifferent look that Josh gave me. They all gave me that judgmental look as if they all knew the dark path I was walking on. As if they all had walked that same path before. These were lost souls feeling empathy for the next person walking straight into the depths of hell. That next person was me.

Once I left the apartment complex, I met Abel earlier than I expected.

"Yo, what's up?" he said as he approached me.

"Nothing. What's up?" I answered.

"Shit, chilling. Yo, I called Andre. He said he had some people coming over to smoke, but you've got to have bud." He puffed on his cigarette and showed me the stash he had in his pocket.

I pulled out the half of the blunt Josh had given me and showed it to Abel.

He nodded his head and said, "That'll work."

We started walking to Andre's house. We walked in silence for most of the way. Abel wasn't much of a talker, but he wasn't difficult to read. He looked like the simplest guy you could think of. He probably liked working on cars and wanted nothing more out of life than to just live. I felt sorry for him. Gina seemed to mean a lot to him from what I could tell at the party.

"How are you and Gina?" I asked.

"Shit, we good. I'm still trying to figure out whether Amiel was trying to fuck with her or not, but I don't know, bruh. I lost her for like a good twenty minutes at that damn party. I keep asking her about it, but she's starting to act shady." He took another hit from his cigarette and shook his head. "I don't know, man. Maybe I should just leave this girl alone."

"Gina doesn't seem to be so bad though; she seems sweet," I said, giving my honest opinion about her.

"Shit, all these bitches look sweet, but they end up being hos, bruh. That shit happened to me too many times. I should know better, dawg." He had a disappointing look on his face.

As we approached Andre's house, I noticed two cars and a moped. I could smell the weed before I even reached the backyard. I knew almost no one there except for Andre, Abel, and the Riley brothers. I was never really comfortable with parties; I was always the more awkwardly quiet type. Then again, no one could peg me as a stoner until just a few days ago. It was weird to think about how quickly the people around me were changing. Abel did look entirely thrilled to be there either. He looked like he was worried about his girlfriend. I didn't know what Charlie and Gina were doing right then, and to be honest, I didn't care. The only thing I could worry about was how I was going to survive the party.

Looking around, I realized I didn't like any of these people. Andrew and I would try to avoid them. They were all loud, rude, and stuck up, and they were all drunk. They all carried themselves with such arrogance; an angel could descend from heaven and not be able to convince them that they were fucked up. To put it frankly, the girls were shallow, and the guys were dumb.

Andre came stumbling toward me with a cup of Kool-Aid. "Yo, Timmy what's up!" He hugged me, damn near tackling me to the ground.

"What's up?" I asked, doing my best to hide my annoyance.

"Yo, we all about to get fucked up! Here, drink some." He motioned me toward his drink. I didn't know what was in his drink, but by the stench of his breath, I could easily guess it was alcoholic. I shook my head, and he shrugged and finished his drink in one big gulp. He left me to go find more entertaining guests. I stood there and watched everyone else having fun. Just as I started to dread the party, an easily recognizable voice lightened up my mood.

"Yo, Timmy. What's good?" Amiel was holding a beer can. His eyes were redder than a demon, and his crooked smile and wavy movements were evidence of his alcohol consumption.

"What's up, Amiel?" I was genuinely happy to see him—even if he was drunk.

Abel was a buzzkill, and Andre was too much buzz.

"Yo, I'm chilling. You know me. I'm going to be real with you though. You look like you don't want to be here on some shit." He took a sip of his beer.

"Yeah, I'm not the party type," I said nervously.

"Shit. I can tell. You know what your problem is? You're too stiff. You need to chill out. Yo, relax. Walk over to that cooler, grab yourself a beer, and start fucking with one of these bitches."

I didn't feel comfortable partying with a bunch of people I didn't like, but Amiel sounded so convincing. I walked over to the cooler and grabbed a beer. Amiel motioned for me to drink it. I opened the can, took a sip of the bitter liquid, and then made a sour face.

"Ha! Yo, you're a fucking freshman with this shit. Yo, it's straight. We about to get hella fucked up." He laughed.

From that point on, the entire night was a blur. There were too many people talking, and even I was talking without truly knowing what it was about. I had been drunk before, but the way Amiel drank was almost inhuman.

Andre didn't limit the party to beers and weed; he had hard liquor as well. There were two big bottles of liquor on a little table in front of the cooler. Once Amiel was aware of that, he insisted I take shots with him.

Amiel was a monster when it came to liquor. He would chug the bottle while everyone was cheering him on. He drank it like it was water. He began to encourage me to drink, but I wasn't sure if I wanted to. I was unable to feel anything. I knew Andrew was mad. I knew Allison was hurt, but after a few shots with Amiel, I couldn't care less. It was almost as good as weed. I couldn't care about anything—even if I wanted to. Everything became a blur. All of my words and all of their words—the entire world— became a blur. The liquor hit harder than the weed and quicker too.

Amiel was already drunk, but he kept drinking with me as if he wasn't. I knew I was drunk after the third shot, but Amiel was relentless. He insisted I keep drinking whether I wanted to drink or not. The more I drank, the more I became a senseless robot. It was as if the words coming out of my mouth were just static. Static was the only way to describe it. I felt hollow, and everything around me was happening on its own. Everything became a blur, and lost touch with myself without really losing who I was. It was as if I was on autopilot. My subconscious started to take over, and who I thought I was became nothing but a fantasy. Who I was, began to come into the light, and I wasn't ready for it—and neither was anybody else. They rejected my sly comments and my observations and decided it was nothing but drunk talk from a drunk asshole.

To be completely honest, they were probably right. I was too drunk to understand the difference between right and wrong. All I knew was the blur; it was the only thing that was real. The blur was the only thing that truly existed. Everything I said and did was nothing but a fantasy; it was nothing but a thing in the past. As soon as I did one thing or said one thing, it was gone. I was incomprehensive. It was as if this was the leeway I was finally waiting for—to say what I wanted to say and do what I wanted to do. In the morning, my excuse could be validated by the fact that I was drunk. I said whatever I wanted, when I wanted, and it felt good. I couldn't filter any of my words or thoughts—even if I tried. I suddenly became a talkative asshole without fully realizing it.

Amiel was the same way, but he wasn't talking as much as I was. When he did talk, he would rant. To be honest, his drunken rants made more sense than anything I was talking about, but no one was listening but me. As drunk as I was, I could hear what he was saying. I understood where he was coming from. He made it easy to do that, but everyone else wrote it off as nothing but drunken talk.

"Yo, like on the real though, this race shit has existed forever. Like, yo listen," he said above all the chatter and laughter. "Yo, like, think about that shit, though like for so many years, that shit had people tripping. Like for real, think about it. How many rappers and like black comedians drew inspiration from that shit. Like, when it's on TV as a joke, people think it's just that. It's a joke that isn't real. Cops don't do that shit. They didn't think that that shit was real, and it is.

"People talk about MLK and that shit, the freedom march, they teach us that in school like that shit is history. Like that shit just ended racism as a whole, like what people don't understand is that we still living that.

Like before things were worse, I understand that, but just because that's true doesn't mean shit is good now. If you go from eating shit every day to drinking piss, like is that any better? Now, people pulling out phones on these pigs, and the news is finally broadcasting that shit, like why? What is different now than before? Before when police were shooting us down like animals, nobody gave a fuck, but now when the media can make money off that shit, they broadcast it everywhere and amp that shit up. Like why everybody so mad for? This is just life for us, man, this is just the shit that we have to go through." He took a sip of his beer.

"Shit, and people are always like 'Oh, but there are good cops out there' and I'm like, bitch, where? Like, yeah, you right, there are some good cops, but to me and all these motherfuckers living in the hood, that will never be true. You know good cops, you pale-faced motherfucker? I've lived for nineteen years and still haven't met one. I know people who died, like why? Why are we the ones getting shot and shit? Why are we the hoodlums? Why are we the people who have to deal with crooked cops and ghettoes, man? My backyard ain't this damn big. I don't have two cars in the driveway. What the hell do I have to do for this shit? 'Cause I'll do that shit. But the way, I see there isn't anything that you white motherfuckers do that I don't do. You smoke, me too, you drink, I do too, you like fucking bitches, I do too. The only difference that will ever matter is the color of my skin, that's real."

Just like that, it was over. Just like that, everything he said turned into smoke. Nobody was truly listening; they were all too drunk to care. Amiel didn't seem to mind though. After he was done ranting, he was back to drinking, smoking, and just being part of the party.

I was left standing there, mesmerized by his reality as opposed to mine.

We continued partying for almost an hour, but I felt like we had been there forever. I didn't know what to do with myself. I was so drunk. I just wanted to lie down for a minute. My head was spinning, I felt dizzy, and I felt like I couldn't stomach any more alcohol. That didn't stop Amiel from pouring more shots.

After I took the sour, painful shot, Josh, Charlie, and Cole walked through the gate. I didn't know what Charlie was doing here—I honestly thought he would be with Gina—but he was high as hell and ready to party.

I really couldn't leave; the only place I could go was Charlie's, and he was right there. I didn't want to go home; facing my mother was the last thing I wanted to do. Even though the party had started to make me nauseous, I decided it wouldn't hurt to stay a little bit longer. Charlie looked like he was already drunk.

Amiel approached me with another shot. "Yo, take this shit. You've got to get right, bruh." He clumsily handed me the shot.

I stopped in my tracks to take the shot, but in my peripheral vision, I could see the three of them walking into Andre's shed. They went to smoke, and I wanted to find out what Charlie was doing with Gina, but then I decided it was too much work. I didn't care what he was doing with her; at that point, I was just trying my best to even walk straight. Amiel was drunk and thrilled with the fact that he had gotten me drunk. When I first hit that blunt, I was looking for a release, a break, an excuse not to care about anything—even if it was for a few hours.

Being consumed by a blur was fun. It was fun when nothing made sense. It was fun when nothing mattered.

My phone buzzed three times in my pocket, but I didn't even think to answer it. It was too much work to grab my phone from my pocket. I didn't know who could be texting or why, but I didn't care. The only thing that mattered was the blur. It was a cloud, it was a hazy vision, it was talking about nothing, and it was a lot of yelling, flirting, and laughing. It was nonsense, but it was bliss. It was the kiss of relief; it was something so beautiful that it had to be ugly. It had to be an illusion. Nothing like that could exist in the real world. We were all facing the same issues, were all outcasts, and we had all decided as a unit that we didn't care. We had decided that we were going to have fun whether the people in our past or present judged us or not.

The only way to truly describe it was by calling it beautiful chaos. It was a dream that wasn't happening; it was bringing the magic of the nonexistent to reality. It was not by what we were doing but by how we felt. We finally put to rest all of our curiosities; we finally knew the secrets that had been hidden from us for so many years. It was the most elegant discovery; that was what our parents, teachers, and authorities tried to keep us away from. That was what they sheltered us from, but they couldn't stop us from feeling the real world. They couldn't stop us from feeling all right.

They couldn't keep their secret to themselves. We finally understood what they didn't want to tell us, but none of us understood why.

Why keep something that feels this good away from us? What are you afraid of? What is the monster that you keep hidden? I couldn't put my finger on it, and by looks of it, nobody else could either. We were all just chaotic, mischievous outcasts, and we loved it. We loved the blur.

CHAPTER

11

After the party, I was left with the curse of walking home. Charlie, Josh, and Amiel decided to stay, but I couldn't take it anymore. I had to get some rest; standing had drained so much energy from me, and I couldn't take it anymore.

The walk home was as dreadful as I expected. I had to focus so much on not looking drunk as I walked down the street that it was making my head hurt. I finally decided to look at my phone to see who had been texting. The long walk was haunting, my head was spinning, and life around me was moving too fast. I felt like I was floating through a dream. I had to keep reminding myself that it was real life.

As I stumbled on, my phone buzzed once again. I finally reached for it to see who it was. That's when I discovered all the previous messages were from my very angry mother. I already knew what they were going to say, and I didn't even bother opening them. I was much more interested in the most recent message, which was from Allison.

Allison: Thank you for hanging out with me today. I'm sorry you had to deal with my shit. LOL.

I didn't want to respond. I didn't know what to say. I was so intoxicated; anything I tried to type wasn't even words. I held my phone and I continued the journey home. Just as was getting too woozy to even stand, I felt a presence approaching me from behind.

Amiel grabbed my shoulders, shook them, and yelled, "Where are you going, bruh?" He still looked very intoxicated, but he was handling better than I was.

"I got to get home, man." I was slurring my words very heavily.

"You need to get right first. Your momma is going to beat your ass if she sees you like this. Bruh, come with me to Benny's. I'll get you some food and then walk you to your crib 'cause you look way too turned up right now. I'm drunk—so I can just imagine what you must feel like." He stopped in his tracks to light a cigarette.

I shrugged and followed him. It was probably best not to walk home alone, especially when my vision was reduced to just pictures of the sidewalk. Being drunk was different from being high—a lot different. I felt good when I was high. I felt like I was floating on clouds. On the other hand, being drunk, I started feeling nauseated. The world moved in waves, and with every sleepless second, I felt sicker and sicker.

We weren't far from the restaurant, but I couldn't stand walking. Benny's was a local burger joint that made our small town seem even more cliché since everybody went there. They stayed open until four in the morning, and it was the designated fast-food place for the seniors in town to eat after a party. They made good food, and the owner was a big, bald Spanish dude who was very nice to customers, but he was the most intimidating man I'd ever seen. Amiel, being the charismatic person he was, could make friends anywhere—even to a tired cashier who was stuck working graveyard shifts.

"Yo, how you doing, my man?" Amiel leaned on the counter a little too much.

"I'm just chilling, man, working," said the cashier.

"Shit, you got to, man. Got to get on that grind, man. Shit is hard nowadays, bruh." Amiel lit another cigarette.

"Hey, man, I feel that. This isn't even my only job. I've got work at noon after a ten-hour shift," the cashier replied.

"Damn, that's crazy. It's hard out here for a pimp."

"You ain't never lie. Yo, can I bum a cig?" The cashier finally revealed his name tag. His name was Derrick.

We ordered our food and sat in one of the booths near the exit. Amiel put in his headphones and started jamming to some loud rap music. I rested my forehead on the table and squeezed my eyes shut, hoping I would sober up soon.

Amiel dropped one of his earbuds and said. "You! So, what's the deal? When are you going to get laid, bruh?" I could smell the alcohol on his breath.

I sighed and shook my head, hoping he would get the hint that I didn't want to talk about it.

He didn't.

"Yo, for real, man, where the girls at? Where's Sophia?" He started laughing, mocking me, and I didn't even have the energy to sneer at him. I kept shaking my head and sighing.

"Man, I'm about to call somebody, yo. I feel good." He pulled out his phone, scrolled through his contacts, and dropped his phone on the table when he realized it was too late for anybody else to be awake. I sat back and just watched Amiel being Amiel.

Derrick was nice enough to bring our food to our table, entering and exiting our lives with just a nod. Amiel started eating quickly and furiously, but I stared at my food and wondered what it was. I didn't remember ordering anything.

"Yo, eat. It'll make you feel better," Amiel mumbled. "It makes me feel better. I come here every time I'm drunk." He started laughing. "Yo, I think I drank too much. Did you hear all that bullshit I was talking about to all those white boys?"

I nodded my head, still feeling too revolted to speak.

"Them motherfuckers don't understand people like us, bruh. They're in their own little privileged world, man. I know everybody's got their trials, but they act like that shit don't exist. They ignoring the problems, bruh. I'm not. I can peep everything. I can read people so well, like, shit, them boys are stupid. Like, I can't fuck with them sometimes. Yo, like, why fuck around like this when everything was handed to you?

"Shit, they haven't experienced the real shit. I have. Bruh, like the people I used to fuck with, they were worst. They were much worse. Like, those kids at that party think they hard. The people I used to fuck with will let them know like yo, you pussy. Shit, man, I was losing myself fucking with them, man, like. All right, so when me and my bro Calvin started chilling, you know, we started smoking weed together and shit, and like, he was moving it, but I was burning. I mean, I would sometimes help him find customers, but like, shit, we smoked every day. Like, every fucking day, like before school, after school, before work, after work, before I went to bed, and when I woke up. Like, that shit was crazy. I used to have bread, bruh. Like I had a job over at a convenience store, and my step-pops worked in construction, so I would be making bank. I spent all that shit on two things: clothes and weed. Shit, the only thing I would worry about was making money, fucking bitches, and getting high. Better yet, making money so I can go get high and fuck girls.

"Well, anyway, I started hanging with his boys more often, yo, and they all were like drug pushers, so the weed never ran out, bruh. Like, it was frustrating when there was a drought. Like, that shit would have me so mad because we smoked every day. But, yo, like they were fucking crazy, like they were the type to fight you and then shoot you if they lost. Like, yeah, they always stayed strapped—even if they went to football games and shit.

"I fucked with them 'cause they were hood-ass niggas, and I'm from New York, so like, I could relate. You know what I'm saying, like everybody here and their brother are some preppy white bitches. Like even the dudes, like, hearing some of them talk, like, they sound like bitches. I always fucked with them, and I was bad. I had my mom tripping, dawg, because my mom was a church head, like, she was always in church. She'd be telling me, 'Yo, Amiel, don't hang with those boys. They no good for you.' On the real though, I didn't give a fuck. Like, I wasn't hearing it, yo. Like, I was riding around town with the boys holding pistols and shit. Like, if we got pulled over at any time, we would have been fucked 'cause they always stayed strapped, and they were drug dealers.

"Shit, I had a falling out with them boys like you wouldn't understand. Like, I had people telling me that they were no good for me, like, even people I didn't even fucking know, bruh. That's how I know God is real. Like, one time, we were at a football game, right, and honestly, like, bro, listen. We were at this football game, like, it wasn't even for our school, like, it was a big-ass school, but anyway, we were just walking, and like, one of my dudes bumped into somebody. They were like 'watch your step,' and you know we wasn't taking that shit. They start arguing, like, but we kept walking, so the whole night, everybody's like, yo what's going to happen them dudes over there talking shit. So, my dude, Calvin was like 'no let's go to the car, they about to see.'

"Nobody was saying shit, but I was, like, damn, are we about to do this? But, shit, I didn't want to say anything because I respected it, you know what I'm saying, so we went to the car, right. He pops the trunk, right, and my dude, there was an ass of cops there, bruh, like, that would have been the end of us. So, we pop the trunk, and this old head comes out of nowhere and touches all of us on our heads and is like 'Whatever it is you're about to do; don't do it. You are all better than that God bless.'

"Yo, but when he touched Calvin's forehead, I could see the change, like, I could see the look in his eyes change after the man touched his head. After that, we were out of there. That shit is so crazy, like, when I think how different everything could have gone down if that man hadn't shown up. Instead of talking to me, you'd be reading about me. Some of us ain't so lucky. So, why was it me? There's gotta be someone up there looking out for me, bro. That's the only way this could make sense." He stopped talking to play with his fries. "How many times will he save my life before he forgets about me?"

The rest of the night was nothing but mind-numbing silence. Amiel must have been thinking of all his horrid memories, but the only thing I could think about was how little I knew about him. How little I knew about everything.

The next morning was one of the worst experiences in my life. I woke up to my mother screaming at me to get up and go to school because I was going to be late. I had a migraine from hell, and my mother's shouting wasn't exactly easing the pain. Every movement I made was accompanied by a groan. I felt sore, I felt sick, I felt bloated, and I also felt regret. I regretted drinking at that party. If being drunk was a crime, the hangover would be fair enough punishment.

Hungover or not, I knew I had to make it to school. There was no escaping it this time; at least now when I told everybody I was sick, they'd believe me. Getting dressed was painful, but I didn't have to suffer through walking there. My mother wanted to make sure I got to school this time and was driving me there. Any other day, I might have had a problem with it, but I didn't feel like walking.

The entire ride to school, my mother wouldn't shut up about how much trouble I was in. I honestly wasn't listening. I was more focused on the fact that I had no idea how to function hungover. The numbness the alcohol brought to my brain didn't fade; it was only amplified by the sickness.

My mother dropped me off right by the front office, and after I got out of her car, she drove off without another word. I looked at the school and sighed. *I don't want to go in there.* Nevertheless, I started walking up the stairs; I was a little bit late, and the ladies in the front office were giving me death stares. I didn't look back; I continued slowly walking to my class.

I knew the late bell had just rung because the hallway wasn't fully empty, kids were scrambling to get to class, and some of them were walking just as slowly as I was. The teachers were letting the last of their students into their classrooms and shutting the doors. Even though I hadn't been in school for two days, I still couldn't feel the urgency.

As I approached my first class, which sadly was American History, I noticed Gina entering the room. She wore a light pink sweater with lightly faded blue jeans. She caught me looking at her, and she turned and waved with a big smile on her face. I smiled and nodded in return.

I walked into my classroom a few minutes late. The morning announcements were still playing, but that could not silence one obnoxious kid from shouting, "Where have you been?" I gave him a dirty look before taking my seat.

Mr. Nelson approached me with a stack of missing work. He didn't question why I was absent, probably since I looked so sick. "Just remember to bring in your doctor's notes." He was a pretty cool teacher.

Luckily, after that loud kid's outburst, everyone else sort of forgot I was gone or that I was even there. It was weird. Even the people sitting around me didn't acknowledge me. As much as I don't want to sound like every teenage girl who ever existed, I had to admit I felt invisible. Not that it bothered at the moment; I kind of appreciated being a loser.

I felt horrible, and once Mr. Nelson started teaching, it was all static to me. I couldn't understand a word of it. I started to look around and couldn't even think without hurting. I started to think about the guy next to me. To be honest, I sort of started judging him. How lousy of me, right? Yet, even though you can't judge a book by its cover, it's still always the first impression. I mean, how many people out there are putting Nazi signs on the covers of Bibles to make people believe you don't judge a book by its cover.

Thinking back, I didn't even truly see it was judging. I sort of thought I was trying to study him. He was dressed in a white polo with khaki shorts. He wore a gold Rolex on his wrist and his class ring on his middle finger. However wrong it was, I couldn't help but think. *Fuck this guy.* He looked like he had it all, and I didn't have shit. I never really thought of myself as poor. I was fully aware of my mother's struggles, but we had food, most of the time, and we had cable. I had clothes, and we had shelter. I supposed I never noticed mainly because I never really needed much. My mother always gave me my needs and left my wants for someone else. Another reason would be because I would always see what real poverty looked like—and then I'd feel guilty for complaining.

My mother would bring in real poor people, with real problems, and try to feed them when we had barely anything to eat ourselves. Why was my mother sacrificing the little she had while this prissy fuck could afford gold? The thing that made me so angry with my oblivious classmate was that I bet he complained all the time. I was willing to bet that he would run and cry to his parents the second everything went wrong, and they would listen, and even worse, they would fix it. This guy's parents could afford a gold Rolex, a class ring, name-brand clothing, and a new car. It's funny how they say, "Get a job and work for your first car." Well, why do I have to break my back for a crappy used car while this guy is just expecting a brand-new one for his birthday? I hate to sound bitter, but fuck him. His normal life is everything I dream of, and he doesn't appreciate it.

As soon as he caught me staring, I turned away as quickly as I could and started to focus on the maps on Mr. Nelson's walls. The rest of the class dragged on, but it was nothing but an eternal blur. When the class bell rang, I wanted nothing more than to bolt through his door. Instead, I slowly walked out with a crowd of my classmates. We were all eager to leave his class.

As I slowly walked to my next class, I caught a glimpse of Sophia. She was entering the library when I saw her. It was only a moment, a second, but my feelings for her came pouring over me like a waterfall. I hated how much I liked her. I hated that I had to force myself not to walk into the library. I also hated the fact that it really wouldn't have made any difference to her if I did. Being hungover sucked, but I felt a slight depression come over me.

Just before my illness was challenged by my sadness, I bumped into Allison. She happened to be going the same way. "Hi, Timmy." Her smile almost reached from ear to ear. It was a greeting I had never seen from Allison before. You would have thought she hadn't seen me in years from the way she looked at me. I was mesmerized by it. I always knew she was pretty, but having someone pretty look at you like you matter was a special kind of beautiful. I found myself at a loss for words, which was strange. I had spent the past few months hanging out with this girl every single day. We talked and laughed, but I was frozen solid.

"You okay?" she asked after I didn't respond.

I quickly shook my head and said, "Yeah, sorry. What's up?"

She sighed. "I thought you weren't going to talk to me."

"Why would you think that?"

Andrew walked by and gave both of us the dirtiest of looks. He walked by and shook his head.

Allison looked crushed by his gaze, and I couldn't help but think I was glad he was gone. He looked at me as though I was taking his girl. He looked at me like I had done him wrong; if anything, I was hurting myself. It made me angry that someone I considered so close could be so judgmental.

"Forget him," I said more to myself than to Allison.

"It's not him I'm trying to forget."

I gave her a questioning look.

"Are you doing anything Saturday? My mom is going out of town, and I don't want to be alone."

"No. Do you want to chill?" I don't know why I was so used to asking dumb questions. Of course, she wanted to chill.

"I can pick you up," she responded.

I nodded, and she smiled—and that was the end of that. She walked away, and I stood there dumbfounded. The rest of the school day was just another boring school day, with the same dull teachers and the same annoying classmates. I didn't see Andrew, Allison, or Sophia for the rest of the day, and my brain just sort of went on autopilot.

After school was over, I had to make the journey home. I didn't feel as bad as I did in the morning, but I still didn't feel like walking. It was the first time I wanted to go home. I didn't want to see Charlie and hang out with Abel, but I knew that was his plan. I knew Charlie wanted to see Gina again, but I was tired of the entire situation. I didn't like knowing something about someone when that person had no idea. It seemed cruel.

Halfway home I caught Gina waiting to cross the street.

"What's up, Gina?" I said as I walked up behind her.

"Hi!" She hugged me before I could even wrap my arms around her. "How are you?"

I walked across the street with her. "I'm good. You know me," I replied.

"I kind of don't though. We never hang out."

"Yeah, well, that's 'cause you're always hanging with Charlie," I said with a chuckle.

She gave me a half-smile and then looked at the sidewalk.

"You ever think you loved someone, even though you couldn't be with them?" She looked deep into my eyes. She wanted to see the truth in my pupils. I shrugged, and she shook her head. I figured I didn't want to talk about whatever was bothering her.

"What do you and Charlie do when he sneaks over?" I asked.

"We talk. That's it. My mom usually doesn't bother me in my room, and I keep my door locked. I sneak him in through the window, and we just hang out in my room. We talk just like we used to, about stupid stuff." She didn't look at me when she talked about Charlie. She looked ahead of herself—far ahead—as if she was trying to see something in the distance. It was like she was trying to see something so far away that it couldn't exist. "I don't know, Timmy. Everything is so complicated. I never felt like this about anyone, but everything is so hard. Abel is so sweet, and we've been together for a while, but I like Charlie so much. I hate what I'm doing to Abel, but I don't know what else to do." She sighed, looked at me, and smiled.

"You seem like such a nice guy, Timmy. You seem like you don't belong with those kinds of guys."

"What do you mean?" I asked.

"Charlie and Josh are kind of like cousins, so I know why they're friends, but why you? You seem like the kind of guy who would avoid people like them and Amiel." She looked concerned for me, as if she felt sorry for me—but also like she knew something I didn't.

"Why Amiel? What kind of people are they?"

"I saw you hanging out with Amiel at that party; he isn't what you think he is. None of them are; the best person is Charlie. He isn't going to stop hanging with Josh, but you should." Her voice got less peppy and darker. "Whatever it is you're doing with them, it isn't going to end well.

It never does." We reached her street, and she turned and walked the rest of the way by herself.

She left me there without another word. She left me there questioning the people I trusted. She made me question why I decided to trust them in the first place. I didn't have many friends, and the ones I did have never lasted very long. I never had a childhood friend who had been through thick and thin with me. I had friends then, and I have friends now, but they were all different. I thought Andrew could stick with me, but even he was fading into a memory. Charlie was the only one who almost remained constant. We hung out a little, and he'd disappear, but then he'd come back, and it would be like nothing changed. I couldn't stop thinking about what I knew—and what I didn't know. I didn't know if whatever Gina was talking about was even worth knowing. Why were they so bad?

"Yo, Timmy!" Charlie shouted from a distance.

He was standing with Josh and Amiel—all people I didn't want to see. They were all guys I didn't feel comfortable being around. It was like I couldn't trust anyone anymore.

CHAPTER 12

"What's up, Timmy?" Amiel pulled out a cigarette out of his pocket.

"What's up, everybody?" I shoved my hands in my pockets and tried desperately to look normal as my suspicions slowly crept to the surface.

They all stared at me for a moment without saying a word.

Amiel glared at me with one eyebrow raised. "You good? You look shady as fuck."

"I'm straight. What do you mean?" The more I spoke, the more nervous I felt. I hated that I was bad at hiding my emotions.

"You look like you're hiding something," Josh said as Amiel passed him the cigarette.

I had no idea Josh even smoked cigarettes.

"Fuck is you hiding, Timmy?" Charlie yelled and then laughed to lighten up the mood.

Josh shrugged it off, but Amiel's suspicious looks remained.

"Yo, call Abel, bruh," Charlie said as he nodded at Josh.

Josh passed him the cigarette, which was nearing its end.

"You going to see that bitch again? You need to chill. Abel's going find out—and then what?"

"I guess I'll have to fuck him up then," Charlie said with a cheesy smile.

"Yeah, you say that it's whatever. I'm out. I'll holla at you later, Josh."

Josh nodded and watched as Amiel left. Josh and I turned to Charlie, and he still wanted to see Gina.

"Abel is at Andre's house, and they asked me to come through," Josh said.

"Can you go and make sure he doesn't come back?" Charlie asked.

"Shit, I guess. Come on, Timmy," Josh said.

I followed Josh and watched as Charlie went to go do whatever it was that he did.

Josh walked coolly with his hands in his pockets, and his eyes never left the path ahead of him.

We walked in silence for a little while, and Josh finally said, "I saw the girl you were talking to in the hallway today. That's the same one who dropped you off, isn't it?"

I didn't respond right away. I was still skeptical about whether I should trust him with that information—or with any information. Then again, I didn't know why a couple of random questions from a girl I barely knew would cause such scrutiny.

"Yeah, she is," I said.

"She's cute. I think she likes you too." He didn't look at me when he spoke; it was almost as if he was going to great lengths to avoid my gaze.

"Why do you say that?" I asked.

"Just the way she was looking at you—and talking to you. I'm not surprised you didn't notice it, but I did notice it. She likes you, Timmy. What are you going to do about it?" Josh asked almost sarcastically.

I didn't know how to answer him. I didn't know the answer. Allison was stunning and was everything any guy would ever wish for, but it didn't seem right. What bothered me was that it wasn't the first time I thought I could like Allison. When we all started hanging out before they started dating, I flirted with Allison just as hard as Andrew did, yet she chose Andrew. It bothered me for a while that I lost to the likes of Andrew, but I would just smother my envy with my feelings for Sophia. I didn't want to like Allison. It was enough to have a heart-aching crush on a girl I only knew in my dreams, but it was another thing to like a girl you knew. Allison was my friend. If she didn't like me back, it would hurt so much more. Sophia might not have liked me because she didn't truly know me. Allison knew me, and if she didn't like me, I would have to face the fact that I was a loser. "I don't know," I said. "She's my friend. I don't want to jeopardize that."

"Ha!" He finally turned to me. "You sound like a bitch," he declared between chuckles.

"Fuck you! Just because I value her friendship doesn't make me a bitch."

He continued his snickering. "No, you're right. It doesn't, but if she was fat and ugly, would you still value her friendship? Better yet, if she was fat and ugly, would you even care if she liked you or not?" He looked me dead in my eyes.

I didn't answer him.

"That's what I thought. Timmy, you've got a good heart, and I respect that and all, but just remember you're still a guy. You're still as shallow as the rest of us."

I hated how right he thought he was. His cool and arrogant way of speaking made my skin crawl because he wasn't always right—he thought he was. "That isn't true!" I was never good at arguments or confrontations, but I had to say something.

"Come on, Timmy. Don't be so naïve. We like girls off of looks. You tell me otherwise, and you're a fucking liar. We're dudes—better yet, we're humans. Do you think girls are out there searching for personality? I mean, I know they claim they do, but that's a bunch of bullshit. Girls are like guys, you know? They want the dude who has the most swag or who can sweet-talk the best. That's why you can't get girls, Timmy. You have neither of those things. Shit, you'd be a hell of a boyfriend probably, but I doubt you'll ever get to that point."

We were approaching Andre's house, and I didn't want to carry out the conversation in front of Andre and Abel. "Whatever, man."

"Don't get mad that I'm right," Josh said arrogantly.

I rolled my eyes as we entered Andre's driveway. In the backyard, Andrew and Abel were taking turns boxing a punching bag that Andre had hung from a tree.

There were two pairs of boxing gloves in front of the punching bag—along with Andre's cup of Kool-Aid.

"What's up? Josh?" Andre walked over to his cup, breathing heavily and sweating like a fat kid in the summertime.

Josh nodded indifferently and walked over to the punching bag.

"Yo, you want to throw on the gloves?" Andre said with a devilish smile.

Josh's smirk was more evil than Andre's; he chuckled and responded, "Nah, I don't want to hurt you, Andre."

"Come on. Don't be a pussy," Andre spit back.

Josh's grin turned bigger and bigger. He raised an eyebrow and picked up one of the gloves without another word.

Abel walked over to me to watch from a safe distance.

Andre started stretching as he put on the other pair of boxing gloves. He started jumping around like a real boxer before a fight. It seemed like Andre was taking it a bit too seriously. Josh wasn't taking it seriously at all. I started to see a hint of worry in Andre's eyes while the cool, emotionless eyes of Josh were staring into his soul.

Once they both were ready, they touched gloves and put their guards up.

Andre kept dancing around Josh, attempting to move in rapid motions, and Josh leisurely circled him with his right hand close to his chin and his left arm closer to Andre. Andre tried to hit Josh with a quick jab only to be deflected by Josh's left hand. Andre threw more jabs with an uppercut, which were all either dodged or blocked. Andre continued to dance around Josh, attempting to find an opening; he tried to go for another jab but was quickly stunned by a quick left jab to his face. That's when Josh started to pick up the pace. He kept leading with quick left jabs that barely landed, only to surprise Andre with a powerful right hook to the chin. Andre did his best to retaliate, but Josh was a lot quicker than he looked. He ducked every punch Andre threw, and the ones Andre did land seemed to have little effect on him. Josh started dancing around with Andre. Andre kept a smile on his face but had a scared look in his eyes; he tried to throw a wild blow with his right arm. Josh ducked and returned with a monstrous blow to Andre's eye. The hit nearly knocked him off his feet.

"Shit!" Andre grabbed the side of his face.

Josh finally put his guard down and started to peel off his gloves.

"Man, I'm not fighting your big ass no more, man," Andre said.

"I told you." Josh was panting and sweating heavily. "You got water?"

"Yeah ... in the house." Andre was still clutching his eye, which had a big purple bruise on it. Abel began laughing as he approached Andre.

"The fuck you laughing at?" Andre spat. "I want to see you take on that big motherfucker."

"Nah," Abel said. "I like my face and my life." He picked up Andre's cup and took a big swig. He offered it to me, but I shook my head.

I was a little disgusted that they were so willing to drink out of the same cup, but then I considered the fact that the two of them had probably done nastier things in their lives.

Josh walked out with a bottle of water and a paper towel to wipe away the sweat on his face.

"Shit, you need to do UFC or some shit," Andre said as he reached his fist out for a respectable fist bump.

"Nah, I got bigger plans," Josh replied with a smirk on his face.

Andre grabbed his cup and started walking to the shed. The rest of us followed him. We all knew what was in that rusty shed. There were only three seats, but Abel volunteered to stand. It was a little crowded, but we didn't mind.

Andre pulled out his big box of paraphernalia, a big bag of weed, a small scale, and two packs of Swisher Sweets. "My friends, we are about to get more stoned than a motherfucker." Andre pulled out one of the cigars and started to split it in half.

"You know how to roll yet, Timmy?" Andre asked.

"Hell, Nah," Josh answered.

I sneered at him even though he was right.

"You can't be a stoner and not know how to roll, man. Josh, how come you don't teach this man." Andre split the cigar, emptied the tobacco into the box, and started licking the inside of the Swisher. "Man, I'm going to tell you one thing, man. There is nothing like smoking your blunt by yourself. It makes you think about everything." Andre sounded so enthusiastic about it. He passed a cigar to Josh and Abel.

They began to break down the cigar. He didn't even have to ask them. It was like muscle memory.

"You think you can try to roll this one?" Andre asked.

My phone buzzed in my pocket before I could give him an answer. Andre shrugged and put down the pack of Swisher Sweets.

Allison: Hey, Timmy.

While everybody was focused on rolling blunts, I decided to shoot her a text.

Me: Hi, Allison.

I tried to set my phone down, but it buzzed before it even reached the table.

Allison: I miss him. I miss us.

If this wasn't the universal sign for friend-zoned, I didn't know what was. I still felt the need to comfort her.

Me: You'll get through this.

Damn, I sounded like one of her female friends. Josh was right. I was terrible at flirting with girls. She wanted to talk about her feeling for him; I wanted to talk about her feelings for me.

"Yo you still got that bowl I gave you?" Andre asked.

I thought for a moment before reaching into my pocket and discovering that it was on my person the entire time.

Josh practically read my mind. "You took that shit to school with you? Are you fucking stupid?"

I shrugged and thought about how many teachers and administrators had walked past me that day.

"School is the worst place to have weed. A fucking teacher or some shit catches you with that shit, it'd be like having cocaine on an airplane. You'd be expelled on the spot if not arrested," Andre added. He grabbed the bowl from out of my hand and started to break up nuggets of weed into smaller nuggets of weed. He shoved the smaller nuggets into the bowl and returned it to me with a bright yellow lighter.

I felt my phone buzz again but decided to ignore it until after I took a hit. While everyone else was busy rolling, I took one of the longest hits of my life. I guess I wanted the high more that day. I pulled in so much smoke that it burned my lungs, but I endured the pain. I sucked in so much that holding it in was not an option. I coughed like a dying old man. I put down the bowl, sat back, and started to feel the effect of the marijuana's glorious high. That's when I decided to pull out my phone.

Allison: He used to be so sweet to me. When we first started talking, I thought he was the nicest guy on the planet. But now he's treating me like I'm a ho.

Me: He doesn't know what he's losing.

That was a good response. I suppose I was going to figure it out one way or another. After everyone was finished rolling blunts, I passed Andre his lighter. Abel and Josh had their own. While they started smoking, my phone buzzed again.

Allison: I guess.

Crap, that wasn't the response I was hoping for. I had to come up with something.

Abel passed me the blunt he had rolled after he hit it a couple times.

A little voice in my head, which kind of sounded like Amiel, screamed, "Chill out and hit the blunt. You'll think of something." It was a little hard to argue with that logic. I did what that little voice commanded. I grabbed the slow-burning blunt and began to cough more and worry less. The coughs started coming with laughs and curses.

"This is some good shit, bruh. This shit is that purple Kush," Andre bragged.

"This shit doesn't even look like Kush," Josh commented.

"You don't know what you're talking about. I got this shit from Cali, man," Andre retorted.

"Don't disrespect California like that, man. You don't have to lie about your weed, man." Josh passed the blunt to Abel.

"Believe what you want. I mean, shit, you don't have to smoke it." Andre sounded upset, and I didn't blame him. Josh kicked his ass at his own house and then judged his weed. Josh kept his composure while Andre looked like he was losing his cool with every insult. Josh blew a puff of smoke in Andre's direction and said, "Them's fighting words."

I could see the rage in Andre's eyes. "You know, if you weren't so damn big, I'd probably fuck you up."

"You're probably right. It's a crying shame, isn't it," Josh replied sarcastically.

The tension was far thicker than the fog that filled up the room.

Abel and I quietly got high while Andre was getting mad. I might have been a bit concerned if I weren't so stoned. I couldn't tell if this was Kush or not. All I knew was that it was had me floating in a canoe on a river of marijuana smoke that was taking me far away from my worries and my stresses. I decided to text Allison.

Me: Just try to keep your mind off of the whole situation.

Allison: How?

I wanted to text her back and say smoke some pot, but I didn't know how serious she was about trying it. After the blunts were passed around a couple of times, I couldn't feel the tension anymore. I really couldn't feel anything anymore. I could barely see two inches in front of me. There was so much smoke in that little old shed. All of the smoke that came out of the blunt and our bodies was suffocating us. It was hot, and all I was breathing in was more smoke—even when I wasn't smoking. My eyes weighed a ton, and the struggle to stay awake was unreal. I couldn't help but shut my eyes; it was like with every breath, the world got a little darker. I got to the point where I couldn't keep my eyes open anymore. I would only open them to grab the blunt and hit it again.

Luckily, the weed calmed down Andre and Josh.

"Shit, this some good shit, man," Josh finally admitted.

"Yeah, I told you, man. You still think it's not Kush?" Andre replied.

"Honestly, bro, like you could have told me it was dog shit, and I wouldn't care at this point." Josh exploded with uncontrollable laughter. It was kind of nice seeing the biggest guy finally as high as I was.

Abel said, "Shit, I haven't been this high since my little sister died." He silenced Josh's laughter quick; it silenced all of us.

"She was five years old, you know, and we were living at my grandmother's house at the time. My mom was in jail, and shit, I don't even know my damn dad, that piece of shit. Anyways, I was in school at the time, I think, or I was coming home from school. I don't really remember. I can't remember shit nowadays. My grandmother was kind of old, you know, so she forgets shit, and she liked to smoke. She went to the store, it was just around the corner like maybe five minutes away, she did it all the time, you know, and thought nothing of it. My sister was smart, you know, if my grandmother told her just to chill for a couple of minutes, she would listen." I couldn't see the tears, but I could hear his voice beginning to break.

"She left my little sister watching TV, and when she came back ... when she came back ... the living room was on fire, you know, she screamed her name and everything trying to call her. She tried to run back into the house, but she couldn't get in from anywhere. The whole house was up in flames, and by the time the fire department came, it was too late. They couldn't save her ... and it was because my grandmother left a lit cigarette near the drapes." He took a long pull from his blunt. "I don't blame her;

she's just forgetful. I couldn't deal, you know. I was going crazy. I had to smoke or lose my mind. My sister's name was Madison."

We were all speechless. He had to be lying. Things that horrible don't happen to real people, but when the smoke cleared enough for us to see the look on his face, he looked broken. He looked horrified by his tale, and he looked high. Something that terrible wasn't ever going to change the fact that he smoked, and why should it? He needed to cope somehow.

Abel walked out of Andre's shed, letting out a wave of smoke once he opened the door.

Andre was staring blankly at the wall and clutching his cup of Kool-Aid. Josh didn't look high anymore; his eyes were still red, but he looked angry. He stood up and walked out of Andre's shed.

"Come on, Timmy," Josh said as headed for the exit. We were dismissed, and Josh was the only one who spoke after Abel's story.

As we walked down the street, I couldn't help but think about it. It was haunting me. "Abel is a strong dude," I said.

Josh chuckled and said, "Abel's a piece of shit."

"How can you even say that?"

"Wake the fuck up, Timmy! Do you think he's the only one out there who has suffered a loss? Do you think he's the only kid out here with enough baggage to be a fifty-year-old man? Are you really that naïve? I told you everybody has a fucking sob story, everybody, just because he lived through some shit, that makes him strong? Tell me, Timmy, how is he strong? He's out here smoking dope just like the rest of us. Life isn't pretty, it's never what we expect, and it's never what we wish it'll be. Look around you; this is a fucking ghost town. This is an endless library of sob stories, and the only way they can come to terms with it is by doing the very thing that caused so much pain. It's the curse of life, man. You're just so used to all your friends being oblivious to how horrible shit really is. They cry over grades, boyfriends, and drama with their friends, while we don't cry. We smoke, we drink, we keep drowning our sorrows in the very thing that keeps killing us because we have too much pride to cry. Look around, Timmy. Look at this ghetto. There is a reason there is one in every city." Josh kept walking and did not look back. His eyes were fixed on the path ahead of him.

Josh went home, and so did I. I was lucky enough to make it there before my mom did, and I did what any kid who's baked out of his mind would do. I went into the kitchen and started to cook a feast. I turned on the TV and put on some cartoons I had recorded on the DVR. I made two packs of Ramen noodles and a sandwich on almost-expired wheat bread, and I filled the biggest cup I could find to the top with orange juice. It wasn't a five-star meal, but it was enough to fill me up to the point where getting up was too much of a chore to even contemplate. I ended up sleeping on the couch that night, which was fine. I was used to sleeping on the couch. When I was younger, I would always stay up late watching TV and end up passing out on the couch. Every time I would wake up, I'd be back on my bed without really knowing how I got there. Being older now, I realized it was my mother every single time. She would scold me for staying up watching TV—and then take care of me despite how annoyed I probably made her.

When I woke up the next morning, I realized that the plates of food were gone, the TV was off, and I had a blanket over me. It was surprisingly early when I awoke. Even though she was probably upset at my attendance and the fact that I have barely been home, she was still taking care of me.

I started getting ready for school before realizing it was Saturday. By that time, I had already gotten dressed, had my book bag over my shoulder, and had walked out the door. It wasn't even the time or the date that made me realize I had no school; it was the beauty of the day. Even on weekdays, when the weather musters up spectacular scenery, it is always shunned by the ominous radiance that surrounds the school. That is my obnoxious way of saying that the day can be nice, but if you've got school that day, the day still ends up shitty.

I walked back in the house, a little embarrassed that I almost made a twenty-minute walk for nothing, and I turned the TV back on. I always loved the way Saturday mornings felt; it was a relaxing sensation to know I had nothing to do and nowhere to be. I had no responsibilities and could just watch Saturday morning cartoons the way I did when I was ten.

My mother woke up a couple minutes later and started making coffee and frying up eggs. I always loved this routine; she'd make me breakfast and then sit down with me and watch me eat. She hated all the shows I loved, but she still watched them with me, sipping her coffee as she sat on the chair closest to the window. I ate my little plate of breakfast, and she sipped her coffee. Mornings like those never got old, and it put me in such a good mood. I knew it was going to be a good day.

I hung around my house for a long time before deciding to walk to Charlie's. I knew he wouldn't be up at eight in the morning and waited until noon before leaving my house. I knew there was still a chance he was sleeping, but it was more reasonable to wake him at noon than at eight.

When I got this apartment complex, I noticed that all the cars that would usually be gone at that time weren't. People were inside their houses, spending their own Saturday mornings with their own families, in their way. I'm sure that half the nation would probably agree that Saturday was the best day of the week.

Charlie spent his Saturday morning the same way he would spend every other morning, facedown on his bed with a half-eaten burger beside him. His mother wasn't home when I walked into his apartment. Charlie didn't wake up the first few times I shook him, and I sat on his computer chair and waited.

Charlie woke up for a moment to see who had disturbed his slumber. He looked at me through his squinted eyes with saliva still on the side of his mouth, "The fuck?" he said. Charlie looked around his room as if the explanation for why I was sitting in his room, uninvited, would be somewhere on the wall.

"What's up?" I said.

He sighed and said, "I'm fucking sleeping." He remained motionless for five more minutes before he finally got up and walked into his bathroom to get himself together.

As I waited in Charlie's bedroom, I heard the alarm on his phone go off. I searched through the cluster of blankets and sheets and found it. I quickly hit dismiss and noticed he had six text messages from Gina. I had to admit I was curious as to what they could be talking about, but I wasn't about to start digging and find something I didn't want to see.

Charlie walked back into his room and sat on his bed. He looked stoned; his eyes weren't red, but they were glossy. He had a blank expression like his very existence was confusing him.

"Dude, I smoked so much weed yesterday. I think I've been high for the past three days, bro." He looked around his room with wide eyes and did his best to clear the fog from his head. I looked over to his desk and noticed a little bit of weed next to an empty pack of cigarillos. He saw me staring at them and shook his head. "I can't smoke right now, man. I can't even think straight." He put his face in his hands and took a deep breath.

"Who'd you smoke with yesterday?" I asked.

"I got high with Gina, man." He was trying to conceal his grin, but his face lit up after saying her name. It made me smile as well. Charlie glanced at me for a second and realized I knew what effect she had on him.

"What?" he yelled.

I shrugged and kept the same look on my face.

"The fuck is you looking at me like that for? You gay, bro?" Charlie began to giggle, but I never changed my expression.

"What?" Charlie exclaimed.

"Nothing, man. What did you guys do together?" I could feel my smile becoming more mischievous, and I'm sure Charlie could see it too.

"Nothing, man. Why? Why do you want to know? Mind your business!"

"Shut up, man. Just tell me."

He smiled nervously before finally saying, "All right, shit."

He paused took a deep breath of air and then started his story. "She asked me to come over, and like, you know, that's when you and Josh went over to Andre's house. I walk over there, and she meets me halfway. She was crying, man, her face was like red from tears and shit. I asked her what's wrong, but she didn't want to tell me. She said she wasn't going to tell me until she got home. Her parents were out of town or some shit, but when we got to the house, she still didn't want to tell me. She said she wanted to smoke so she could calm down. So, we went to my house.

I had like two grams, and we didn't have any wraps, so we ended making this cool little bong out of an old plastic bottle of vodka, a pen, and some aluminum foil. I got her so high, dawg, like we almost hot-boxed my whole room. She was geeking, like, for five minutes, I couldn't get her to stop laughing. When she did, you know, I asked her again why she was crying, and she told me it was about Abel. She said he was going crazy, he lost his little sister I think like last year, and she was really worried about him. She said he kept having mood swings, he would start crying over nothing, and like, he would always talk about killing himself. She said he started smoking spice."

"Spice?" I asked.

"You know spice. It's a weed, but it's not weed. It's like fake weed, but it'll get you high as fuck for fifteen minutes and shit, but it can put, like, holes in your brains. He started smoking that shit at her house. It doesn't leave a smell, and you can't see it in a drug test. She told me that she and her mom want to kick him out, but then he'd have nowhere to go. She told me she wants to be with me, but she's afraid of what Abel might do to himself. Her eyes started watering, so I pulled her in close and just held her, man. I don't know, man." He pulled out the homemade bong from under his bed.

"I thought you didn't want to smoke," I asked.

"I didn't, but you got me talking about all this romantic bullshit, man. I can't not be high." He started to pack the weed into the aluminum foil.

"I mean, it sounds like she likes you," I said, trying to comfort him.

"Yeah, but she's with Abel now. I mean, I know they fucked, he fucking lives with her, but that shit makes me want to fight him." Charlie couldn't make eye contact with me. I always noticed when my friends wouldn't look me in the eye. They would stare at whatever was in front of them and tell the story to themselves.

"If she still likes you, that's all that counts, right?" I wondered what was making things so complicated, and then it dawned on me. "Wait, aren't you dating that one chick?" I quickly got in my question before Charlie had the chance to respond.

His face changed from one that was madly in love to one that looked sexually frustrated.

"Yeah, I'm still fucking that bitch, man," he said, not realizing he hadn't answered my question.

"I asked if you were still dating though", I tried to wrap my head around this odd love triangle. Charlie liked Gina, Gina liked Charlie, Gina was dating Abel, and Charlie was dating whatever her name was. I didn't understand. It wasn't even a love triangle; it was just two people in relationships they didn't want to be in who were justifying cheating by calling it, love.

"Yeah, we still dating, but like all we do is fuck," Charlie explained. He finished packing the bong and put it down. "If you could get laid by someone—even if she wasn't the person you like, really liked—would you still do it?"

I pondered that for a moment. *Any moral person might say no, but deep down, any guy would say yes. As a guy, I think about sex a lot, not because I'm a man ho—I am far from that—but because I'm a dude. I'm someone who thinks about sex every twenty seconds without really trying to.* I wanted to say no—that I wouldn't take advantage of a girl like that—but rather than hopping on my high horse, I gave him the truthful answer: "Probably."

"There you go. She's a ho anyway." He lit the weed in the aluminum bowl and pulled smoke in from the top of the bottle. He inhaled smoke until the entire bottle was a grayish-white. He pulled out the aluminum bowl, which was being held up by the pen, and completely cleared the entire bottle of smoke. It didn't take him long to start coughing. He handed the bottle to me.

"Light the weed, hold the carb, and then pull that shit out to get all the smoke." His coughs continued.

Before I could start smoking, the door swung open, and Amiel and Josh walked in.

"Yo, what's good?" Amiel took a big whiff. "Damn. It smells good in here. Smoking on that good good, huh?" He sat right beside Charlie, and Josh stood by the door with his arms crossed like a bodyguard.

"Let me hit that, man," Amiel said as he reached for the bottle.

"Let me hit it first. Damn." I pulled the bottle away from him. I hit the bog and was almost instantly stoned. It was like the high reached over and smacked me in the face.

As the bong started going around, so did the stories. We mainly talked about other times we'd gotten high, and since I'd only really ever smoked with them, the stories I had were very limited. The three of them had endless stories that I could hardly believe. They didn't limit their tales to just their smoking habits. They talked about parties and fights, and then the conversation reached to every guy's favorite topic: girls.

I always wondered how girls spoke about guys. It's common knowledge that when girls hang out with their friends, the topic of conversation was mainly boys. I wanted to know how they talked about us. What did they talk about? I wondered if they praised our body features in the same way we did theirs.

"Bruh, I was at this party, and there was this fine-ass white girl. She was wearing these yoga pants, like, her ass was out of this world," Amiel recalled. "Yo, like, I don't remember her name though, but I started talking to her and shit, and you know, for a minute, it didn't look like she was into it, you know, she looked kind of like she never been to a party before. So, we start drinking, she didn't want to at first, but we started drinking, and after she got a little drunk, I got a little drunk, bruh, it was over. We went upstairs to a room, and shit, you know, I'm finessing."

Josh stopped Amiel before he could go any further. "So, did she laugh when you whipped your little dick out?" Josh joked.

"Shit, your sister wasn't laughing when she saw that shit the other day," Amiel said.

Josh and Amiel both looked at each other with straight faces before laughing at each other's insults.

"But, for real though, I think she was a virgin, yo, like, I had no idea. I kind of thought she might have been before, but I didn't know until I was in there, you know." Amiel shook his head. "That shit was crazy."

We smoked in silence for a moment before Josh had to bring up Allison. "Yo, who is that white girl you were talking to?" He gave me one of his infamous evil grins.

I sighed in frustration. I didn't want to talk about a girl I might like while they were all talking about girls they all slept with.

"Her name is Allison," I answered. "She's just a friend."

"Damn, you got friend-zoned by another girl? That's tragic." Amiel hit the bong again.

I shot daggers with my eyes and flicked him off.

Amiel chuckled as he struggled to keep the smoke in his lungs. "I'm just asking if you have a shot with this girl or if you are going to follow her around like a lost puppy until she shows you attention out of pity." Amiel released the smoke.

"Do you even hang out with this bitch?" Charlie asked.

I wanted to huff and puff and say that I didn't want to talk about it, but even if I did, they wouldn't listen. They would just laugh and call me a pussy.

"I mean, we're supposed to hang out tonight," I stuttered.

"Oh, word! Where you guys going?" Josh asked.

"Well, I mean, we were just going to chill at her house, I think. Her mom is out of town."

"Hold on!" Amiel exclaimed. "So, you're going over to her house while her mom is out of town? What about her dad?"

"I don't think she lives with him. She never mentions him." I never questioned why she never mentioned her father. I knew her for this long but never thought to ask her about him.

"Okay, so she has daddy issues," Amiel said as if he were stating a definite fact.

"I mean, I don't know. She never told me anything," I replied in an attempt to defend her.

"Look, I'm telling you, bro, just listen to the master. She's got daddy issues. That's a good thing though, I mean, not for her, but you. Damn, I just realized how fucked up that shit sounds." He looked ashamed to have said what he said.

Josh said, "But it's true."

"Yeah, it's true. I mean, it's fucked up, but it's true," Amiel said.

"Look, all we're saying is that this is the perfect opportunity," Josh added.

"For what?"

"To fuck, you idiot!" Charlie shouted.

I didn't like the pressure they were putting on me. It wasn't like I hadn't thought about it. I knew that the chances of that happening were very slim, but the chances weren't slim if it was Amiel, Josh, or even Charlie. The thing that kept me up a night was as easy as buying weed to them.

"So, did she invite you—or did the two of you just agree to chill there?" Amiel asked.

"She invited me," I answered.

"She wants the D!" Charlie shouted.

Amiel shook his head in disbelief. "Nah, he ain't going to do it—not even when she's practically throwing it at him."

I hated the way he said it. He said it like he meant it. It lit a fire inside of me, and it made me angry. I always hated it when someone told me I couldn't do something. It made me even angrier knowing that Amiel believed it, he didn't believe in me, and he wasn't afraid to share that information. "I told you we are just friends," I said.

"Nah, while you're busy being 'just friends,' someone else is getting ready to do what you're too afraid to do," Amiel replied.

I hated how right he was. Allison may have been a shy girl at school, but that didn't mean she didn't get attention. Whether she knew it or not, boys were just dying to get a chance to talk to her—and now I had that chance. Amiel might be an asshole, but he was right. She didn't just invite me over for nothing. To be honest, I didn't know what her intentions were; all I knew was that out of all the dudes at our school, I was the only she was giving actual attention to. I had to make a move. I had to get over this slump. I was sick of being the best friend. I wanted to be the boyfriend or the one-night stand. I wanted, for once in my teenage life, to feel like a man. Amiel could get any girl he wanted without breaking a sweat; he never once went about anything with the same level of insecurity as I did. He waltzed around with this "you can't tell me nothing" attitude because, at the end of the day, it was hard to make fun of the guy who just stole your girlfriend.

I spent the rest of the day in silence. Charlie, Josh, and Amiel kept rambling on about nonsense, but I was thinking about how I was going to act, what I was going to say, and how I would react to her reactions. I wanted to ask Amiel for advice, but that would mean he would go back to ridiculing me. As all of this was going through my head, I received a text from Andrew.

Andrew: Hey, man. Can we talk?

Andrew was the last person in my brain right then. I didn't want to talk to him. He hadn't spoken to me since he drove off in a fit. What was the point? I could have been dead in a ditch somewhere, and he wouldn't have known about it. I ignored his message and decided I would be the one to text Allison first.

Me: Hey.

After a few minutes of waiting for a response, I began to grow impatient. I did not want to text her twice, but the fact that she didn't reply within five minutes made me nervous. I didn't keep smoking after we hit the bong. They had a lot of weed, but I did not know if going over there high was such a great idea. She did tell me she wanted to smoke with me, but I didn't have any weed to bring her. I realized I was broke. Josh and Charlie always had weed or booze, but I never once asked them how they could afford it. The supply never ran out. I didn't know if they would give me some, but I highly doubted it.

Allison finally responded after thirty minutes.

Allison: Hey.

Me: What's up?

I was a little embarrassed that she waited thirty minutes to reply when my responses went back to her within seconds. I didn't know what I was doing. I didn't know what to say. It was hopeless. I started to lose faith until she texted back.

Allison: Did you still want to hang out? My mom just left, and I'm all alone.

Reading that was like a breath of fresh air after almost drowning. She still wanted to hang out with me. I hoped she liked me and that it wasn't some trick. Allison was gorgeous and a huge catch. I would finally be over Sophia, and I would finally be proud of myself. I sat there for a moment as the feelings of excitement and nervousness swirled around in my head like a tornado.

Me: Yeah of course. LOL.

I waited for her to respond with a goofy grin on my face, and Charlie noticed. "Look at Timmy's high-ass cheesing."

They all looked at me and ridiculed my smile. I didn't care as long as they didn't know the real reason I was smiling.

Allison: Where are you?

Me: At my friend's house. I'm about to be home though.

Allison: Okay.

I wanted to head over there as soon as possible, but I also didn't want to be there looking like a bum. I quickly said my goodbyes and promised I'd hang out later. I rushed home as fast as I could without actually running. By the time I left Charlie's, it was almost dark. I knew my mom wouldn't be home, and I didn't have to worry about her seeing me like that.

When I got home, I ran to my closet to pick out the best outfit I could find, which was almost impossible. A majority of my clothes were hand-me-downs my mother got from the church, and a lot of my clothes were either too big or too small. I only had three pairs of pants, including a pair of dress pants. I didn't have anything to wear that would wow anybody. It was either wear a church attire or dress like I would normally dress. So, I picked whichever smelled the least dirty and hopped in the shower.

After I undressed and the water was warm enough, I got in and let the warm water wash over me. It felt amazing. I didn't know what it was about taking showers that made me feel like a new person every time I stepped out. I also noticed that I didn't feel as high as I was showering. It was as if the water was washing away the dirt from the outside and the inside as well. It was washing away all of the weed, all the alcohol, all the lies, and all the secrets. When I stepped out of the shower, I had none of those things to weigh me down anymore. When I stepped out of the shower, I was fresh, new, and unsoiled.

When I finished getting ready, I texted Allison that I was home. It took me all of fifteen minutes to get ready, and in those fifteen minutes, I went from the stoner to just the kid who didn't know how to talk to girls. I started to miss those days when the only thing weighing on my heart was Sophia, when I didn't wonder about the world around me, and when I didn't have doubts about the people I called friends. It was as if the reality was finally revealing itself to me, but I wasn't ready to accept it. I was afraid that Allison would be another person who I thought was fine, but then I'd have doubts about it. I was even more afraid of the fact that I had started to doubt myself. I wasn't the person I thought I was, but then again, I didn't know who I thought I was in the first place. As painfully cliché as it was, I started to ask myself, *Who am I?*

When Allison showed up, she honked her horn and parked right outside my window. I could see her waving. She wore a smile that I hadn't seen in a while. I knew she was going through a hard breakup, but she didn't seem bent up about it. I ran out of my house and jumped in her car.

"Hey," she said.

"What's up?" I replied.

"Nothing much. Just driving around this old town," she answered.

"So, where are we going?" I asked.

"I want to show you this cool place behind my neighborhood." She kept her smile through the entire ride, which started to attract my curiosity. It looked genuine. It looked like she was happy to see me, but I couldn't help feeling that it was forced.

When we got to her neighborhood, she parked by her house and led me to a small opening by the woods behind her community pool. We walked on a small dirt path that only seemed to be fit for bikes. We arrived at an enormous meadow with a giant boulder in the middle. She walked up to it and sat on the very top. "Well, this is it," she announced.

"What is this place?" I asked.

"When I first moved here, I found this place after a fight with my mom. I followed the little dirt path, and it led me here. Now every time I need to find a quiet place, I come here. I've never shown anybody this place," Allison said with a warm smile on her face. "You like it?"

"It's beautiful, but it seems a little cliché, don't you think?"

She laughed a little at my response and then hopped off the rock. "Well, maybe if you didn't watch so many movies, it wouldn't be."

"How do you know I watch a lot of movies?" I asked.

"Because you're dramatic, Timmy. You take everything everyone says to heart and expect the same thing in return—without realizing that life isn't really like that." The way she spoke was hypnotizing, and every word had me gazing at her lips. I was on the edge of my seat and wondering what she might say next.

"Am I that predictable?"

"A little," Allison replied with a giggle.

There was something different about her. She was acting differently, but I couldn't put my finger on it. I couldn't keep my eyes off of her. I always knew she was pretty, but it was different this time. This time, she had my attention to the fullest. This time, I didn't look at her like my best friend's girlfriend. I looked at her like the beautiful girl she was. Every feature on her face, every curve on her body, and every small and irresistible movement made me wish that moment would never end.

"Why are you looking at me like that?" Her smile never left.

I didn't understand what she was so happy about. I couldn't help but look right through her. I'd seen her smile a thousand times, but this one didn't seem real. At that point, I didn't care. All I knew was that she was smiling at me; whether it was real or not, it was stunning.

I whispered, "Because you're beautiful."

Her smile faded for a moment, and her pale cheeks turned pink. She looked afraid or surprised. She didn't expect that from me, and I could read her face like a magazine. Her brief moment of weakness didn't last before her forced smile returned. "Do you want to go swimming?" Allison asked a bit nervously.

My heart was pounding, and my mind was blown in so many directions. The only thing I could do was nod.

The night started to creep upon us. It wasn't dark, but the light blue sky began to change shades.

"I have to grab my bathing suit—just wait for me by the pool. I can bring you a towel. Do you need shorts?"

I used head gestures to answer her questions.

We walked back down the dirt path in silence—that pure, wonderful, compelling silence that drew me closer and closer to her with every unspoken word.

She walked me to the pool and left me waiting by the restroom, right next to the water fountain where the water hardly drips above the dispenser. I didn't have to wait long, but standing there alone made my mind wander. I knew Sophia would always be in the back of my head, but this time, she was only there as a sense of pride. I was proud that I was finally moving on from a girl who hardly gave a shit about me. I was with an amazing girl, and she was probably doing the same boring thing she always did. The funny thing was I didn't know her well enough to know what she would be doing at that very moment. She was still a mystery to me, but at that point, she was a mystery that wasn't worth solving. I was on the verge of uncovering a different mystery, from a different girl, and I was closer to the answers than ever before.

Once Allison returned, I was so deep in my thoughts that I barely realized she was walking up. I turned fairly quickly, and time slowed down.

Allison was in a green bathing suit that revealed so much of her body that my tongue just died. I couldn't speak. Her muscles were perfectly toned, her hair fell flawlessly on one shoulder, and her exotic eyes dragged my big stupid eyes right to their doom.

"Are we going to swim or what?" Her smile started to look more and more genuine.

I nodded and almost ran into the bathroom to change. The gym shorts almost didn't fit, but I tied the strings together. By the time I got out of the bathroom, she was already in the pool.

The way she danced in the water was magnificent. Every movement she made had such elegance and grace, and I was almost amazed it was her in the water and not the queen of England. It was so smooth, and the water complimented her beauty so much that I had to jump in the pool before my true intentions became apparent.

Then again, my true intentions began to change once I got in the water. Amiel's cruel words stuck with me, but I couldn't keep my mind off of how amazing she was. I didn't care what Amiel thought at that point. If she wanted to be with me without all of the physical attachments, I still would have taken it. I didn't care how weak it made me look. I wanted the beauty, this splendor, this love—even if it didn't exist.

I didn't keep track of what we talked about because we talked about a little bit of everything. It was all nonsense, tired jokes, and gags that still made us laugh. I learned a little bit more about her, and she learned a little bit more about me.

She was from Maryland, and her mother worked as a columnist for a newspaper for almost twelve years until she moved down South to become a teacher. Allison wanted to become a doctor, not a nurse. Even though she respected what nurses had to do daily, she thought becoming a doctor would be more rewarding. Allison wanted to make a difference in people's lives; she met a few doctors when her father was diagnosed with cancer.

She finally revealed the mystery that was her father. Amiel was right. She did have daddy issues, but not the ones he expected or I expected. When someone says they have problems with their father, they usually mean they have a deadbeat dad. The number of fathers like that was constantly increasing, but Allison was the exception. Her father did everything right; he was a good man who was gone too soon.

Allison's father joined the army straight out of high school once he realized that Allison's mother was the love of his life. He served three terms in Afghanistan as a marine. He was almost fictional. It was like I could hardly believe a guy like that existed. Her tales about her dad's life made me think of all the people they sent over there. I was convinced people joined just for the benefits, but he was more than a man. He was a warrior, and his daughter was amazing.

"I don't know if cancer was the way he wanted to go. He'd been shot so many times, and you can only evade death for so long." Allison was doing her very best not to cry.

My eyes never left hers, and I set my hand gently on her back.

"You remind me of him. My mom always said he was never a tough guy, and she was surprised when he said he'd enlist. My mom always said that through it all, he didn't change. He got a little rougher around the edges." She turned and gave me a look I had never seen before.

I didn't understand.

Her eyes went from my eyes to my lips and back again. She wanted to kiss me, a part of me was sure, but I was so uncertain.

My heart was racing, and I finally decided to stop overanalyzing things. I leaned in and kissed her. I hadn't had much experience kissing girls, and a part of me wished Allison had been my first because that's what it felt like. That was all I wanted. I wanted Allison to be my first—my first kiss, my first love, my first everything—and at that moment, it felt like I was finally getting what I wanted.

Then reality hit. Allison pushed me off and pretty much leaped out of the pool. "I'm sorry. I have to go." She grabbed her stuff.

I couldn't speak. I stood in the cold pool water with a stupid, confused, and probably hurt look on my face.

As she opened the gate, she looked at me one last time and whispered, "I'm sorry." She meant it—I could tell by the look in her eyes—but it still didn't answer any questions I had. It also didn't kill the pain I was feeling, but I knew what would. I needed a ride.

14

CHAPTER

Andrew picked me up after an almost forty-five-minute wait. I couldn't complain since he was cool enough to pick me up randomly. I had to say it was awkward. He drove and made odd small talk like I was some stranger. I didn't know what to say, and after the pleasantries wore off, we were driving in a thick, uncomfortable silence. He did his best to avoid looking at me. He finally sighed and said, "You were with her, weren't you?"

I nodded my head.

"So, I guess she's your best friend, huh?"

I gave him a sour look and said, "Come on, man. Don't be so dramatic."

"Dramatic? Are you fucking serious? You're supposed to be my best friend, and lately all you do is smoke weed and hang out with my ex. You bastard! How could you do this to me?"

"Chill out, man! The fact that I smoke weed has nothing to do with you. Quit being so self-centered."

He clenched his jaw and continued driving. "Did she tell you why we broke up? Do you even know?"

"She didn't tell me anything," I replied.

"At that party she went to, she didn't just have one beer. She fucking lied, and I wish that was the worst part, but it isn't." He stopped for a second and then said, "She fucked some guy."

There was a silence between us. A thick, dead air stood between us like another person. It was mocking us and forcing us to believe what we didn't want to believe.

"I don't know who he is, and she doesn't either, but when she told me, I ended it. She tried to say she was drunk, she couldn't fight him off, all this bullshit, but I couldn't believe her. She was supposed to be mine, you know, she was supposed to be something special for the two of us and no one else, and she ruined it. She called me an asshole for not believing her, but, shit, if I got drunk and slept with some random chick, she wouldn't be so quick to forgive me. I'd still be an asshole. I was always the asshole, you know? I was always the scapegoat. Blame everything on the boyfriend; it's his fault. One of her friends had to nerve to say that I shouldn't be mad over this small bump in the road? A small bump in the road? That's what she fucking called it. If Allison stabs me in the back, I shouldn't cry, and she shouldn't be held responsible, but if I leave so much as a paper cut on her, I deserve to be fucking crucified.

"Allison is a slut. She is exactly like every other girl looking to have sex with the more damaged people because those guys are more fun. They say they want Prince Charming, but they are so ready to give it up to Shrek for a dollar and a ride home. I'm not mad at you for being there though; she's like a mermaid drawing innocent guys like us into her trap. Then when we survive, we're the animals. I hope you went and got what you came for. After all, that's all she's good for." He pulled up to Charlie's apartment complex. "I know you didn't ask to come here, but this is where you were going anyway. Have fun—for the both of us." He turned his head and said nothing.

I got out of his car and stood right by his door as he drove away.

I almost forgot I had gone swimming until a cool breeze passed right through my clothes. I did my best not to shiver as I approached Charlie's open door. Lights and music were pouring out of it.

As I stepped inside, I saw some people I had never seen before, and Josh was the only recognizable face. He stumbled toward me with a dumb grin on his face, "Aye, this is the greatest guy I know, like out of all us. Fucking Timmy, man, what's up?" He was drunk.

I noticed two very large vodka bottles and a half-empty case of beer on a table along.

"How much did you drink?" He was the only one acting drunk.

"Enough, Timothy. I drank enough." He hit me with a smile that was warmed by all the alcohol he had ingested.

"Where's Charlie?" I asked.

"He's downstairs with his girlfriend. I use the term very lightly. Hey, you think she'll find out about Gina? That shit'll be funny."

I almost forgot Charlie had a girlfriend, but I didn't want Josh's drunk ass to get anybody in trouble. "Shut the hell up—and go sit down."

He raised an eyebrow. "You know I can still kick your ass, right?"

I rolled my eyes and proceeded downstairs.

The door right under the staircase was open, and Charlie was smoking a cigarette in the doorway. "Timmy!" Charlie greeted me with a hug, which indicated that he was drunk as well. "Why you all wet, man?" he mumbled.

"It's a long story. Do you have a change of clothes?" I tried my best not to show that I was freezing.

Charlie nodded, and I followed him upstairs to his room.

"Who are all these people, man?"

He grinned and said, "Everybody here is a stoner, bro. Get ready to be higher than you have ever been in your life." He handed me a big red sweatshirt and some old blue jeans. I looked like I was getting ready to paint someone's house, but I wasn't looking to impress anyone out there and didn't care.

"Come on. Chelsey's parents aren't home, and we're partying up here and down there." He led me out of the crowded apartment. The noise started to build, the music was the only thing causing it at first, but people started to talk and interact. The sounds of the party started to build as more people started drinking, which led to more conversation, which led to louder music, which led to louder conversations.

I wasn't in the mood for a party. I felt wounded, like someone had punched a hole through my chest. I looked around with nothing but distaste and envy. As pathetic as it sounds, I couldn't stand that everybody else was happy except for me. I didn't hate them for it, but the stupid laughter and all the happy party music was mocking my emotional state. I didn't know if I could stay here without losing my mind. I felt restless. I felt like I had to do something about Allison and Andrew, but I couldn't do anything. What could I do or say to possibly change anything that had happened?

Everyone around me was so oblivious to my pain.

I sat on a stranger's couch, watched everyone else have fun, and wallowed in self-pity.

Josh ran clumsily down the stairs to bring me some good news, and I started to cheer up.

"We about to hit a real bong, kid." He almost lifted me off the couch and practically dragged me upstairs.

One of the strangers in Charlie's living room had been inhaling smoke from what looked like a large glass tube.

"Sit down," Josh commanded as he sat me right next to the man.

"He never hit a real bong before," Josh said.

The dude looked at me and said, "Get ready to get high as fuck, bro." He passed me the bong, and I held it with the ignorant clumsiness of a child for a few seconds before Josh rightfully snatched it from my clutches.

"Here, I'll do it for you. You're going to break something." He pulled a red lighter from his back pocket. "Just hit it, and when you form a cloud in this little tube here, I'm going to pull the part out, and you suck that entire cloud in, and I mean all of it, you suck that thing like you're a pretty boy in prison, you hear me?"

I scowled at him but did as he asked. I put my lips gently at the opening of the tube, doing my best not to let my lips touch the glass. Who knew whose lips had been on that thing? Once Charlie lit the weed, I started pulling in smoke.

The cloud started to form at the bottom of the bong, and the smoke crashed against itself in swirls and waves. Once the fog-filled up the tube, Josh pulled out the part of the bong that looked like a bowl, and all of a sudden, the cloud I helped create came rushing into my body like soldiers rushing into battle. The smoke that once moved slowly and eloquently inside the glass tube, rapidly and angrily forced its way into my lungs. I was coughing and choking before the bong was even remotely clear of smoke.

Luckily, Josh grabbed the bong and took the rest for himself, and the weed wasn't wasted.

The high hit me like an uppercut from Mike Tyson. The coughs and the chest pain disoriented me, and the high settled in like the lights you see on the ceiling before truly blacking out. All that surrounded me was white noise. I was happy, and so was everybody else. I couldn't hear what anybody was saying because I refused to listen. I focused on the feeling I got from it. It was beautiful tranquility. I was so anxious before—so ready to jump up and try to fix a problem that couldn't be fixed—but none of that mattered now. All that mattered was the calm, even if it was just the calm of the storm. All of a sudden, that big pain in my chest started to melt away.

After a few more minutes, I heard a knock on the door.

One of the girls opened the door, and a short, skinny man came hustling through the door. He found an open spot on the couch and took out two large glass bottles from a black plastic bag. He grabbed a Swisher Sweet packet from inside the bag and started rolling a blunt.

For a second, I thought everybody would be happy, but they all stared at him with angry, disgusted, and confused faces.

He looked up and glared at everybody, testing them, trying to figure out why they were all staring at him.

Josh finally broke the thick and awkward silence. "Yo, TJ, what the fuck are you doing here, man?" He spat out the sour words with a coldness that could be felt like a breeze.

TJ sat up and looked just as confused and just as angry as everybody else. "What the fuck do you mean? I came to smoke." He shot daggers out of his eyes to everyone who was staring at him. "Is there a fucking problem?"

"Why don't you go downstairs and talk to Charlie?" Josh stood up, towering over the frail but furious stranger.

That's when it hit me. He was the guy who had drugged Charlie. It took me a minute to process that. I knew Charlie had threatened to fight him the next time he saw him, and Charlie had spent four days in the hospital after he took TJ's mystery pills.

TJ shot up like a bullet and raced downstairs to see Charlie. As soon as he left, the whispers started. Some of them were retelling the story of TJ and Charlie, some of them gossiped about a possible fight, and some of them debated the idea of jumping him.

Charlie had more friends than I thought he did. It didn't even seem as though they were genuinely angry at what TJ did; they all were too excited to see a fight, and my heart started to pound as well.

I wanted to see a fight too, and I followed half the people in Charlie's apartment out to the steps. Josh was right on TJ's heels as he knocked on Chelsey's door.

Charlie opened the door, and the big, drunken smile on his face quickly faded into disbelief and panic. Charlie looked horrified, but he didn't look angry. He looked hurt and betrayed, but he decided to do nothing.

TJ said, "Aye, man, is there something wrong, bruh? Your people are tripping." He looked at Charlie with gentle and forgiving eyes.

Charlie slammed the door shut.

TJ made his way past the spectators and gathered his things.

Cole snuck through the crowd and found Josh. "What are we going to do?" Cole whispered.

Josh yelled, "Aye, TJ. Come here, man. I want to talk to you."

TJ stopped in his tracks and took a deep, exaggerated breath before coming back down, stomping on every step with a mean and ugly look on his face.

Cole gave Josh a questioning look before realizing that Josh was taking matters into his own hands. Cole silently stepped aside as TJ approached them. They both glared at each other with their chests out and their chins up, sizing each other up. Josh towered over TJ, but it didn't bother TJ one bit as he stormed over to where Josh was standing.

"Is there a problem?" TJ asked in an almost professional manner.

"Yeah, I got a fucking problem," Josh said.

TJ sneered at Josh without trying to hide his facial expression.

"Then what's up? You squaring up like you want to fight?" TJ raised one eyebrow high to the sky and looked Josh up and down. He shot laser beams of anger from his eyes, daring Josh to make a move.

"You know you sent my friend in there to the hospital, right? How stupid do you have to be? What pills did you give him?" Josh asked while returning TJ's threatening gaze.

"They were just some of the pills I have to take. He wanted to take them. I told him they'd fuck him up, but he didn't listen." TJ didn't seem to show any remorse or concern, which made Josh a little angrier.

"He was drunk—and a kid—and you're a grown-ass man." Josh stepped a little closer to TJ, and their noses almost touched.

"You right. I am a grown-ass man, so what are you going do, boy?"

Josh stared at TJ with his fist balled up and his jaw flexed. Josh remained motionless.

TJ said, "Nothing to say? So, you scared now?"

Josh grabbed TJ's shirt and shoved him so hard that TJ almost lost his balance.

Once his equilibrium had returned, TJ retaliated by throwing three quick punches to Josh's stomach.

Josh quickly threw his arms down to guard his stomach, leaving his face exposed to TJ's right hook. Josh tried to come to his senses and protect his face from TJ's speedy and furious attack. After a little while, Josh began to realize that TJ's punches had little effect on him. He started to block more hits and continued to shield himself as he waited for an opening.

TJ was relentless and continued to shower punches on Josh.

Josh surprised TJ with a powerful left jab that landed right on the bridge of his nose. The blow knocked TJ's head back in an explosion of blood, nearly knocking him to the ground again. TJ was a lot quicker than Josh, but Josh was a lot more powerful. Josh started moving his hands and feet and started to look like the boxer he was in Andre's backyard.

Josh and TJ circled each other each, trying to get the right angle, and Josh delivered a deadly right hook that almost knocked TJ down.

TJ kept his composure and his head in the fight.

Josh tackled TJ to the ground, TJ wrapped his arm around Josh's neck and put him in a headlock. As TJ's tiny arms tried to keep Josh's thick neck in his armpit, Josh started to feel for TJ's face. Once he found it, he hammer-punched it.

TJ's head bounced off the cement, and he quickly let go of Josh.

It was Josh's turn to rain down punches. Unlike TJ's fast and useless punches, Josh's punches were heavy, and he dribbled TJ's head on the concrete.

Josh didn't stop until Chelsey's drunken uncle stumbled out of their apartment and pulled Josh off of TJ. Josh breathed heavily and began to pace in circles as his adrenaline rush slowly died down.

TJ remained on the floor until Chelsey's remarkably short and remarkably drunken uncle helped him up. "All right. I've seen enough," the uncle said in a raspy voice. "Look, I don't know why you two were fighting—and frankly I don't care—but from what I understand, you're a grown man." He pointed at TJ. "That boy over there is sixteen years old."

TJ quietly took a switchblade out of his back pocket and started to move toward Josh. Luckily the very intoxicated adult stepped in front of the very intoxicated teenager to defend him.

"Hey, hey, come on now. Put that away. Now, he kicked your ass fair and square. He's a minor, and you're an adult. Now, this could go one of two ways. I can get the police involved, and you can explain the situation to them—or you can leave, and we'll call it a night. The choice is yours." Although he reeked of alcohol and cigarettes, he seemed coherent enough to be the responsible adult at the moment, however short that moment might have been.

TJ stood there with an even angrier look on his face as the blood dripped from his nose to the floor. He slowly turned around and marched away with the switchblade in his fist.

After TJ disappeared into the night, the small crowd began to cheer for Josh's bravery. Josh didn't seem impressed by all the compliments he was getting.

Charlie walked over, put his arm over Josh's shoulder, and said, "That's what happens when you mess with family!"

Josh shook his head and continued to drink.

The party was back on—and even louder and more exciting than before. Everyone murmured about the fight and talked about other fights. They still discussed the idea of finding TJ and jumping him—as if Josh's beating wasn't enough—but I didn't say much for the rest of the night. I listened, observed, and drank.

When the liquor started to hit, the people around me started to sound funnier, smarter, and more down-to-earth. I felt an undeclared bond with these strangers, and I didn't even know their names. As we all destroyed our livers, we all confided in each other like long-lost friends. The alcohol gave us all loose lips, making us tell old childhood stories, more recent endeavors, and our histories. We unintentionally revealed the truth about who we were. No one was listening—not even ourselves. We were once again strangers to the world and ourselves because it was hard to see the truth through blurred lines and foggy memories.

Charlie snuck out to talk to someone on the phone while Chelsey and Cole snuck into a bedroom. The apartment was too chaotic to notice anybody coming or leaving.

Josh was the center of attention at the party, but once all the hype died down, he snuck outside. When I looked around, I realized I was at a stranger's house and that I belonged outside with Charlie and Josh. I made my way out of their apartment and heard Charlie screaming at his phone. I gave him a confused look. Josh was sitting on the steps with his face in his hands.

"You all right, champ?" I patted him on the back.

"Ugh, I think I drank too much," Josh mumbled before releasing a painful, smelly burp.

Charlie was laughing and tripping over air as he listened to his phone.

"You don't believe me? Ask her!". There was long a pause, and I could hear the faint screams coming from the other line.

"Oh, you won't do shit, you pussy. Don't make me get Josh to kick your ass," Charlie said.

I walked over to Charlie and said, "Who are you talking to?"

Charlie turned to me with his bloodred eyes and gave me the most demonic look I'd ever seen on a human face. He laughed manically and whispered, "Abel."

I finally realized what was happening and why it was happening. After a few too many drinks, Charlie thought it was a brilliant idea to call Gina—but Abel picked up the phone. I wanted to tell him to hang up, but I didn't know what Abel already knew.

"What are you saying to him?" I asked.

"Aye, you can be mad at me all you want, but you aren't going to do anything." Charlie was too drunk, and watching Josh beat the crap out of TJ made Charlie want to get violent. After another long pause, Charlie said, "Oh, yeah? Fight me then, bitch. That's why I fucked your girlfriend."

"Why would you say that?" I asked. I didn't understand why Charlie was risking everything he had with Gina. He was revealing his secrets instead of keeping quiet and continuing to see Gina discreetly. Charlie wanted to start a fight, but in doing so, he would lose his chance with his dream girl.

Josh seemed to be one more burp away from vomiting. "What is he doing?"

"He's telling Abel everything we had to do to keep him away while Charlie sneaks away to his girlfriend's house. Abel will get mad and break up with Gina, and then they can be together. It's not going to work, but when you're drunk, any idea is a good idea."

Josh said, "TJ had a knife on him. He could've killed me."

15
CHAPTER

S unday slipped away as one of those lazy, uneventful days that remain in an ocean of useless and unobtainable memories. When the worst day of the week came, I was actually kind of ready for it. I had not seen anybody who had made my life stressful for the past few weeks—or in at least twenty-four hours. I didn't smoke or drink on Sunday due to the massive hangover I had to endure, and I felt ready. I went to school with a good attitude, but Allison's face still hung at the center of my thoughts like a portrait. My feelings for her were sweet and sad; I wanted to embrace the pain even though it was killing me. At that moment, I started to wonder when I had become such a masochist.

The day dragged on as usual, and though I hadn't seen any of the people I was trying to avoid, a part of me wanted to see them, confront them, and fix whatever was wrong, but I could honestly admit that doing so would be so overbearing that the hole I felt like in my chest might have given me a heart attack. I went about my day, laughing lightly here and there, and I socialized with the people who only seemed to be friends with me at school.

As I roamed through the hallways on my way to lunch, I caught a glimpse of Gina by her locker. I stopped in my tracks to go talk to her.

As I approached her, I realized she had been crying. She was packing all her books into her book bags as if she about to leave, and when she saw me standing there, she almost burst into tears again.

"Are you okay?" I asked.

She slammed her locker, turned to me, and shot death rays out of her teary eyes. "Were you at that stupid party on Saturday?" Gina's sad face was morphing into one of fury and rage.

"Yeah, why?"

"What the hell happened? Why did Charlie call Abel? What did you say to him?" She was doing her best to yell without being loud.

"I didn't say anything to anyone. What the hell is going on? I thought Charlie called you?"

"He called Abel!" Gina screamed, attracting unwanted attention. She started crying again and hid her face.

I gently placed my hand at the center of her back to calm her down. "Hey, it's okay," I whispered.

"No, it's not okay," she answered between sobs.

"What's going on?"

Gina slowly calmed herself before answering. "Charlie called Abel and said he and I were having sex, which isn't true because Charlie and I never did anything like that. Abel got hysterical. He started yelling, cursing at me, crying, and asking how I could do that to him. I kept saying nothing happened, but he wouldn't listen to me. I don't know … he took some pills or something like that. He was on something, but I don't know what it was. He kept yelling at me, and he started threatening Charlie and me. He kept saying how he was going to kill us." Gina's voice broke, and the tears started to flow once again. "Abel hasn't been home since Saturday. I'm scared that he's going to do something stupid. What if he does hurt Charlie?"

"Come on. Abel's not crazy," I said, convincing no one—not even myself.

"You don't understand. You didn't see the look in his eyes. I'm afraid he's going to hurt somebody or maybe hurt himself." She walked away without another word.

I could feel myself starting to panic. I knew what Abel had gone through, and if Charlie's life was at stake, then I knew I had to do something. I began to walk through the hallways, searching for Charlie, but I knew he probably wasn't in school. If there was a slim chance that he did decide to go, I had to warn him.

Once I was sure that Charlie wasn't at school, I decided to leave. I had two more classes to get through, but I couldn't wait that long. I rushed to the lunchroom; I knew I could escape through there.

As I approached a crowd of teenagers, I was abruptly stopped by one of the guidance counselors. She seemed to be waiting for me. "Timmy, could you come to my office for a moment?" Ms. Rodgers had such a sweet beauty about her. She wasn't anything jaw-dropping, and her modesty reminded me of a mom in a TV commercial. She didn't wait for me to respond.

I followed her into her office and sat in the chair that was closest to her desk.

She typed something into her computer before turning to me with a warm smile. "How are you, Timmy?" she asked.

"I'm good," I mumbled.

"Are you sure? Some of your teachers are a little concerned about you." She turned to her computer and started to pull up my grades. "Lately, you haven't been coming to school, and that's really been affecting your grades." She typed something into the computer again, and I heard her printer starting up.

"I know. I'm sorry. I'll pull them up." I was trying to end the conference as soon as I could so I could go talk to Charlie.

"You need to talk to some of your teachers about extra credit and maybe even ask if you can still make up some of the stuff you missed. You also need to turn in some doctor's notes or parent notes for some of these absences."

"Are they that bad?"

"Well, take a look." She handed me the paper with a list of the classes I was currently taking, and by each class listed, there was a number. That number represented how much of a fucking idiot I was. I had no idea the numbers would be so low. I had been so used to just slipping by with okay grades that I didn't realize how quickly those grades could slip into the gutter. I could honestly say that I was surprised. My grades were never perfect, but the grades she handed me didn't even look like mine. I wouldn't have believed her if my name wasn't plastered at the top of the paper.

"These grades can improve significantly if you do all of your makeup work—and if you stop skipping school." She looked right into my eyes. "We're concerned about you, Timmy. You have been letting your grades slip, and your teachers say you've been coming in late. You haven't been misbehaving, but a lot of us are concerned that something might be going on at home." She stared at me and waited for a response.

I quietly shook my head. I was still at a loss for words after seeing my grades.

"If there is anything wrong, or anything you want to talk about, you can come speak with us. It's our job to talk to you guys—not just about grades but about anything that could be causing you trouble. If it's something at home, something that has to do with your friends, anything that you might be going through, you can talk to me or any of the guidance counselors. I know you're a smart boy, Timmy. I know these grades can improve. You just have to try a little bit harder, okay?"

I almost mistook the concerned look in her eye for empathy, but deep down, all I saw was pity. I nodded my head in agreement.

"You can go, but remember that you can talk to me," she said.

As I walked out of her office, all the urgency to see Charlie vanished. I could almost feel my blood pressure rising, my heart beating a little harder, and a small dark gray cloud of depression forming above me.

As I heard the school bell ring to end lunch, I started dragging my feet to my next class. I knew it was stupid to leave school right then, especially after seeing how much I needed to do. I barely did any schoolwork before, but now I'd have to work like a brainiac just to get my grades up to passing.

As I sat through my next two classes, I couldn't help but wallow in self-pity. There were so many things wrong that I didn't know what I was most upset about. Allison was a pool of sorrow, and throughout the entire day, I was tiptoeing on the edge only to have the news of my grades knock me right into it. I was so angry. I was angry because I was confused. I knew I had made mistakes, but I couldn't piece together what I had done to come to this.

I always found solace in knowing that everything happened for a reason, but at that moment, I could not figure out what that reason was. Life was too complicated to ever be a straight line; the plan had too many moving parts, and the bigger picture was just too big. The weight of my problems was too heavy, and as I thought back on everything that had happened to make sense of it all, all I saw was a mess.

I was fortunate enough not to see any of my friends or Gina as I walked home. I caught a glimpse of Sophia turning on her street, but for once in my pitiful life, she was the least of my concerns.

When I got home, I thought I was through hearing bad news, but hearing bad news wasn't enough for that godforsaken Monday. My mom had been waiting for me as I stepped through the door to my room.

"What is going on with you?" She didn't even give me a chance to sit down.

"Nothing," I replied.

"Really? Nothing? That's the story you're going with? Are you kidding me?" She was pissed.

"What's the problem?" I tended to ask my mother stupid questions when she was really mad.

"The problem is your grades, Timmy! When I get a call from the school telling me that you're not coming to school, that you don't do any work, and that you're in danger of failing, I consider that a problem! Not to mention the fact that you're never home, and when you do come home you come home, you come home late. Sweetheart, when was the last time you even looked at the shower? You look like all of those bums you hang out with. Do you think I'm dumb? You don't think I know that you hang out with Charlie and all those trashy-looking kids who stay up there? So, you think I haven't noticed that all your clothes smell like cigarettes or alcohol? I've been doing your laundry for years, Timmy.

"Timmy, explain to me what's going on with you because I don't understand. Do you really want to be like those kids you hang around? Those kids who probably never go to school, probably treat their parents like crap and don't care about anything unless it has to do with smoking and drinking. You're not like those kids, Timmy. You're smart, you're sweet, and you can go to school, go to college, and make something of yourself. All those little punks you surround yourself with just spend their whole lives cursing their parents' names just so they can grow up to be just like them. Is that what you want?" Her eyes began to water.

I didn't want to see my mother cry; it would just add to all the things I had to feel guilty about.

Her tears quickly dried, and her fury resurfaced. "Now here's what you're going to do. You are going to do all of your makeup work, you're going to go to school every day, you are going to stop hanging out with those boys, and you are going to stop looking like you live on the streets because you don't. Do you understand me?" She spit out her words like venom.

"Yes, ma'am," I answered in a small voice.

"Now go take a shower. You smell like dirty underwear." With those final words, she went to her bedroom.

I started to do what she had ordered me to do. I took a quick shower and started on my missing assignments. I stared at each sheet of paper for thirty minutes before concluding that I had no idea how to do any of it. The history assignments were about periods I didn't know existed, the English assignments were about a book I hadn't read, and the math problems looked like hieroglyphics. I was so overwhelmed by all the work I had to do, and I didn't know where to even start.

I attempted a few math problems, tried to read something in my history book, and tried to figure which book we were reading for English. All in all, there wasn't any way I could finish any of my missing work. I closed all my books and collapsed on my bed.

I went to sleep, and then I started to dream. I dreamed that I could sleep for one hundred years. I dreamed that I didn't have to live my life without dying. I was never one to contemplate suicide. I would love to say that the reason would be because it's a selfish act, and I would never do something like that to my mother, but the real reason was quite the opposite. The real reason was that I was too afraid of death. I would think about jumping in front of a train, jumping out of a building, or poisoning myself, and I would think about who would miss me. What would they say about me? Would they cry over me? I'd think that'd be the only way to feel loved. Honestly, I'd just want the attention, but instead of being petty, I realized that I wouldn't feel any love. I wouldn't feel anything because I'd be dead. The attention I would get from all the grief would be useless to me because I'd be in the dirt. I knew that wasn't the reason some people became suicidal. I knew the weight of some people's problems was too heavy, that the dark cloud of depression that formed over their heads turned into a hurricane, and that they just wanted to escape it. The attention didn't matter to them. They just got tired of living the hellish minefield that was life. They just wanted not to deal with what they had to deal with, and I could understand that. I knew I was being stupid. A lot of people have it a lot harder, and I knew that times would get better, but I was not those other people—and the good times weren't there yet. Life just sucked, and I was doing nothing about it.

The next day, I had to get up and do something to get out of my slump. Instead, I was wishing I could sleep for one hundred years. *Maybe in one hundred years,* I thought.

16
CHAPTER

J osh and I continued to smoke until it hurt our lungs to even reach for more. We both sat and almost sank into the couch, staring into nothingness. We were motionless and silent. I felt almost incapacitated; no matter what I did, I could not move an inch from where I was sitting.

Our conversation kept dying down every time one of us hit the blunt, and we kept tapping each other on the knee to make sure we were both still alive. I kept drifting in and out of consciousness, catching only glimpses of the world around me and hearing only parts of conversations I didn't know were going on. I couldn't differentiate real life from my dreams. My dreams were so vivid that I gave up on figuring out if it was happening to me. If it was, I let it happen to me. I didn't fight it. I let the allure of my imagination entrap me into a reality that I knew could never exist. It was a place where I could be with whomever I wanted; it was a place where the curse of bad grades could not reach me. I could love, laugh, and wonder without worry. It was a place I could run away from life.

Waking up was like dying and waking up to your worst fears. It was like being struck down from heaven into a pit of horror and fire with demons instead of angels. My eyelids weighed a ton, but with the power of will, I opened them to find that I was still at Charlie's place.

Charlie was sleeping next to me on the couch, but Josh was nowhere to be found. I struggled to stand up. I felt slow and lethargic. I held a confused and almost angry look on my face, but no one was awake to see it. I quickly pulled out my phone to see what time it was. It was still dark outside, so I knew it couldn't be morning. When I checked my phone, I stared in disbelief. It was four in the morning. I was a bit relieved because I could still walk home. I was awake in time to go to school.

I shook Charlie lightly to tell him I was leaving. He groaned, and I decided to leave. The night was cold and dark. Sadly, I didn't feel high anymore; otherwise, the walk home would be less stressful and more fun. Instead, I was left with the after high, Josh's stupid name for the feeling you get after your high has passed. I chuckled at the idea. He was right; there was this weird buzz after the heaviest slumber of my life. It was like I was high—just not as high as I was before. I was coming down, and the stairs I used to step down were the same stairs I used to come up. The effects before and after were the same; you fell in and out of your high. The THC can only free you of gravity's clutches for so long. I walked and did my best to clear my head on my own. My mind was too crowded by all the smoke, all the stress, all the problems, and all the emotions, and it made me wonder if there had ever been a time in my life when I could think clearly.

When I got home, I snuck in through my window. The papers and the mess on my bed had vanished. My room looked neat, and I was a bit confused since my room hadn't looked like that when I left. It had to be my mother. It didn't take me long to realize that, but the fact that she cleaned my room wasn't what surprised me. What surprised me was that she never called when I was at Charlie's. She didn't yell, and she didn't lecture. If I made noise breaking into my room, she didn't wake up. It was a relief, but it was a peculiar behavior. My mother always complained when there was something wrong. I suppose she was tired of yelling at me. I started to realize what a strain I was putting on her.

If I fell asleep, I knew there'd be no way I would wake up in time for school. I pulled out all of my makeup work and tried and get something done. It all looked like a different language to me. I put it down, remaking the mess my mother just cleaned up. I kept pacing around my room and trying to think of something I could do to get the work done. I knew I could probably ask someone in class to copy their work, but that would still leave the extra credit assignments. I began creating a plan of attack. I didn't know how to climb out of the hole, but I knew that fixing my grades would be a start. In hindsight, the bad grades were the only hole I had to climb out of. I didn't have any problems of my own—or at least problems that adults like my mother and the guidance counselor would notice. I never truly thought I'd ever be caught up in high school drama.

I almost hated the word *drama*. If it wasn't used to describe a genre, then it was used by loose-lipped girls who gossiped about everyone, including themselves. The word *drama* made me think about reality shows. I hated reality shows. They were always far too dramatic to ever be like real life. The problems were always the same. Everybody was too honest for their own good, someone was always out to get someone else, and everybody was a victim. No one ever took the fall for anything wrong, almost no one apologized, and when they did, it was a big dramatic scene. The person who apologized always gets victimized again.

Josh was right; everybody had a sob story. I was just so tired of living in everyone else's sob story. I was tired of going through everything with everyone else; it was exhausting. *How many people do I have to make happy before I'm happy myself?* I started to question if there even was happiness left to pursue. Chasing after Sophia was like running after the moon, but at least that had a destination. Even if I never got there, at least there was a place to get to.

I felt like I was just waking up every day for the sake of waking up. I was living for the sake of living, and I still couldn't figure out what made the Riley brothers so happy. I liked feeling high and liked the escape, but what was the point if you just had to go back to all your problems. You returned to all your issues after you woke up, and sometimes it was messier than you left it. There was no one to clean up my mess after I went to smoke—not even my mother, who would if she could. The saddest part was that my life before wasn't so bad, but I still had the same underlying problem. I had nothing to fight for. I had nothing to look forward to. I existed.

My lonely thoughts were interrupted by a rapping at my window.

Charlie was watching me pace around my room—and almost gave me a heart attack. I jumped and checked the time again. *Five thirty? I left Charlie's house an hour and a half ago, and he managed to wake up.*

I opened the window and motioned for him to be quiet.

He entered my room, laughing silently the entire time.

"What the hell are you doing here?" I whispered.

"Dude, you left your bowl at my crib, man," he said.

"So, you come to my house at five in the morning to give me a bowl? This couldn't wait until tomorrow?"

"Who cares? You was up anyways. I watched you leave," he countered.

"Yeah, but what if my mom woke up? She's mad enough. I don't need another reason for her to yell at me."

"All right. All right. I'm sorry. I wanted to talk," Charlie said.

"To talk about what? And don't you dare say, Gina," I said.

"No, bro. Chill. Jesus, what are you so irritable for, man?"

I didn't know if I was angry or just annoyed. Maybe my mother was right. Maybe my problems would lessen if I stopped hanging around Charlie. "I just ... I'm trying not to get in trouble, man. What do you want?"

"Yesterday, I was on the phone with my brother, and I don't know, I wanted to talk to someone about it," Charlie said softly.

I couldn't endure another sob story, but I suppose my curiosity got the best of me. "He's the one in jail, right?"

"Yeah, Sean is um, that's his name, but he, I don't know, I guess I kind of miss him, you know," Charlie said. "He looked out for me a lot, and now I'm kind of on my own."

"I heard from someone that he went to jail because of cocaine or something. I don't know ... it was just what I heard."

"Yeah, I don't know. I told a lot of different people a lot of different stories. Barely any of them are true—some of them are partially true, but not what happened." Charlie looked distant, but he still managed to stuff some weed into the bowl.

"What did happen?" I asked, ignoring marijuana.

"Sean wasn't ever what people thought he was. Everyone saw him as the coolest fucking guy or some bum, you know, there was never any in-between. Everybody wanted to be his friend or his enemy. Sean's biggest enemy was my dad. My dad was a big dude, and my dad liked to drink, but he got real aggressive when he drank. When he wasn't beating me or Mom, he was beating Sean. Sean did have a girlfriend, she was pretty hot, and her name was Alicia. Alicia met Sean through a couple of drug deals. She hooked him up one time with an ounce of weed so Sean could get started. Pretty soon, Sean was making a lot of money.

"Sean was pretty good at selling weed—almost as good as he was at smoking it. You know, he could do every trick in the book: French inhale, making the little Os, all that shit. The first time I smoked, I was with Sean. Smoking with him was so cool; he made you feel like a hippie. He'd play old music from, like, the Beatles, and he'd play reggae sometimes just to get you into the spirit of smoking. He was always real mellow. My dad found out he was selling weed, and I thought he was going to curse him out and stuff, but he didn't. They talked one day in their room, and after that, Sean started making real money. He would walk around with stacks of money, he had guns and shit, he was on some next-level gangster shit. The truth was that my dad had Sean pushing other drugs. He only sold weed and maybe some pills to the people he went to school with, but Sean sold the real hard shit to some people I will never know. He sold it all though. Sean was the type of kid who could get his hands on anything, and once he had it, he'd sell it to the highest bidder.

"Well, shit hit the fan pretty fucking quick. My brother threw a party, and some of his friends came over. I remember I got fucked up and ended up passing out on the floor in my room. I never even made it up to my bed. Meanwhile, in the bathroom, my dad was snorting enough cocaine to fucking give King Kong a heart attack. My dumb-ass dad left the bathroom and left all his shit out. All his coke was on a tray by the sink, already lined up and everything. Everyone else at the party chose a different kind of white powder. It was hydrocodone, and my brother likes to crush them up so they can snort them and shit. So, then Alicia, the life of the party, the one chick who could out-drink and out-smoke anybody who wasn't Sean, had to take a piss. She walks in the bathroom, sees the tray, and snorts some of pure fucking cocaine. The entire party, she had been taking shots and snorting hydros, and so that one line of coke had her foaming at the mouth. Her friend freaked out and called 911 and everything got busted. The cops came so quickly … it was like they were waiting just around the corner, or at least that was what my brother said. I woke up when the cops busted in. The ambulance took Alicia away, and that was the last I saw of her. My dad and my brother got arrested. It was as simple as that." Charlie walked over to my window and lit the bowl. He blew the smoke outside, holding the bowl out the window as well.

"Why did you lie?" I asked.

"After he got arrested, it was all over the internet. People Sean went to school with kept posting the news article, police report, or whatever the fuck it was. They kept talking about it, and it pissed me off. They all laughed at him and commented on him like they had any fucking clue what they were talking about. After his class graduated, people still asked about Sean, but they didn't know what happened. They heard rumors, but they wanted me to tell them the truth. So, I told them more rumors. Fucking people will believe anything about somebody—as long as it isn't something good." Charlie hit the bowl again and then motioned for me to smoke.

"Why'd you lie to us though?" I asked as I reached for the bowl.

"Because it's easier than explaining myself," Charlie said.

We smoked until my mother woke up. Luckily, she didn't smell the smoke, but she knew I was home. She hammered at my door and yelled for me to get up and go to school. I waited to get ready until after she left.

Charlie and I kept smoking. We got a little more careless after my mother was gone; instead of blowing the smoke out the window, we left the window open. I got ready pretty quickly so I could keep smoking before I went to school. I suddenly realized that I had never been to school high before. It didn't hit me until I looked in the mirror. My eyes were red, glazed, and barely open. I might as well have walked into school smoking. "Shit, dude. I'm stoned. I have to go to school," I said.

"So? Ho to school," Charlie replied.

"I can't go to school looking like this."

"It's called eye drops and coffee. You'll be fine." Charlie grabbed all his things and climbed out my window. "Hey, can you do me a favor?"

"What?"

"Could you hit up Abel after school?" Charlie gave me a huge mischievous grin.

"I thought you told him about all this already. He's going to know what I'm doing," I said as I looked frantically for eye drops.

"I didn't say anything about you. He knows me and Gina have been sneaking around. Come on. One last time—I have to see her," Charlie pleaded.

I rolled my eyes, but I agreed to find Abel. Gina had said he was missing, but he was probably just hiding from her.

Charlie left, and I was stuck trying to figure out how to sober up in thirty minutes. Luckily, my mom made coffee. I poured some into a plastic cup and started walking to school. All I could do about my eyes was pray no one would look me in the eyes.

I drank my coffee slowly on the way to school. It burned my hands a little to hold the thin plastic cup, but I sucked it up as I hurried to school. I walked as fast as I could. I even spilled some of the coffee on my hands. I cursed, threw the cup out on the street, and started speed walking. I didn't know why I was rushing. The opportunity to get to school on time had already escaped me. As I rushed to the school, my mellow high was turning into paranoia. I looked behind every tree, by every bush, for someone who was out to get me. I knew I was late, and being late made me more noticeable, and for once, I wanted to go unnoticed.

I got to school a few minutes after the late bell. My teacher didn't say much as I hurried to seat with my eyes glued to the floor. I pulled out a binder from my book bag and started reading old notes, doing my best to act natural.

Gabriel Hastings, a soccer player who sat in front of me, was the only one to notice my strange behavior. Gabriel wasn't exactly my friend, but he was obnoxious enough to talk to anyone—even if they weren't talking back.

"The hell is wrong with you?" he asked, attracting the attention of a few of my peers.

I tried my best to ignore him and kept my eyes in my binder.

Gabriel would not be ignored. "Aye," he said a little bit louder.

I sighed before making the dreadful mistake of looking up.

His eyes met mine at the same time, and then it was too late. The split second it took for my eyes to reach his was all it took for him to notice what was wrong. As soon as his gaze met mine, a wicked smile formed on his face, and an evil laugh followed right after. "You look high as fuck!"

I soon got all the unwanted attention I could want.

Gabriel laughed at me and gave me a thumbs-up as if there were some secret joke between us. The people close enough to see my eyes all laughed with Gabriel. I quickly hid my face and continued staring at my notes, hoping that everyone would go away if I stayed in between the covers of the book for long enough.

My worst fears were realized when the teacher walked over to Gabriel's desk to see what all the commotion was about. "What seems to be the problem?" Mr. Nelson asked with his arms crossed.

Gabriel continued to giggle before fully calming down.

"Mr. Hastings would you please inform the class what is so funny that you had to disrupt my lesson?" Mr. Nelson's face grew more serious the longer he stared at Gabriel.

Gabriel still couldn't fight a smile, but he calmed down enough to say, "I'm sorry, sir. I, um, I got gas."

The entire class laughed.

Mr. Nelson rolled his eyes and said, "Please just be quiet, Mr. Hastings. Some students actually care about their educations."

Gabriel shrugged off Mr. Nelson's insult and winked at me. I was grateful that he had diverted the attention from me, but I was also annoyed because he had attracted the attention in the first place.

The day went by terribly slowly, and by the third period, my high had left me to face the boring day sober. I was a bit lonely at school. Andrew had ceased any connection with me, Allison had moved or gone to great lengths to avoid me, and Charlie never went to school in the first place.

I said hi to people and made small talk with whomever I sat near in class, but it was easy to tell the difference between friends and classmates. My conversations with classmates only lasted about five minutes. They were almost always about schoolwork, and it was almost always about how we didn't want to do it. The smarter kids would complain for about thirty seconds before starting on their assignments and finishing them, and the other guys, myself included, would slowly and reluctantly do the work.

School was as boring as it was depressing. Most of the time, if the strain of schoolwork doesn't get to you, it's the social life you're watching everyone else have except for you. It was like the social groups were just there so you can fully understand that you don't belong anywhere. I hated those groups—or I envied them. They all went through high school together, drinking the same kinds of drinks, talking to the same kinds of people, and doing things so similar that you often couldn't tell them apart. I didn't ever think that any of those kids in a *squad* understood the concept of friendship, but who was I to judge? I barely understood it myself. I realized that Andrew was a smokescreen. He was concealing the fact that I didn't have any friends. I was truly alone.

I was no better than Charlie, Andre, or the Riley brothers. They were all outcasts, all belonging to the social group that no one ever had a name for. A part of me was happy I was an outcast; it meant I couldn't be labeled by my peers. I was different, but if history proved anything, it was that it fucking sucked to be different.

After school was over, I made my way home, knowing very well that I probably wouldn't reach home. As I walked, I noticed Andre standing in the middle of the sidewalk. He was saying hi to the few friends he had at school. He stood there with a tank top, showing off muscles that weren't there, and smoked a cigarette with his cup of Kool-Aid in his right hand.

"What's up, Andre?" I said as I approached him.

"What's good, Timothy? You trying to smoke later? I got this shit called green crack, bro. It'll fuck you up … I'm telling you." He kept his eyes on the people walking by, hunting for someone he knew.

"I'm kind of broke at the moment," I replied.

"You can smoke with me, man, free of charge. Just when you have money, bro, hit me up." Andre winked at the girl walking by, and she gave him the most disgusted look I'd ever seen.

"Have you seen Abel?" I asked.

"Yeah, he's been staying with me the past couple of days. Did you hear about Gina and Charlie? That's kind of fucked up, man," he said between coughs.

"Yeah, I heard. How'd you hear about it?"

"Abel told me, bro. Charlie is about to get his ass beat."

"What do you mean?"

"Abel said he's going to fight Charlie, dude. Abel just doesn't want Josh to play bodyguard like he did with TJ. I don't even know why he even fought the dude. It wasn't any of his business, and it wasn't like TJ force-fed Charlie those fucking pills. One of these days, Josh is going to fuck with the wrong person—and he's going to get fucked up. Just watch."

Before I could respond, I turned to see Sophia and Grace. My heart stopped, and I stood still as a statue as she walked by. She saw me standing there with Andre. All of a sudden, I was on the outside looking in. I was the outcast, and I realized that Sophia was an ocean away from me. I was too different, too flawed, too damaged. I was a whole island away. I was on a different level—a lower level. I was on an ugly, dark, and lonely level. I realized all this by looking into her eyes, and I didn't know if what I saw was what she felt or a reflection of how I felt about myself. No matter what it was, I didn't like what I saw—and neither did she.

17

CHAPTER

Andre and I went to smoke in his backyard. He gossiped about people I didn't even know and Josh and Charlie. He talked about the Riley brothers and almost everyone he invited to the party. He also spoke about Gina. I was a stranger to her. The stories surrounding her always involved a lot of alcohol, a lot of drugs, and someone always got lucky at the end. It was all fun and games to Andre, but to me, it was a little unsettling. He made her seem as careless as he was and as relentless as he was. If Andre was the perfect asshole, he made Gina into the perfect tramp. A lot of what he told me sounded a bit too exaggerated to be true. However, when I asked about the football players, he confirmed it to be true.

It was sad. What he revealed about her seemed like he was talking about a different person entirely. To Andre, Gina was just another number in the long list of girls he'd been with, girls his friends had been with, and girls he knew were willing to give it up. He lived in a different world than I did. A bad day only meant he didn't smoke or get laid that day. He didn't stress about his friends, his grades, or his problems; instead, he embraced them. Rather than trying to get over his slump, he rested at the bottom of the pit and enjoyed it as much as he could. He didn't aspire to do better. He didn't regret his ways. He was just him, and that was enough of an excuse for him to be an asshole. The truth was that if it were between Andre and me, Andre would always get the girl. He grew up wanting to get laid, and I grew up wanting to be in love. If anything, I was a scapegoat. After they'd mauled through as many assholes as they could, they would end up with a guy like me—a guy who would never hurt them. I didn't want to be that guy, but I lacked the arrogance that females found so attractive.

These thoughts swirled around my head as Andre and I smoked. Andre never shut up, but I wasn't paying attention. I kept smoking almost to the point of passing out. Andre would touch my shoulder to keep me awake or pass me the blunt. Andre was informing me about his friend who lived across town and had good weed plus some females. I didn't understand what he was saying until he told me to get up.

"Where are we going?" I asked as I slowly rose from my comfortable beanbag chair.

"We are going to my dude's house. I'm just about to serve this dude real quick and then maybe smoke a blunt."

"Another blunt?" I said.

Andre laughed and said, "Man, if you can't handle it, you can always go home."

"Nah, I'm good." I floated through Andre's backyard. I was so high the air thickened as my eyelids slowly closed like theater curtains. I couldn't tell if I was walking slower or if time disagreed with me. I lacked the motivation to even move. I think being high was the only time I'd be okay with becoming a vegetable. At least I wouldn't have to move. I could just eat, sleep, and dream.

It was kind of funny how stressed out I was only a few short moments ago, but the stress had vaporized in all the smoke. I was stress-free, hungry, happy, and sleepy; being high started to get redundant. Smoking weed was getting old. When I was high, my dreams were too vivid—and reality wasn't vivid enough. I didn't want to smoke any more. I was already too high, but I was never good at saying no. I wanted to escape it, but I was too high. I was too deep within the clouds, and the fall back down would take an eternity. I never thought I'd be afraid of heights, and while my mind exploded with thoughts, memories, and hypotheticals, I couldn't put them into words. It was like I was a deep thinker for nothing—like if Socrates kept his philosophies to himself.

Andre led me to his friend's old minivan, which had four people in it already. I was stuffed into a hot car that smelled like cigarettes and urine with a bunch of strangers who looked either too old or too young to be in the car with us. Luckily, I was fortunate enough to be sitting by the window. I couldn't fall asleep; they were all too loud and moving too much to let me sleep. The driver was a heavyset guy in his late teens or early twenties. He was tall, and his untrimmed mane made him look like a bear. Besides being kind of big, all of Andre's friends looked like that. What they lacked in muscle tone, they made up for with five o'clock shadows, bloodred eyes, messy hair, and dark bags under their eyes. It looked like they all wore makeup.

The driver played loud music, and everybody else in the van made it their mission to talk over it. I stared out the window and shut my eyes whenever I got the chance.

"Aye," Andre shouted. "Wake the hell up. We haven't even got there yet."

I sat up and did my best to keep my eyes open.

"Your friend looks high as fuck," someone said. I didn't try to figure out who said it; I kept wiping the imaginary crust out of my eyes.

"He is high as fuck. Still a rookie, I got him smoking weed and shit, and now that's all he does. Shit, let's see if we can get his cherry popped too."

Andre and his friends laughed at me, but I was too high to even give them a dirty look.

"Here." Andre passed me a joint. "Hit this shit."

I slowly and almost involuntarily grabbed the joint and used my old, dried-out lungs to inhale it. My mouth was starting to get dry, and my coughs were harsher and more painful. After one hit, I passed it back to Andre.

"Aw, look at him. He's so fucked up," said the girl sitting shotgun. She was a blonde with green eyes and was pretty in a strange way. The darkness under her eyes was makeup, and her eyes weren't exactly pearly white. They were red like the rest of us, and she fit in perfectly with this weird group of people.

"He's my friend, and it's my job to make sure all my friends get fucked up with me," Andre announced proudly.

"He's so cute. He can't even talk," the girl said.

"Hey, Lauren, why don't you come back here and slide him a kiss or maybe some head?" Andre teased.

"Maybe ... if he can stay awake," she replied.

"You hear that, Timmy?" Andre screamed in my ear and hugged my shoulders with one arm. "If you wake the fuck up, you might get laid. Wake the fuck up, Timmy! Here." He passed me the joint again.

"Oh, sweetheart. Don't hit that. Andre, come on. He's done," Lauren cried.

"Don't listen to her. Timmy, hit that shit. Don't listen to that bitch. You take that shit like a man. Do you hear me? Hit that shit. Hit that shit." Andre soon had all the guys in the car chanting with him.

Lauren shook her head, and I grabbed the joint and took the biggest hit my chest could take.

They applauded and cracked jokes, and I coughed and wheezed like an asthmatic old man.

We stopped by a gas station, and everybody rushed out of the van, forcing me out as well. While the hairy dude pumped gas, the rest of them entered the store as a group. I waited by the car and tried not to pass out.

Watching all of them in the store laughing and enjoying each other's company made me miss the friends I once had. I missed our simple, innocent fun. I didn't know what friends I still had left. I didn't know if I could even consider Josh, Charlie, Andre, Abel, Amiel, or anyone else I hung around since I started smoking actual friends. Then again, I didn't even know if Andrew was a true friend either—or perhaps it was me who wasn't true. I wasn't sure about anything; nothing made sense anymore.

Despite my depressing thoughts, it was hard to think. I had inhaled so much smoke that it had snuck its way into my mind, stuffing all the empty spots with a thick sense of claustrophobia. The air around me was suffocating.

To my surprise, Amiel walked out of the gas station. By the time I looked up, he already had his hands up. "Timothy, my man!" He tossed me a bottle of water.

Out of sheer luck and reflex, I caught it.

He stopped in his tracks to take a good look at my eyes. "Damn, I don't think I've ever seen someone look so high, dawg. The fuck did you smoke?"

"I'm so fucking stoned," was all I could muster.

"Yep, you sure are. Come with me, man. You look like shit." He motioned for me to follow him.

"What about Andre?"

"That's why you're coming with me. He's throwing a party or some shit, but he said for a fact that there'll be girls there—and you like ass, man, I'm telling you."

I nodded my head and followed him.

Andre just waved and shouted that he'd see me later.

Amiel walked fast, and it slowly burned my high to have to hurry behind him. He led me through a crumbling neighborhood to get to his house. I sipped on my water quietly as my thoughts inched their way to clarity.

"Bro, you need to chill with that smoking shit, man. Like you just hit your first blunt, and every time I see you now, you're either high or about to get high," Amiel mumbled with a cigarette in his mouth.

"Is that bad?" I asked.

"Well, let me tell you this, if you were a girl your age and just lost your virginity, and every time I see you, you are either about to get some dick or are getting dick, would you consider that a problem?"

"Why do you have to be so graphic?"

"'Cause it's real!" Amiel shouted. "How does it feel to be the equivalent of a ho?"

"I'm not a ho," I said.

"I didn't say that. I said you're the equivalent of a ho," he replied.

"How?"

"That's just how it is, man. People want kids to stay in school so the girls won't turn into hookers and the boys won't turn into crackheads." He lit his cigarette and blew a puff of smoke in my face.

I ignored him and said, "Being a stoner isn't as bad as being a ho."

"Why the fuck not? So, a girl who sleeps around as much as she wants has a problem, but a guy who spends all his time fucking high doesn't? Get the fuck outta here. You know sometimes girls are going to fuck, bro. If it doesn't start in high school, it'll start in college. If not there, then after. There's going to come a time in your life that when a girl tells you she's been with more than one or two guys, and it's not going to be that big a deal. She did her freaky shit when she was young, and when she grows up and becomes somebody's mom. End of story. When girls become hos, however, and I mean real ones, the ones whose headcounts are higher than their ages, they fuck just for the sake of fucking. They fuck because it makes them feel good, and it's a few minutes or hours away from the mirror, so they don't have to realize who they are or what they are. So, tell me, Timmy, why does that remind me so much of you?"

"I'm not a ho. I'm not a girl. Why are you comparing me to a slut?" I asked.

"The same reason people compare Coke and Pepsi, bro. Girls and guys are the same, but like different, you know what I'm saying? Like, we want the same shit. I mean, fuck, it's hard to explain." He paused and took a long drag from his cigarette. "Everybody wants to be happy, and when they're not, they hurt, right, and that hurt, a lot of the time, makes people do dumb shit. They're not dumb people—they just in pain. Like what I heard about Gina, and I know you and dude had this thing going with her calling it love and shit, and who knows, it might be, but sometimes shit just isn't what you think it is. Love, like real love, isn't what you think it is. Like Josh told me, and he called her a ho an ass of times like he had no more respect for the girl. Like, I guess what I'm trying to say is, we're all the same, you know. We all have to live, we all have to go through shit— even though it's different shit—and even though that's the same for all of us, bro, like, we all create different demons out of our problems. You can't judge people off of what they do. Like, you don't know what they have to deal with, and you don't know why they do things they do—and a lot of times, they don't know either."

"So, if you can't judge them off their actions or their words, how can you judge them?" I asked, breathing heavily as I hurried along his side.

"You can't."

When we arrived at Amiel's house, he led me to his room. His room wasn't that different from Charlie's room; it wasn't as big, but it was just as cramped. He had a big TV just like Charlie did, and just like Charlie, it seemed that the television was the only thing appealing about his room.

Amiel slipped away to talk to his mom and told me to wait. I was starting to feel a little less high, but I was still so tired. Every movement was a chore, and I wasn't motivated enough to accomplish them.

When Amiel returned, he rummaged through his closet, pulled out shirt after shirt, judged each of them with a serious face, and mumbled to himself.

"You don't have to give me clothes, man. I have clothes at home," I said.

"Bruh, let me help you, dawg. There will be girls at this party, and I know for damn sure you can't spit game, so the only other option is to get you swagged up real nice."

"Swag isn't everything," I replied.

"What?" he shouted. "Man, I can pull bitches with Jordans and a bucket hat. If not, I got words smoother than cream cheese, baby." He laughed as he tossed me a couple of shirts. "Try them on, man," he said.

I studied the shirts and said, "So, I'm supposed to put these on—and girls will magically talk to me? Getting girls is as simple as having swag?"

"You'd be surprised—and don't think of swag as just the clothes you wear. Think of it as a mindset," he responded, undeterred by my sarcasm.

"A mind-set?" I asked.

"Yeah, man, like, you look better, you feel better. You feel better, you get more confident. Girls like a confident dude. If you go and get a hoodie just to hide behind the hood, girls ain't going find that attractive. They're going to think you're creepy, like you're hiding some dark evil secret when you're probably going to be the least creepy dude at this party. Every guy in there is going to be trying to grab-ass or titties, and the guy who doesn't look like a rapist. Does that make sense to you?" He scowled at me and waited for an answer.

"I guess."

"All right, then, shut the fuck up and let me put you on, bro. Don't undermine the swag. Trust me. When you pull bitches like you pull blunt hits, then you'll understand."

I tried on a few of his shirts and pants before Andre made the final decision of dressing me in a red and black Polo shirt and some khaki jeans. He didn't have any shoes that would fit me, so I was stuck wearing my old run-down Converses, but for the most part, I looked good. I had a plain white T-shirt under the Polo shirt, which made me a little hot, but Andre insisted on it.

"See? Now you look good—or at least decent. I can only do so much," Amiel bragged.

"So, what do we do now?" I asked.

"Now we pregame." He slowly pulled out a bottle of vodka from under his bed. It looked like Amiel had already started drinking out of it. He walked to his kitchen to grab a red plastic cup. He handed me the cup and poured it until it was a quarter of the way full. He held the bottle up for a toast, and I raised my cup to meet his bottle.

"Here's to getting fucked up on a school night." We raised our drinks, and Amiel took a big gulp out of his bottle.

I didn't drink mine. The smell was intoxicating enough—not to mention the taste.

"Ah!" Amiel shouted after drinking. "You ain't drinking, dawg?"

I shook my head and put down the cup. I was still fighting drowsiness with everything I had. Amiel had succeeded in getting me dressed—but failed at waking me up.

"Bro, I'm about to get some ass. That'll make my night." Amiel nodded his head in agreement with himself.

I chuckled and then took a small but painful sip from my cup. "I'm not going to lie. I'm fucking high," I said as I stared at the cup on his floor.

"You need to chill, man, for real. Too much of anything is never a good thing," he replied as he took a big sip from his cup. "Come on," he said, and as he stood up, he stumbled a little.

I slowly followed him out of his house. Abel walked a lot slower this time; he walked with confidence, taking every leisurely step with purpose.

I scurried behind him like a rodent.

Abel was such a good-spirited person, especially when he was drunk. He walked by every single person and nodded at them, knowing very well that they were all strangers. He walked those treacherous streets like no one could hurt him, like nothing on earth could kill him.

I was in awe of his confidence. I liked Abel. He wasn't arrogant. He was just comfortable in his skin, and he didn't care what anyone else thought of him. At least that's how he carried himself.

As I analyzed my charismatic friend, I got a text message.

Allison: Hey, can we talk?

Me: Sure.

I tended to stare at my phone for a whole minute after I sent a text to see if she responded as quickly as I did. I don't think anyone responded quicker than I do. It was so rare for me to even receive text messages from anyone other than Andrew or my mother that I dreaded even opening text messages.

Allison took her time—or perhaps she was busy—but I kept staring at my phone and waiting for a buzz that I knew I would still hear or feel if I put the phone in my pocket.

Amiel continued his jolly walk down the street. He was almost a complete block ahead of me. I did my best to hurry after him without fully running.

When I caught up to him, he put his arm around me and said, "Timmy, my man, there ain't nothing like taking a stroll through the ghetto when you tipsy as hell."

I smiled and nodded. I never really considered that part of town to be the ghetto, but as I looked around, I began to notice things I hadn't before. I didn't feel at all threatened or scared to be there. I always thought I'd be afraid for my life if I walked through a tough side of town—or afraid of getting robbed or something—but I wasn't scared.

Amiel wasn't scared either; he walked the streets like he was talking a stroll through the park. I was a little nervous when I walked with Abel before, but now I was not even ready to flinch.

The people Amiel nodded at—all the old weary-eyed people—didn't look threatening to me. They just looked really sad and really tired. They still greeted Amiel nod with a smile or a "what's up" and continued on their way. Everyone I saw seemed to understand each other to a certain extent. It seemed like they all knew the weight of each other's problems. I realized Amiel was the same way; he had this calm, understanding way about him that made you wonder what he'd been through. Everyone out there knew each other's pain and empathized with one another. They all knew how difficult it was to grow up in a place like that or how terrible the events must have been to end up there. I was a stranger in a strange land, but I was no stranger to strife. By the looks of all the people around me, I couldn't help but think that maybe I was.

"Aye yo," Amiel said. "You want something from the store before we go? I ain't making no late-night burger trips again, man. Too many cops out here for that."

We were approaching a corner store that looked as though it was once somebody's house. There were a lot of people smoking cigarettes or drinking forties outside of the store. A lot of the women looked undesirable to anyone who wasn't in the store.

"Aye!" Amiel said. "You want something or not?"

I shook my head.

"Aight, you ready to get fucked up? You think you can make it through the night?"

"Why wouldn't I?" I asked.

"Shit, you never know. We freaks of the night, man. Anything can happen," Amiel answered ominously.

18
CHAPTER

When we got to the house, I had a sick feeling in my stomach. It looked old, broken down, and even haunted. There weren't many cars outside, but I could hear loud murmuring from the sidewalk.

When Amiel opened the door, they shouted his name. He raised his bottle of liquor to the sky, and they cheered for him as if he was holding up a championship trophy.

Lauren was sitting on Andre's lap, and as she pulled in smoke from her blunt, she held the smoke in for a little while before turning Andre's head toward hers and blowing the smoke into his mouth. As I watched this transaction, Lauren kept her eyes on me the entire time. I didn't know if she was taunting me or flirting with me.

Andre blew out the little bit of smoke, turned to me, and shouted, "Timmy! Aye, someone bring me a blunt and let this man show you how to hit that shit!"

I hadn't realized that they were impressed by how I hit blunts.

Lauren passed him her blunt; he grabbed it and passed it to me. "Here, my friend, hit that shit like a fucking G!"

Everyone in the living room had their eyes on me. Part of me wanted to be offended that I was considered a novelty to a bunch of idiots, but the truth was that it was nice to be the center of attention for a change. I took the blunt and pulled in as much smoke as fast as I could for as long as I could. When my lungs wouldn't allow any more smoke, I did my best to hold it in. It was like trying to hold your breath underwater. My cheeks were puffed out, and I could feel the strain bringing out the veins in my neck. Once I started to feel dizzy, I coughed up the rest of the smoke and dropped on the couch.

I could barely hear their muffled cheers. I felt like someone had punched me in the face, and that was the limbo between consciousness and being knocked the hell out. I sat down next to some guy with dreadlocks, shades, and a lot of jewelry. He smiled a big, cheesy grin and put out his fist for a fist bump. "You ever smoked purp?" he asked.

"I don't even know."

He laughed at my response and then slowly pulled a blunt out of his pocket. "Here," he said. "Hit that shit." He gave me the blunt and a lighter.

I lit the blunt and hit it carefully. The pull still made me cough a great deal. I passed the blunt back to the guy, but he told me to pass it to the person on my left. I did as he said, and after that guy hit the blunt, the guy with dreadlocks pulled out another blunt and lit it. I could feel a grin creeping its way onto my face.

Andre said, "Look at Timmy smiling. You about to get high as fuck, Timothy!"

I ignored his obnoxiousness and continued to smoke with this strange kid with dreads.

His name was Dre—or at least that's what they called him. He and I didn't speak—I mean, we did, but we hardly used words. Dre continued to pull blunts out of his pocket. It was like a never-ending pocket; every time I decided I was high enough, Dre silently disagreed and passed me another blunt.

Dre and I were the only ones who weren't moving. We sat on the couch motionless and smoked ourselves nearly to death.

Amiel kept walking around and talking to any female he could find; there weren't many at the party. Andre paid more attention to his friends and his Kool-Aid, and Lauren could only pay attention to him or her cigarettes. The only time Andre gave her the time of day was when Amiel got too close. I could tell Amiel was amused by how territorial Andre was; every time Andre pulled Lauren away, Amiel laughed or smiled to himself.

I was only there as a witness to the madness. I couldn't move, and even so, I didn't want to. I was perfectly fine being half dead with my buddy Dre. No matter how high I got, he continued to pull blunts out of his pocket. I had never seen someone with so much weed, and I had never been so high in my life. My eyelids were closed; all I could keep hold of was the blank slide that appeared right before the real picture because the real picture kept constantly changing. Every time I blinked, I saw either fewer or more people arriving. If I shut my eyes for even a moment, it was like an hour went by. I must have been falling asleep because every time Dre passed me the blunt, he had to shake my shoulder a little bit.

I watched the chaos, the loud, meaningless chatter, the never-ending substances, the dim lighting, and the thick, lingering smoke that made everything I was looking at hard to see. The noise reminded me of the parties I used to attend as a child. I was reminded of the hectic birthday parties; no matter how chaperoned they were, they remained frenzied. Somehow, this one was no different. We were all just kids trying to have fun at any cost—just like when we were eight. I was very sad to think that our idea of fun had to change. Of course, it would be very weird and almost scary if we all still play like we did when we were eight, if we all still pretended we were superheroes or pirates—or if the only thing we needed for a decent party was imagination and a lot of sugar.

The truth was we were still those kids playing pretend. We were all pretending it was normal because maybe it was. We were all pretending it was fun because maybe it was. It was fun to watch and probably even more to fun to be a part of, but if it was anything like those birthday parties, we'd realize in a few years how pointless it all was. We were never really pirates or superheroes; we were just kids being dumb. By that logic, we were still kids—and all of it was just fucking dumb.

It was easy to get lost in it; it looked like so much fun. All around the room, there was nothing but smiles. I still couldn't fight the feeling that an impending darkness was ready to snatch whatever was left of our innocence. I couldn't blame them though. All the music, the sweet noise, the sweet highs, the lack of sobriety, and the lack of truth made everything so blissful. That bliss could only come from the sweetness of not knowing.

They all just let the music flow through them, drank, and enjoyed each other's company—even if they didn't know the person. They just loved the sweet, dark pleasures of the night; they were craving the dark world we would soon live in. The world was just out of our reach. It was the end of our beautiful youth and our heavenly adolescence. They craved the cruel, unforgiving adult world that would soon consume us and engulf us in its blurred lines.

When you are young, it is very clear what is right and what is wrong and what is good and what is bad. It was as easy as black and white. In that world, in that shadowy realm, there was nothing but gray. Right and wrong only existed as points of view and could only be determined by perspective. If not, then the wrong thing shouldn't feel right—and doing the right thing shouldn't be so hard. People don't even know what the right thing is anymore. I don't know what the right thing is anymore. There was only this, only the smoke, only the high. Nothing else mattered. Nothing else was real. I remained in the smoke of it, swallowed by the beautiful, fraudulent gray.

I was soon woken up by someone who dropped their body right next to mine. I turned to see who it was, and it was Abel. He wore a big, goofy smile and reeked of alcohol. "What's up?" He handed me his drink.

I refused, and he laughed along with the rest of the party. I wanted to talk to him. I remembered what he had said, but nothing seemed to be bothering him. He was very drunk and very high. We had nothing to discuss that pertained to anything that would ruin the buzz.

As soon as I realized Abel was there, I kept a close eye on him. He was wasted, but he continued to drink. He almost finished Amiel's bottle and kept asking for more. He stumbled and slurred his words. It looked like he was just aiming himself in whatever direction and throwing himself there. Abel looked awful, and it didn't take much to realize how annoying he was getting. He kept jumping on Andre and begging him for some of his Kool-Aid.

Andre kept cursing at him and was very protective of his purple drink. The more Abel drank, the more he kept begging for Andre's Kool-Aid.

"Man, who keeps giving this dumbass drinks? Man, come on, Abel!" Andre shoved Abel to the ground.

Abel did nothing but laugh, and everyone around him was rolling their eyes or shaking their heads.

"Come on, Andre. Give me that good shit!" Andre laughed maniacally.

"If it'll shut you the fuck up!" Andre finally handed the cup over to Abel.

Abel grabbed it appreciatively and sat right next to me. At first, he drank it slowly, but once Andre left the room, Abel started chugging it. It didn't take a genius to figure out there was more than just juice in that cup, but I didn't care enough to ask what it was.

Abel was soon silenced by whatever was in the drink, and I returned my focus to the rest of the crowd.

Dre kept handing me blunts, and I soon lost track of how many I had smoked. I was half asleep, and if it wasn't so loud, I would've forgotten where I was. While I struggled to stay awake, I looked around the room and caught Lauren staring at me. I didn't know where Andre had gone, and I was way too stoned to wonder if it meant anything. She soon made her way over to where I was sitting. With Dre, Abel, and I taking up the couch, I was curious about where she was going to sit.

Without thinking twice, she solved this problem by sitting directly on my lap. "Hey," she said as she stole the blunt Dre was about to hand to me. She took a big puff and then, using two fingers, she pulled me closer until our lips touched. She exhaled and forced all the smoke into my lungs. I quickly spat the smoke back out in a loud and painful cough, and Lauren just smiled at me.

"You okay?" She rubbed her hand on my cheek.

I nodded, completely hypnotized by her. At that moment, she could have asked me to kill a man—and I probably would have done it.

"You're not like these guys, are you?"

I stared at her—confused and way too high to speak.

"Are you one of the good ones, Timmy?" She smiled at me.

I couldn't muster up any words. My eyes were locked on hers, and I could only nod.

She giggled before taking another hit and whispered, "Good." She blew all the smoke in my face, and I turned to see Dre smiling at me and putting his fist out in agreement. I touched his knuckle with mine and then laughed. I was at a loss for words. My mind was racing, but my mouth could not move.

"Hey," Lauren whispered in my ear. "Do you want to take a shot with me?"

I honestly didn't want to drink, but she had control now. Nothing—no logic—could interfere with my desire to be close to her. I was almost brain dead. My actions were my own, but reason, judgment, and the voice in my head were shouting, "This is wrong!"

White noise filled my mind. It was as if I went on instinct, but it was not survival instinct—or perhaps instinct isn't the right word. Desire is what drove me. Desire is what had control of me. I was hooked like a fish to whatever could make me feel good. I was even dumber than the fish. A fish will always be tricked into biting that hook; it almost always takes the bait. I wasn't baited. I wasn't tricked. I chose to be there, and at that moment, I decided not to leave. I didn't care about anything else. I didn't have anything else: no Andrew or Allison and no Sophia. It was even sadder knowing that I had nothing but this. I wasn't smart like Sophia. I wasn't an athlete like Andrew or Allison. *Do I have anything other than this? What do I have other than the present?*

I had no future, and compared to Amiel and Abel, I had no past. All I had was what I was feeling right then. In a few hours, I wouldn't feel that way. I would feel the same way I felt before—or worse. I realized that the white noise I was hearing, the white noise that clouded my thoughts, was me. I was nothing more than white noise, meaningless, pointless noise. I was born only to die; I suffered only to suffer again. Where was my paradise? When would I be happy? Was everything I was going through just a passing smoke—or was I trapped in my downfall?

The party was as much a drug as the ones we were taking. This was a child's party, like the one we used to attend. The only difference was the games we played. The only difference was the party favors, the hats, the piñata, and the balloons had transformed into weed, liquor, music, and Lauren. Even the girls they invited were as much party favors as the rest. Without party favors, there was no party. Without girls, there was no party. I hated to think that I was the slightest bit sexist, but I didn't hold a candle to every other guy at this place. At least I felt guilty about it.

I followed Lauren to the hallway that led to the bedrooms. I didn't question her. I followed her like a hungry dog.

Before we reached a bedroom, Andre came out of the bathroom with a bucket of water. "Who wants to hit the jeeb?" he shouted.

Lauren quickly turned to me and asked, "You want to hit the gravity bong first?"

"What's that?" I answered.

"You never hit a jeeb?" Andre said as he set the bucket down on the dining room table.

"Bring your ass over here, Timothy!" Lauren grabbed my hand and led me to him. No one else got up because no one else cared. Andre was the only one who ever made a ceremony out of me.

"You, my friend, are very high, probably on cloud nine or some shit, but this right here will send you to cloud forty-five. This, amigo, just might kill you."

All I saw in front of me was a bucket of water, a lighter, an empty two-liter bottle with the label ripped off, scissors, and a pencil.

"What is it?" I asked.

"You about to see some fucking science shit, dawg. Watch." Andre went to work. He cut the two-liter bottle in half, took the cap off of the bottle, and placed the top half of it into the bucket of water. He moved his attention to the pencil. Using his teeth, he ripped the eraser off of the pencil and used the scissors and his teeth to try to separate the eraser from its metal holster. After nearly ten agonizing minutes, he finally got it out. He picked up the bottle cap, lit the center of it with the lighter, and used the pair of scissors to make a tiny hole. He grabbed the metal part of the pencil and carefully bent the bottom of it inward. Andre squeezed the empty eraser into the bottle cap, after struggling with it and finally making it fit, and he screwed the cap back onto the bottle.

Andre placed his invention at the center of the bucket of water, put tiny pieces of weed in the empty eraser, sealed the cap, lit the weed, and slowly pulled up the bottle. As he did, the smoke began to fill the bottle in milky swirls. When the bottle was a thick and silky white, he quickly removed the cap, letting tons of smoke out in the process, and sucked in almost of the smoke while he was pushing the bottle back into the water. Before he could clear it, he choked and coughed like a dying old man, letting the rest of the smoke rise from its container like a chimney.

"Your turn, Timmy!" Andre shouted between coughs. He pushed the bucket in my direction.

Lauren packed it with weed. "I'll help you." She lit the jeeb, and the bottle started to fill again.

I didn't know if I could even stand that much smoke since my throat and chest still burned from all the smoking I had done already. I still hit it.

Once Lauren was done filling it with smoke, she took the top off, and I leaned in to inhale the smoke that was racing out of the bottle. I put my lips on the top and let the smoke enter my lungs. As soon as it did, I started choking, coughing, and wheezing like an asthmatic. I couldn't take all the smoke—not even half—before I started to almost die.

Everyone laughed, especially Andre.

It was like being hit in the head with a bat. My brain rang, and the dizziness knocked my equilibrium loose. I dropped to the floor, and tried my best not to cough anymore. It hurt to cough, but it also hurt not to cough. No matter what I did, my chest and throat were in flames. I was in another world. I was a ghost, and the only thing that reminded me that I was still human was how much my lungs burned. I slowly stood up and giggled like a guy on laughing gas. My head was a balloon full of hot air.

"You like that shit?" Andre asked as he helped me find a place to sit. I was finished. There was no way I could smoke any more weed; if I breathed in secondhand smoke, I'd probably croak.

I felt my phone buzz in my pocket. It was probably my mom, but on the off chance that it was someone else, I pulled it out and read it.

Andrew: Yo!

I was way too stoned to answer him. It was a level of high that I had never reached. My problems were irrelevant and incomprehensible. I didn't know anything at that moment other than how I was feeling. I could stare at the ceiling and feel like I was falling into it somehow.

While everyone else stood up to hit the jeeb, I sat at the table with my head in my hands and tried my best not to worry. How high I was almost didn't seem natural. Once everyone had hit the jeeb at least once, Andre took another hit and then tried to get Abel's attention. "Hey, asshole. Wake up and hit this," he shouted.

Abel didn't move.

"Yo, Dre. Wake his ass up."

Dre shook Abel's shoulder, but Abel fell face-first onto the couch.

"He out," Dre stated indifferently.

Amiel walked over to Abel, lifted his torso, and sat him up straight. "Yo!" Amiel started to shake him violently, but Abel still did not respond.

I could feel the tension building; everyone else could feel it too. The reckless thrill of the party was being replaced by something a lot deadlier: fear.

"Yo!" Amiel slapped Abel's face, and a stream of blood slowly dripped out of his nose. "He's fucking overdosing!"

Amiel's words muted everything and knocked us back into reality. It was almost like throwing us off a train.

Dre stood up, calmly put his hands up like he was surrendering, and said, "I'm out."

Everyone else followed except Amiel, Andre, and the guy who drove the van. Amiel continued to shake Abel as much as he could, but Abel remained unresponsive.

"Yo, what the fuck did he take?" Andre rushed over to Abel.

"He snorted some Xanax with me, but that was it. We only had one!" the furry driver shouted.

"Nah, that shouldn't knock him out like that. How many did he take?" Amiel checked for a pulse.

"We just had one. He said he'd never done it before!"

Andre looked over to his empty cup on the floor and picked it up. "Yo, he drank all my lean."

"Lean?" Amiel shouted. "You had fucking lean? How strong is that shit?"

"It's pretty fucking strong. I never drink the whole thing. Holy fuck!" Andre was afraid of the possibility that Abel wouldn't wake up.

"We have to take him to the hospital!" Amiel tried to pick him up.

"No! That shouldn't be enough for an overdose, right? I mean, he barely had anything!" Andre cried.

"Do you want to wait around here to find out? Are you willing to take that chance, Andre? This is your house, your weed, and your fucking lean that might've killed him. Do you want to stay here and wait?"

"Fuck!" Andre ran his palms through his hair and paced around his living room.

Amiel ran up to the guy who drove the van and shouted, "Can you drive right now? You have a van, right? Can you fucking drive right now?"

"Yeah," he stuttered. "Yeah, I can drive. I can drive!" He didn't seem too sure about himself, but at that point, it didn't matter to any of us. The only thing that mattered was Abel's life.

"Andre, help me get him up!" Amiel commanded.

Andre and Amiel lifted Abel off the couch and struggled to get him to the van.

I stood in the center of the living room, frozen in shock.

"Timmy!" Andre shouted. "Come the fuck on!"

I snapped out of it and hurried to the van. A part of me knew there was no way Abel was about to die. *This doesn't happen!* A part of my brain couldn't comprehend the possibility of Abel dying. As selfish as it sounds, I wasn't as scared for Abel as I was for myself. I was with them. I was guilty by association. I couldn't get over the trouble we all were probably about to get into. *What will my mother think? What will she say? The word will get out soon to people all over school. What will they think? What will Sophia think?* Those were the thoughts running through my brain, and I knew how pathetic they all were.

CHAPTER

19

"How the fuck do we get to the hospital?" Amiel shouted as he shoved Abel into a seat.

"I don't fucking know. Do I look like a fucking GPS?" Andre said.

The driver pulled out of the driveway, and the tires screeched as he sped down the street.

"I don't know where I'm going!" the driver screamed as he continued to drive in any direction that felt right.

"Just get on the interstate," Amiel said.

"What?"

"Get on the fucking interstate. Hurry up!" Amiel continued to check for a pulse, and he finally gave up and just put his ear by Abel's mouth. "Okay," he whispered. "He's breathing."

I couldn't tell if Amiel was scared, but Andre and I were frightened. Amiel kept his composure. If he showed any emotion, it was anger. He looked like he was cursing himself for letting this happen or for putting himself in that situation. I felt the same way.

Go home. All I had to do was go home; it was that simple. I had smoked until my lungs were nothing but shriveled up pieces of cardboard. I didn't need to smoke anymore; it was a school night, and I should have been home. I wasn't, and now I am in the car with a kid who possibly overdosed and a drunk driver.

"Drive faster!" Andre cried.

"Drive the fucking limit; there are cops out!" Amiel said.

"We can't have him in the car, man!" Andre pleaded.

"He's not going to fucking die, you moron. If we get pulled over, we are all fucked—so can you calm the fuck down?" Amiel's attempts to calm us all down were failing to say the least.

Paranoia was all I could feel. My heart was beating out of my chest like a vibrating cell phone about to fall off the counter. I felt like I was going to have a heart attack, and in all the madness, I realized something. I was completely sober. The high had left me as quickly as everyone left the party. I hadn't been drinking, and my chest still hurt, but it was like I had smoked all of that weed for nothing. I was scared. I felt fear, guilt, regret, and every other emotion I smoked weed to avoid.

"Turn here," Andre said, and his friend turned onto the interstate.

I looked out the front window, but all I could see was darkness.

"Turn on your headlights, dipshit!" Andre cursed.

"All right!" I could hear the alcohol in his voice. His speech was sloppy and slow. He was drunk, but he was our best option.

Amiel kept trying to wake up Abel, but nothing was working.

Once we were on the interstate, we drove as fast we could, going at least ten miles over the speed limit.

Andre frantically searched his phone for directions.

Amiel did the same, but his screen went black. "Fuck! My phone died. Does your phone have a GPS?"

"I don't know" I said. "I don't think so." Amiel snatched the phone from me and started to look through my apps.

"I got it!" Andre cried. "I got it. You're going to make a right turn in two miles."

"You hear that? We almost there, man. Wake your dumb ass up, man. Come on," Amiel said.

Abel wouldn't budge.

I didn't know what to do. All I could do was wait, but I still didn't know what the plan was for when we got there. If we brought him inside, there was almost no doubt in my mind they would question us or call the cops to do it.

"What are we going to do when we get there?" Andre asked.

"I don't know."

"Amiel," Andre pleaded. "Amiel!"

"What?"

"Are we going to leave him at the door? Man, we could just leave him there. They'll find him."

"Are fucking stupid?" Amiel spewed.

"Man, I can't go to jail. If we leave him there, they'll find him. I'm telling you," Andre replied.

Amiel said, "No one is going to jail—just chill out and let me fucking think."

Everyone stopped talking for a minute.

"Okay, listen. We are not dumping him in the front. When we get there, you're going to park the car—but keep it running. Don't get out or nothing," Amiel said. "Timmy and I are good, but the two of you are too drunk. We will carry Abel inside. Do you understand?" Amiel was looking me in the eyes. "We are going to bring him in and ask for help. As soon as they got him, we walk out. Don't talk to anyone. Don't make eye contact. We leave. If they call for us, just pretend we don't hear them. If they follow us, walk a little faster. Don't you dare run? We're trying not to look suspicious, all right? After we give them Abel, he's their fucking problem. Our main concern should be not getting arrested."

"You're going to take the next exit," Andre said.

"Are you up for this?" Amiel looked me dead in the eye. I nodded my head but was not being completely sure of myself. I imagined the transaction in my head, and I could feel the adrenaline pumping through my veins.

In all the confusion, I tried to compose myself. I had a job to do, and I needed to be confident enough to do it. I went through all the possible scenarios in my head. *What if they try to stop us? What if Abel doesn't make it? What if we have to run?*

We were getting close, and I had conjured up all the courage I could to handle the task at hand. The van was completely quiet. I tried to calm myself down, but I couldn't. My blood was pumping, and I couldn't fight the feeling that it was all going to go wrong.

All of a sudden, Abel jerked up, scaring Amiel and me. His nose had stopped bleeding, and it looked like he had barely come back from whatever world he disappeared to.

"He's up!" Amiel shouted. "He's fucking up!"

Abel mumbled something we couldn't understand, and Andre and his friend looked back—and that's where it all went wrong. We had been speeding for so long that we couldn't even feel how fast we were going. The driver took his eye off the road for a second to look at Abel, but when his eyes returned to the interstate, we were way too close to an SUV that was in front of us.

It all happened in a second. It was like blinking, and then all of a sudden, the world ended. The only thing I could grasp was the sounds of the car. First, it was the screech of the brakes trying their best to stop the car, then it was the crash, and the big bang when the car rammed into a tree. It happened so fast that all I could do was listen—and not even watch—as my life was nearly stripped from me.

Before we could hit the SUV, Andre screamed, "Look out!"

The driver tried to slow down, but crashing his old minivan was inevitable.

Andre grabbed the wheel and jerked it, and we missed the car in front of us. The car flew into a tree, and the only people with seat belts were Andre and the driver. Abel was launched like a rocket into the radio, opening a big cut on his forehead and probably knocking him out if he wasn't out already. I felt the jerk forward, but I also felt a jerk back. Amiel's arm raced to meet my chest like a baseball bat. My head hit the back of Andre's headrest. Amiel jerked forward but had a seat belt on, which confused me because I was pretty sure he didn't have one on before.

He was just that fast. Once the back of that enormous van was in our headlights, Amiel had strapped on his seat belt. Once Abel went flying, Amiel went over him, trying to stop me from going through the window. It was the back of Andre's seat, however, that stopped me. Amiel was good, but he was not God. He couldn't stop this. It was too late. We were doomed the second we left that old haunted house—and we all knew it.

I could feel my head starting to hurt and something burned on my arm. I had probably been cut, but it didn't matter. As soon as the car stopped moving, I kept my eyes shut and squeezed them together, hoping I'd be home when I opened them—and I could shake off this scary dream. I couldn't because it was no dream—but I still couldn't open my eyes.

Amiel grabbed me. "Timmy! Timmy, wake the fuck up! Are you good?"

I slowly looked up and noticed the terror in his eyes.

"Timmy, come on, dawg. Answer me." Amiel continued to shake me.

I slowly opened my eyes.

"Are you good?" he asked as he helped me out of the car.

I didn't respond. I couldn't speak, and I could hardly breathe.

"What the fuck?" It was all I could squeeze out of my broken voice box. After we got out of the van, Amiel started to drag Abel out of the car.

"What the fuck!" Andre yelled as he struggled to open his door.

Abel wasn't waking up, and we had no idea how we could escape. There was no escape; no amount of weed or alcohol could make it not exist. It was not going away. I finally realized what I had been doing for the past few weeks. At that moment, I had to do what I hadn't been doing. I had to face reality. The real world jumped in and ruined our perfect oasis. We were all so isolated from what the reality was, so when the reality came, we weren't prepared for it. I wasn't prepared for it. I didn't want to face anything. I didn't want to work for anything. I wanted so much for my life to have purpose, but I did not search for one. The only thing I ever really wanted was the attention of a girl who was too busy with her own life to worry about mine.

I kept hunting for approval, for sentimentality, for someone to come and tell me that I mattered, but I didn't. I was there because I deserved to be there. No one forced me to be there. I had every chance to just go home. It was painful how easy it could have been to avoid it all. The past mocked me, laughed at how simple the answer was, and in a symphony of a hundred voices, sang to me that I couldn't change a thing. I couldn't go back. All I could do was swallow the lump in my throat and wait for the police to arrive.

There was a car parked on the other side of the road, and a man walked over to us with his cell phone to his ear. Andre's friend was passed out in the front seat, Andre and Amiel looked like they were just shaken up, I had a few minor cuts on my leg from the glass, and Abel more than likely had a concussion.

The rest of the night happened like most nights: in a blur. The police questioned everyone; we had to take a Breathalyzer, and they put us in handcuffs. We all shared the same expression—eyes wide in disbelief—and we hung our heads in shame. Our hands were shaking from the fear of almost dying. The lights were what scared me though. The lights made me uneasy. I was ashamed—just like we all were—and the cops interrogating us didn't help. They constantly reminded us that we could have been killed—or could have killed someone else—as if we didn't already know that.

The medics took Abel to the hospital on a stretcher; he never woke up from his daze. They took the driver away first. After questioning Amiel and Andre, they took them away in the same car. I waited in handcuffs on the hood of a police cruiser for them to finally take me to jail too.

A police officer walked over to me. I recognized his face, but I couldn't figure out from where. He looked just like all the other police officers: hard, relentless, and indifferent.

"Is your name Timmy?" he asked in a booming voice.

"Yes," I whimpered.

"What happened here?"

"We thought he was dying ... we tried to take him but ..." I was one word away from crying, but I wanted to at least pretend I had dignity.

"Can I ask you something?" He didn't show any sympathy, not that I deserved it, but it still would have been nice. "Why is it that when your friends breathed into our little toy, they were well over the legal limit, mainly because anything over point zero is over the legal limit for them. The kid in the front seat is a grown man, and he's getting a DUI. Your buddy Andre had weed in his pocket along with being drunk. That stupid ass tried to get rid of it—we didn't even search him. Your friend Abel might need his stomach pumped, and he has a concussion, and Amiel was just plain drunk. You must be special because according to our little toy, you haven't been drinking at all. All your friends say that you weren't drinking, that you were just there looking for Abel. So, tell me, why the hell are your eyes so red?" He stared at me and waited for a response. He was peering deep into my soul and studying every facial expression I made. He was like a human lie detector.

I couldn't answer. I knew he would be able to tell if I was lying, and I also wasn't about to incriminate myself either. I tried to find the words, any words, any form of response that would make him leave me alone.

"Nothing?" he asked without taking his eyes off of mine. "Are they just sensitive to light? You got allergies? What is it?"

"I've got allergies," I whispered.

"Okay, so what's your story ... just at the wrong place at the wrong time?"

"Yeah," I whimpered.

"Okay, you're coming with me. Let's go." He grabbed my arm and led me to his patrol car. He opened the door to the back seat, sat me down, and shut the door. After a few words with other police officers, he got into the driver's seat and drove off.

I was certain I was getting arrested until the officer turned around and asked, "Where do you live, kid?"

I gave him a confused look and said, "You're taking me home?"

"You're a minor out late on a school night. You haven't been drinking. I assume you haven't been smoking, and according to your friends, you didn't get there until they were rushing to the hospital. Is that true?"

I couldn't believe my ears! I was going home. After everything, I was going home, and all I had to say was "yeah."

"Okay, well, I am going to have to let your mom know what happened. Does she know you were out this late?"

"No," I replied. "I snuck out."

"Okay, well, tell me where you live, son," he said in a calm voice.

I gave him directions, but it was hard because I had never been to that part of town.

The officer took the nearest exit and turned around.

The hospital was right by the exit, and the exit was right by the crash. We were a minute away from reaching our goal; we were sixty seconds away from being in the clear. It was amazing how detrimental a few seconds could be.

I sat in the back of a cop car in handcuffs, and never once in my life did I think I would end up there, but part of me knew it was inevitable. I had no idea what would happen next or how it would affect me if it did at all. I wanted to think that I was better than this. In my head, there was a voice that was slowly being silenced by much louder voices. The voice said, "You don't belong here; you're better than this." The louder voices roared, "You deserve this." What scared me the most was understanding that they were both probably right. As shallow as it sounds, I was worried more about what my friends were going to think. I was more concerned about my peers. I wondered what they would say, what they would ask, and how would they find out. *Will this make me look cool or like even more of a loser?*

I felt bad for Amiel. Andre and his friend looked like they were used to trouble. Andre had been expelled, so he was no saint. Amiel was not a saint either, but he didn't deserve to be arrested. He tried to help, and he tried to do the right thing. He manned up when no one else would, but I was still the one going home. I knew he had been drinking, but he had far better judgment than I had. I always imagined that I would be the one to step up in emergencies, but at that party, I was just as scared and selfish as everyone else. Had Amiel not been there, we would have all left Abel right where he was. Even if he didn't overdose, it didn't matter because it wouldn't have mattered to us if he had. I didn't know what was worse: trying to help him when he didn't need it or leaving him when he did.

As we pulled up to the parking lot, I noticed the lights were out. I knew my mom was home. It was funny how much I cared about the opinion of my peers when, in a few seconds, only one opinion would matter. My mother's. Despite not having to enter a cell, I might as well have been with how angry my mom was about to be with me.

"Which one is yours?"

I pointed to my apartment.

"Okay, stay here." He left me in the car and went to knock on my mother's door.

It took a little while before my mom came to the door in her pajamas. They talked for a moment, and she sneered at me through the glass. The officer didn't talk to my mother the way he spoke to me; his face seemed soft and understanding. He walked over to the car and opened the door to let me out.

"All right. Your mom's pretty pissed, so you have to go deal with that. Look, don't think you can miss school because of this. I'm going to call you into my office tomorrow, and we're going to talk, all right?"

"Your office?" I was confused.

"I'm Officer Williams. I'm your school resource officer. You didn't know that?" He looked genuinely puzzled, and so was I.

"No."

"I walk down the hallway every day, and you never noticed me?" A smile formed on his face.

I shook my head.

"Huh, and this is how we meet? What a shame. All right." Officer Williams took off the handcuffs and got back in his car. Before he left, he rolled down his window and said, "Good luck." There was a sneaky grin on his face.

My mom was waiting for me by the door with her arms crossed and a look that could scare the devil back to hell. I slowly walked inside, and before I could even step one foot in the apartment, my mother slapped me hard across the face. It didn't hurt; it hardly ever did. It was mainly the surprise of receiving a beating that affected me. I knew I couldn't just walk away; there was no way I could just go hide in my room—even though that's exactly what I wanted to do.

"Sit down," she said in a stern voice.

I did what she said.

"What is the matter with you? I told you not to go out with those kids, and that's exactly what you do. Are you stupid? No, you're not stupid. You're my son. Why are you doing this to me? You don't think it's hard enough for me to raise you by myself? Huh? Now you have police officers bringing you home? What is going on with you? Please tell me." Her voice started to crack, and I could see the tears starting to build up in her eyes.

A weight started to press against my chest. After everything that happened that night, the last thing I wanted was to witness my mother crying. I shot up from my seat and rushed to my room.

My mother quickly followed, but she wasn't quick enough to stop me from locking the door. "Tell me!" She banged on my door. "Tell me … what did I do?" She kept banging on the door, screaming, crying, and asking me what she had done.

I leaned against the door the whole time, knowing her what she was asking. Where did she go wrong?

CHAPTER

I was never the type of person to always be on Facebook or any other kind of social media. It was not that I was some self-righteous person who thought he was above all that. It was mainly because I had no home computer, and my crappy phone barely ever had Wi-Fi. So, due to the circumstances, I learned to live without it. It was not that I never went online, but on mornings like that, I realized I could go offline for weeks at a time without anybody noticing. I mainly used it to see what everyone else was saying or doing. I never posted anything personal or even said I was currently eating a sandwich because I knew no one cared. If I posted a big long paragraph about how my life took a turn for the worst, people probably would read the first sentence before deciding to not look at it anymore. I knew because that's exactly what I'd do. The only good thing about the internet was discovered that a lot of people had a sense of humor. If I could find something funny as I scrolled through the nonsense, it would almost be worth it to give twelve hours of my life to a website.

That morning, I realized how negative everybody socializing on the internet can be. I had heard of cyberbullying, and I luckily was never a victim of it because no one cares enough about me to waste their status by calling me ugly, fat, or gay. I'd seen a few stories about people who had killed themselves over it. It would happen in a different state or right in my school.

When sending nudes started to become popular, the idea of cyberbullying got a little bit darker. There was this girl, Natalie, who was at the wrong end of a very powerful gun. I didn't know her well; all I knew was her name. One day I—along with everyone at the school with a phone or a computer—soon knew a lot more about her. No one knew who did it, but whatever boy she had been dating with a grudge or a sincere lack of a conscience had posted naked pictures of her all over the internet. The pictures were the talk of the school for about a month, and they didn't go away as fast as they should have either. Every time it was taken down, some other kid would repost it. The cycle went on, and it wasn't like this poor girl didn't have defenders. The comment section was filled with people, mainly girls, disgusted by what they saw and outraged that whoever did it dared to do so. Natalie ended up dropping out of school. Rumor had it that she became homeschooled because she was too embarrassed to show her face in school. I didn't blame her. I have no idea what it's like to be a girl, but even as a guy, I wouldn't want my naked picture up for everyone to see. I'd probably hide under a rock. What happened that morning wasn't anything like that, but it was pretty close.

That morning, I woke up on my own accord. My mother left without saying a word to me. I was dreading school, mainly because if I knew anything about kids my age, I knew that what happened the night before had already become the topic of conversation. It didn't matter because I didn't have to go to school for the suffering to start.

Before I got ready for school, I did what most teenagers do the second they wake up. I checked my phone. The Wi-Fi in my apartment complex was spotty, but on that occasion, it worked just fine. I decided to go online, which was a big mistake. I often agreed with the people who didn't believe cyberbullying was real—not entirely—but in some cases. If you don't want to see it, don't open it. Don't go online. Just shut off your laptop or your phone. The stupidity of people was a sort of drug. I knew most people posted dumb crap and dumb opinions, but I still felt the need to check it. Ignorance is truly bliss because even if you know someone is saying something, even without knowing what they're saying, you almost always assume it's either hilariously stupid or undeniably offensive. It never matters which one it is because everyone still wants to read it. If someone is getting bullied online, and they know they're getting ridiculed online, they still check because no matter what people say about them on social media, their imaginations can come up with so much worse. They don't check it because they are willing to get insulted but because knowing beats not knowing any day.

While I scrolled down, I noticed an article. It wasn't news to me that people liked to share or repost news articles they believed were talking for a good cause. Most of the time, it wasn't even news—it was just bloggers with the same strong opinions as whoever reposted it. It was almost funny how much the internet was filled with opinions as opposed to actual information. That article would not have caught my attention had it not had Amiel's face on it. It was an article from the local newspaper because any arrest in our area is public news—not to mention a car accident. The writing of the article wasn't what angered me or surprised me. Some news reporter doing his job didn't upset me. What upset me was how quickly the people at my school were willing to share and repost it. I mean, it happened in the middle of the night. An article written that quickly was believable, but who is up all night searching through news articles just so they could find someone they know who had been arrested.

The title and article said things like "DUI," "minors in possession of narcotics," and "motor vehicle accident." No one would look twice into it unless it involved someone they knew, and in that case, it did. There was a list of people who reposted it and shared it. The comments included "Damn," "That's crazy," "Anyone you know," "LOL," "So stupid," and "Tsk tsk."

I didn't know why Natalie's story came to mind when I saw that. Being arrested and trusting someone with your naked pictures were two very different things, but it was a shame that no matter what you did out of school, your classmates could still find out about it. Natalie might as well have walked through the hallway without a shirt, and Andre and Amiel might as well have been arrested in front of the whole school. It was the same thing.

I wanted to know if people knew I was there, and even if they did, did they care? I slowly got ready for school, angry at a desensitized generation, and still not fully over the shock of nearly being killed or arrested. The sensations came in waves. It was a relief I almost didn't look forward to. Every second, every thought, everything I saw, and everything I did brought me right back to the night before. I often contemplated my death; I'm not suicidal, but I always thought I wouldn't be so scared of it. The more I thought about how it all went wrong, the more ideas of how it could've gone a lot worse came to mind. What made me even more nervous was visiting Officer Williams.

When I started walking, even the day reminded me of the night. It was a little chilly, the sun was barely out, and the clouds looked thick without threatening rain. It was a normal day for everyone else, for the grass, for the sky, for the clouds. Nothing was different, nothing had shifted in the world, and nothing had erupted chaos, but I felt as though I was walking through ruins. I felt like I had survived a catastrophe, and I was in awe of the rubble left in the aftermath.

I felt isolated from the world without the help of marijuana. The weed set me above everybody else. I walked above them all and watched as they moved through mundane lives—doing what someone else told them to do and living the life someone told them they had live to be happy. I floated above all that and separated myself by feeling something they never felt in their lifetimes. I was here back on earth with the rest of the world, isolated only by the feeling that the day was not a normal one.

When I got to school, I was already late. I was practically dragging my feet as I entered the school. I couldn't have gone any slower if I had crawled. I entered the school with a huge lump in my throat and found that it was just the way I left it. The kids who were left in the hallway were either rushing to class or taking their time talking with their friends. No one even looked at me, which was not unusual, but the usualness of such an unusual day was very unusual.

I didn't know what to expect. It wasn't exactly a national tragedy; it wasn't even a regional tragedy. I half-expected to walk through the hallways and have the whispers of gossip follow behind me like a smoke trail. I thought I'd see people on their phones giggling as they watched me walk past like in the movies, but no one did because no one cared. It was funny how concerned I was the night before about this very moment—only to realize that the only people my near-death experience affected was my mother and me.

My mother had cried herself to sleep that night. She banged on the door for what seemed like hours, begging me to talk to her, but I couldn't. I could hear her sobs through the door, and I leaned against it, feeling every bang against my back. I didn't cry. That's how I knew I was an asshole. It wasn't too long ago that I couldn't even watch my mother tear up without sobbing like a bitch. That night, I didn't sob. I didn't even flinch. I had to be the biggest coward I knew. I didn't even have the balls to let my mother lay into me.

I snuck into a bathroom before I reached the classroom. I didn't even need to use it. I needed to wash my face. I splashed cold water on my face and used my hands to try to wipe the shame away. I tried to wipe away the guilt, but I couldn't. No amount of water could purify me, and when I looked up in the mirror, I got a good look at the stranger on the other side. I looked weak—in every sense of the word.

My eyes were still glazed, my shirt was still dirty, my hair was a mess, and it was longer. I had a five o'clock shadow going on. I didn't even know hair grew on my face. I didn't know why my clothes were still dirty. I had changed them. I had forgotten to do laundry. I forgot I did my laundry. I forgot about a lot of things. I stared at myself and thought, *Is this what I am turning into? What was I before?* That was the question that I couldn't answer.

I was turning into something I didn't recognize, but I couldn't pinpoint the turning point. *Had all of this happened just because I smoked a little?* I didn't feel different. I wasn't itching for a blunt. I wasn't shivering or biting my nails off. I was just me, and as I looked in the mirror, I realized that the person on the other side was always me. I had pretended for so long that I was just a normal kid living a normal life, but I was a drone. I dressed up for school like everyone else. I did just enough to get by, like everyone else, but it was a show. It was a cover-up. It was a shell I wore to convince everyone around me that I wasn't a hot mess. In the history of fucked-up situations, mine was pretty good, but my life was just an endless chain of days that were no different, classes that weren't interesting, and the same faces, the same hallways, the same streets. I was trapped in it all. I think normality drives people to madness. Maybe the person I was looking at now wasn't created. He was revealed.

I snuck into the classroom, the door was open, and I suppose we were working on an assignment with partners because everyone was paired up. I sat in my seat, opened a binder, and pretended to do work.

A few kids saw me sit down, but they didn't say anything. They never did. It didn't take long for Mr. Nelson to see me, and when he did, he made sure everyone else there saw me too. "Timmy, could you come here please?"

As I made the short trip from my desk to his, I could feel everyone's eyes on me.

"You're late again," he said.

I shrugged my shoulders.

"Okay, well, I want to show you something." He started to type something into his computer, and I noticed he was pulling up all the grades for the class.

I was a bit relieved that he wasn't asking about the accident last night. The last thing I wanted was to be patronized by a teacher.

"This is your grade as of today," he said as he pulled up a list of my classwork assignments.

I was a bit taken aback—but not entirely surprised. I hadn't been putting a lot of focus on my academics, and on that particular day, it was the least of my concerns. It was almost comical how low a grade can get before hitting absolute zero. It was like I was exploring all the numbers that could translate into an F.

"You're missing a lot of work that you haven't made up. You never took a couple of tests that you were absent for. You haven't turned in a single homework assignment in almost a month. The report cards go out in less than two weeks, and this will be your grade. Are you happy with that?"

I shook my head, not wanting to verbalize my answer.

"Well, you've got to do something. You've got to put in some sort of effort. Timmy, I know you're a smart kid—a bright kid—so I don't understand why you're letting your grades slip this badly. Is there something going on at home? Is there something that you're going through? Because you can talk to me, a guidance counselor, or someone else. You can't keep going like this."

I stared at my grade. I felt a bit uncomfortable looking him in the eye, and although I knew he did his best to keep his voice down, I couldn't help but notice the students sitting closest to his desk could hear our entire conversation.

"Look, I can help you bring that grade up to at least passing, but you should know that I think you're a lot smarter than just passing. I don't know what you're dealing with, and no one will if you don't tell anyone. You're a bright kid, Timmy. Act like it."

I walked back to my seat and tried not to act upset by our conversation or annoyed by how much work I had to do. I hated doing schoolwork in the first place. *I don't know any teenaged kid who does, but at least before,*

I had only one assignment to worry about before the next day. I now have a stack of papers—and multiple tests—to worry about.

Mr. Nelson gave me a few assignments to do while everyone else worked with their partners. It was mostly questions from the textbook, which meant I had to read or skim through the book to find the answers. *There is nothing more mind-numbingly boring than staring at a history book.*

My morning was off to a rough start, and I couldn't focus on anything I had to do. My worries and concerns were beyond stressing me out. I tried my best to just focus on the schoolwork and be productive, but I couldn't get it out of my head how lucky or unlucky I was. I couldn't stop thinking about Amiel, Abel, or how much my mother cried. Now, along with everything else that was weighing on my brain, I had to worry about failing a class. I felt anxious and disturbed. I couldn't sit still. I had to move. I had to do something, and I left like schoolwork was it.

My mind was a fighting over which worry I should most concerned about. My heart was racing, and nothing about any of it felt right. I tried to relax, but I couldn't. My mind just replayed the terrible, blurry images from the night before. I spent the entire ninety minutes in that classroom wallowing in self-hatred and guilt. I had dug myself into a hole, and unlike Andre—who could sit comfortably in the mess he made without a care in the world—the mess I had made and the hole I had dug for myself were collapsing around me and suffocating me.

I managed to get at least two of the assignments done. There were some unanswered questions, but any grade was better than no grade, right? The bell rang, but before I could leave, Mr. Nelson called me back to his desk. "Come tomorrow after school or during lunch to take your missing tests. We can get you to pass this class. You just have to put in a little more effort, understand?"

I just nodded my head.

"Okay, well, Officer Williams asked to see you. Do you know where his office is?"

I didn't, but I was sure I could figure it out. I told Mr. Nelson and walked into the river of students flowing through the hallways between classes. I rushed to find Officer Williams office, which had to be somewhere near the front office.

Due to the amount of people in the hallways, I knew the bell for the next class would ring soon. I walked the way I usually did—with my head down—and tried not to be noticed. What happened next was another thing I could overanalyze. I bumped into Sophia. It lasted only about a few seconds, and it was merely a touch of the shoulder. It was hardly powerful enough to knock either of us off balance, but it was noticeable enough for each of us to say something.

"Excuse me," I said.

"Sorry," she said at almost the same time.

We both kept walking in the direction we were headed; it was almost like we were strangers. I looked back—I always did—hoping she would look back at me in the same manner, but she never did. She didn't overthink things the way I did; at least, I don't think she did. To her, she had just bumped into somebody before class; to me, watching her walk away was like looking through a glass. Looking at her was like looking through a two-way mirror. It was terrible to think that we were both in the same hallway but two very different places in our lives. It wasn't fair to ignore her like that.

When I stopped and thought about it, I had known her longer than Andrew and maybe even Charlie. We used to laugh together all the time and just talk about all the things other kids would find weird or childish. I used to walk her home every day like clockwork, and then I stopped talking to her. That kind of thing happens a lot in high school. You start as friends, and over the years, you're just strangers in the hallway. It wasn't like we both transformed into completely different people. I wasn't a part of any new social group that didn't allow me to speak with the likes of her. We were both still the same people—at least she was.

It didn't matter; it'd be a curse to bring her into my life. It'd be a curse to bring anyone into my life. I was a cataclysmic event that could only cause agony to anyone who came near me. A tad bit dramatic, but it was true. The sad thing is the only person who was close enough to me to get hurt was my mother. I couldn't bear the fact that I was hurting the only woman who had ever cared about me.

When I reached Officer Williams's office, he wasn't there. The door was wide open, so I took a seat in front of his desk and waited nervously. I looked around at his messy office; there was a stack of papers on his desk and another on his chair. There was a cup of coffee that was still steaming, there was country music playing softly out of his speakers, and there was police equipment on the floor next to the trash cans. There was a vest next to some belts that sort of looked like Batman's utility belt. *If I wasn't about to be lectured by a cop, I'd sort of feel comfortable here.*

I didn't have to wait long for Officer Williams to come into his office. When he did walk into his office, he didn't even look at me. He quickly sat down at his desk and started typing on his computer. He shuffled some papers around on his desk. He still hadn't said a word, and he continued to work around his desk like I wasn't even there. Without looking at me, he said, "What are you doing here?"

"You called me in here," I answered.

"I know why you're here. I'm asking what you are doing here?"

"I don't understand," I replied.

"You want to know how many times Andre sat in that chair before last night?" He paused for a moment but didn't wait for me to respond. "He sat in that chair three times. Your friend Joshua sat in that chair four times—and now, here are you."

"Who's Joshua?" I asked.

"Joshua," he repeated as if saying his name a second time would help me remember. "The guy who was driving the van last night. You're missing the point, kid; you see, that chair that you're sitting in right now is for kids facing real problems with the law. That isn't some seat in the principal's office where'd he'd discuss your behavior and get you a week off from school. If you want to know how many times Andre's been in the principal's office, I'd probably need a fucking calculator. You know how many times you've been in the principal's office?"

"No."

"Not once, at least not in this school, but you're here why?" This time, his question wasn't rhetorical. He was waiting for a response, but I would not give him one. We stared at each other for a few awkward seconds before he said, "Nothing? You've got nothing to say? Timmy, I pulled your grades too. I figured they would tell me what kind of person I was dealing with because I don't deal with a lot of smart kids. I deal with a lot of dumb kids, but as it turns out, you're not one. You had perfect grades in your freshman year. Last semester, you held a steady B/C average, which isn't bad I guess, but this semester, you're just failing everything. I talked with all your teachers too, asking them what kind of kid you were, and they all tell me you're this nice, quiet kid who always sits in the back and would never talk unless forced to. So, what's going on, Timmy?" He got out of his chair, walked over to me, stood with his arms crossed, and leaned against his desk.

I didn't answer him. I didn't even look at him. I had developed the magnificent skill of holding my tongue in high-pressure situations.

"You see, I brought you here today because I don't think you fully understand the enormous bullet you dodged last night. Not to mention the fact that you could've been killed. How old are you?"

"Fifteen," I whispered.

"Fifteen? Do you want to die at fifteen?"

I answered his rhetorical question by shaking my head no.

"No, you don't. I know you don't—and I don't want you to. Look, you seem like a good kid, your teachers think you're a good kid, and your mom seemed like a nice lady. She was pretty pissed last night, wasn't she?"

I nodded again.

"Do you want to do that to her? Do you want to do that to her? She's raising you alone, isn't she?"

"Yeah," I replied.

"Where's your dad?" he asked.

"I don't know. I don't know him."

"You see, that right there is a lot more than most kids have to deal with. That's a lot, and I'm sure your mother is doing everything she can to do right by you. Do you think this is fair to her ... what you've been doing?"

I didn't answer him.

"I don't think so. I think you owe it to her to do better." He stayed quiet for a moment to let his speech sink in. "So, were you smoking weed?"

I refused to look at him, and my tongue remained motionless in my mouth.

"You can tell me, kid. Do you know how many kids I know smoke weed at this school? It's my job, and it's the same thing over and over again. They get in trouble, they talk to me, I get them out of trouble, and then a few weeks later, they're coming to me for help again. Like, dude, it's so fucking simple. Stop doing the shit that you keep getting arrested for. I mean, shit, if you're dumb enough to get caught doing that more than once, maybe you shouldn't be doing that. Maybe it's not your thing. But n—they do it over and over again until bam! I have to lock them up. I try to help you, kids, as much as I can, but, shit, I have a job to do too, you know. I have this conversation with tons of kids, over and over again, and even though I know most of them never listen, I continue to repeat the same message, hoping that one day a kid will sit in front of my desk and not let what I'm saying run out the other ear. I had a thought last night that maybe that might be you. I don't know you very well, but I can tell you're not like those guys. You're better than that; you're better than a jail cell.

"I know life is hard. That thing with your dad would be tough on anyone, but that doesn't mean you can't get through it. Smoking weed and hanging out with those guys isn't going to do anything good for you, and you deserve good, Timmy. I can see that in you. Look, I believe you can overcome anything, I do, and to do that, you have to get over yourself. I think we, as human beings, have this power of making things worse than they are. I'm here to tell you not to end up like them. Andre isn't going anywhere. In a few years, I'll bet you ten bucks he's going to be on the same street and getting locked up for the same shit. That's stupid. Don't be stupid. Be different. Focus on school. Focus on making a difference because being out on those streets isn't going to do you any good. Those streets are a graveyard for people who deserve to be there because you get what you give out of life. Please be the kid who's affected by this conversation. You'd be doing us both a huge favor."

21

CHAPTER

T he rest of the day was just as exhilarating as those first ninety minutes. Every single one of my teachers decided it was time to show me my grades. I did my best not to worry about them, but I had to. They were terrible, and the number of times I had been absent had somehow doubled. I avoided anyone I knew at school. I did my best to keep my head down and not bump into too many people in the hallway.

The day dragged on, making me regret having gone to school in the first place. I wanted to crawl into my bed and hide, but it wouldn't make a difference. No one knew I was there, no one cared, and no one asked if I was okay. I'm sure not many people knew I had anything to do with the accident, but it still would have been nice to have a friend at that point. I don't know how I would have handled being patronized, but it would have been a lot better than just being ignored.

School was almost out, but the final bell was taking its time before letting us free. I sat quietly in my seat as everyone else was packing up their things and lining up at the door. I was the only one sitting in a seat. I played with the broken paint chips on my desk, and I didn't even flinch when the bell rung. Instead of rushing out of class like everyone else did, I slowly stood up and walked out. The hallways were like a rush-hour; the only difference was that it was filled with sweaty teenaged bodies as opposed to just cars. I didn't feel like walking home, but I didn't have much choice.

When I got out of the school building, I noticed a cluster of people forming at the edge of the school. At the center of this distorted circle was a very happy and unaffected Andre. I could hardly hear his conversation, but I knew it was about the crash. He laughed and cursed and even bragged a little. The most annoying phrase Andre's posse kept using made me want to rip my eardrums out.

"That's crazy," they said almost unanimously, and Andre ate it up.

I wanted to know how he was out—and where Amiel was. I regretfully walked in clear sight of Andre, and he called me out like only he can do. "Yo, ask Timmy! Yo, that shit was crazy, right?" Andre shouted.

I ducked my head and tried to hurry past him, but he rushed to me and hooked me with his arm. "Yo, Timmy was fucking with us. He'll tell you. Yo, how the fuck did they take you home? Why did they lock my ass up?"

"I don't know," I whispered as I tried to move away from him. I stopped in my tracks when I noticed Sophia. She had such beautiful eyes; they were big, brown, and hurt.

Sophia shyly smiled the way she always did—the way that would drive me nuts—but her hand came up in a wave. I was in such a shock that I let Andre pull me in, and I hid behind a fortress of idiots. I pretended I didn't see her. I pretended I didn't know her. For the first time since I met Sophia, I didn't look back. Nothing about my life felt right. It was a disaster, and I didn't want Sophia to have anything to do with it. I still couldn't stop my heart from tricking my brain into thinking something meant more than it did. She said hi—that was all that was—but I couldn't help but notice the look in her eyes. It looked like she missed me. *Is that even possible?*

Sophia, no matter much I liked her, was the least of my problems. I was starting to feel resentful, mostly toward Andre who probably had way worse issues than I did. He was smiling, laughing, and bragging about an experience that was tearing me apart. How could he be so carefree? I didn't understand. It couldn't be just weed. I smoked weed, and I was still stressed out. How could he not care? How could he think so highly of himself when he was a lot worse than anyone else I knew. Then the question came—that ugly, horrific question that always knocked me off my soapbox and made me take a hard look at myself: If Andre was so terrible, what was I doing there with him?

I slowly slipped away from Andre and his crowd and began moving toward home.

Andre shouted that he'd see me later, but I ignored him and kept walking.

The kids around me all seemed oblivious to the world around them.

I couldn't help but focus on how bad it all was and how much worse it could have gotten. I almost wanted it to be worse. I almost wanted to be seriously hurt in the accident or arrested. What if Abel never reached the hospital? Maybe I could justify feeling so low. If anything, I should have considered myself lucky, but the feeling I was feeling was not one of relief.

My phone buzzed, and I noticed I had a text message from Allison. I ignored it and continued to walk home. I wanted to talk to her, I did, but I couldn't bear the weight of anything else that might make me snap.

I saw Josh sitting on the steps near the rec center. He was reading a book and playing with a toothpick between his teeth. I slowed down so he would notice me.

He closed his book and raised an eyebrow at me. "You know, you remind me of that kid on TV except he doesn't have fairy godparents so he's just miserable."

"It's always a pleasure to talk to you, Josh," I answered sarcastically.

"I heard you almost died," Josh said bluntly.

"How'd you know I was there?" I asked.

"Amiel told me, and Andre hasn't shut up about it since he got out."

"How did they get out?" I asked.

"I don't know. I guess their parents came and got them."

"What happened to Abel?"

"Beats me, I think Gina and her mom went and got him. I heard he's going to the nuthouse or some shit," Josh responded.

I rolled my eyes at him and started to walk again.

Josh, not missing a beat, followed me down the sidewalk.

His cavalier attitude made me want to punch him in his throat. "How is it that you know everything about everyone, Josh?" I asked.

"Same as you. I keep my mouth shut so people talk," Josh spit out his toothpick and shoved a piece of gum in his mouth.

"Only person out here talking is you," I said.

"What the fuck is that supposed to mean?" He stopped dead in his tracks.

I quickly spun around and said, "That story about Gina … you were the one telling people, right?"

"What about the football guys? Shit, everyone knew that story."

"Well, if everyone knew, why make her into such a saint? Why was

Charlie so in love with her? Why make me go through all that trouble for a so-called slut," I replied.

"Charlie made you do all that shit—not me."

"Yeah, but you told me about her … about them. You made it seem like they were so in love, like they were destined to be together."

"Maybe … I thought they were," Josh answered.

"Then why wait to tell me or him? Does Charlie even know? Why makeup all that bullshit?"

"Are you getting mad over someone else's love life?" Josh asked with a sinister grin on his face.

"No, I'm mad because I went to that party looking for Abel … because Gina said that she was worried about him. She made it seem like he was about to kill himself or Charlie. I didn't have to be there. I didn't have to do all that shit. I thought they were going to fight or something."

"You went hunting for Abel so he and Charlie wouldn't fight? Are you one of those guys who splits up the fight? What a square," Josh said between chuckles.

"Fuck you."

"Oh, come on. Charlie and Abel were never going to fight. If Charlie had enough balls to fight someone, he would have fought TJ, but he didn't. I did, and if Abel was going to do shit, he would have done it a long time ago. It wasn't that serious."

"But why wait to tell me that shit? I don't understand. Why is Charlie in love with a whore?"

"Why are you calling her a whore?" Josh asked.

"'Cause you called her that—and I want to know why?"

"You know why," Josh said.

"Apparently everyone knows why, but why keep it from me?" I shouted.

"All right. I'll tell you." He took a long breath and looked around as if he were searching for an escape. "Okay. Charlie knew Gina before any of that happened. He knew Gina before any of us did, but you see, I didn't know that. Charlie likes to disappear out of people's lives and then come back later. I'm pretty sure you know what I'm talking about. Last year, I hadn't spoken to Charlie—I hadn't seen Charlie in months, and, you know, he was still my friend—but he went AWOL. That's when I met Gina; she was this nice, sweet, and flirtatious. So, I had I crush on her, and if we're being honest, I wasn't any better at talking to girls than you were. So, we became close friends. In other words, she friend-zoned the hell out of me. I didn't mind. I kept being friends with her, hoping one day she'd look at me as more, but she didn't. I made a lot of friends playing football, and I always hung out with the same group of guys, you know, drinking smoking all that shit.

"Anyways, she started to like one of my friends. Dale was a pretty fucking good outside linebacker, and he was even better at getting girls. Bitches loved this guy, and he didn't mind. Having said that, Dale hadn't had a girlfriend since middle school, but he still got more ass than a toilet seat.

"I honestly didn't know what I was thinking. I liked Gina so much. I wanted her to be happy, and I tried to set them up. Dale was always down for whoever when it came to girls. Gina just really wanted to hang out with him. So, I set it up. My people weren't home, so I threw a little party and by little, I mean minuscule."

"Wait," I interrupted. "You were there?"

"Yeah, you going to let me finish?" he asked.

I nodded.

"It was after a football game, I think, or basketball ... I don't fucking remember ... but it was just me and a few of my boys. We were just chilling, smoking some weed ... we didn't have any drinks or any girls, so the party was kind of dead. I texted Gina, and she snuck out— and she managed to bring some drinks over too. I think she stole a bottle of rum from her mom's stash. Anyways, she came in, and we started taking shots. Dale was all over her, and it made me want to stick a gun in my mouth. I thought I could be cool with it, but I wasn't. It was awful. I realized then how much I liked her. I got angry and started ignoring her, but that didn't do much good. She wasn't paying attention to me anyway.

"That's when they went into my room. I didn't have enough balls to stop them. I was afraid of making a jackass of myself, but I guess there was no stopping that. I drank damn near the whole bottle by myself, and I don't even think we were supposed to drink that much of it. I drank so much that I didn't notice how many people were leaving the room. The front door never opened. I didn't notice that everyone was making their way into my bedroom. I didn't notice until I stood up to go to the bathroom. That's when I saw what they were doing to her.

"For a second, I thought the worst. You know, I thought the absolute worst. I thought this was going to be a big small-town thing, but she wasn't fighting them. She wasn't saying no, and she had two shots, so she couldn't be that drunk. The fucked-up part was that the door was wide-open. There wasn't anything keeping me from walking in there and joining them. I think one of my homeboys invited me in, but by then, she told everyone she was done. She couldn't take no more. I think that's when I puked. Not that I was grossed out … I mean, I watch porn, but I did drink that whole damn bottle. I threw up and passed out in my bathtub.

"I woke up to my mom yelling at me for the house being a mess. Luckily, the smell of weed as gone. I didn't even know what to make of the situation. I wanted to do what you do naturally and make it a big deal, but it wasn't—to anyone. I don't even think Dale ever brought it up again … unless it was to brag. Hell, Gina sent me a text a few days later telling me she was mad that I drank all her mom's liquor. I never texted back, her, and I never spoke to her again after that. Me and Dale stayed cool. He didn't know I liked her … no one did except for me. Then he graduated, and that was that.

"It was a bitter pill to swallow, but I got over it. I got over her. I started dating this girl from my writing class. She is pretty, smart, and quiet. She likes cartoons and action movies. I'm her first boyfriend too, so I pretty much hit a home run. So, no harm done." He ended with his normal indifferent tone and started walking again.

I hurried next to him and said, "No harm done? Are you kidding me?"

"What? She didn't complain. High school is when girls start to get a little slutty—so what?"

"I don't know. I just … it doesn't seem right," I whispered just loud enough for Josh to hear me.

"Don't sweat it, kid. I don't think it's right either, but it's common knowledge. Girls just want to have fun, and guys just want to get lucky," Josh replied.

"I still don't understand. Why make me do all that?"

"Charlie found out."

"I thought you said he didn't know," I said.

"No. I said I didn't tell him. He found out on his own. He still wanted to talk to her. He didn't care, and shit, if that ain't love, I don't know what is."

We walked the rest of the way in silence. When we got to my street, and it was time for us to part ways, Josh stopped me again. "Timmy, wait." He reached out to me before I could cross the street.

I paused and looked at him.

"You were right."

"About what?" I asked.

"I shouldn't have called her a whore."

"What difference does it make? That's what she is, right?" I said.

"Nah, man. She's just Gina, man. We shouldn't judge her for the things she's done."

"You know, Amiel said the same shit. Actions are the only thing people get judged for."

"But it's not your job to judge them, is it?" Josh turned and walked away.

CHAPTER 22

The next day was just as painful and dull as the day before. After speaking with Josh, I went home and stayed there, not leaving once to go see Charlie or anyone else. I purposely avoided reading any text messages or anything on social media. I went home and tried to get some of my missing work done. I pulled out each assignment from each class and stared at a couple of them for a few hours. I fiddled with my pencil and got a total of nothing done. The only real thing I got away with was convincing my mom that I was trying. After I gave up trying to do my schoolwork, I decided to watch TV for the rest of the night. No weed, parties, girls, or drinking. I stayed on my couch with my eyes glued to a screen.

It was torture, pure torture. I had nothing going on. All I had was a lot of schoolwork that I kept procrastinating with—even though they were all way past their due dates. I was going to fail. I was a failure. The worst part about realizing that I went I little too far with the things I was doing was realizing that, without them, I had nothing to do.

I didn't know what went by slower: the entire week or each day that week. The days happened the same way. In each class, it was a new lesson but the same boring lecture, and then it was going through the halls to see all the friends I didn't have, then it was walking home and catching a glimpse of the girl I was too scared to talk to, and then it was just home. The small apartment with four depressing white walls always smelled like the same meal—even though my mom hadn't cooked all week. It didn't matter. I ate snacks, noodles, and anything that didn't take longer than five minutes to make. Watching TV was the only thing I could do to entertain myself before I realized that, no matter how hard I looked, there were never any good shows on. I started to doubt that good shows existed.

I was going insane and was slowly moving toward a state of depression. I had to think of something to do.

Sitting at school was almost as bad as sitting at home. It was just as painful. While I sat at my desk, I wished I was home. Home was boring, but at least it was comfortable. For the last thirty minutes of the day, I stared at the wall instead of the work I was supposed to be doing. I still had makeup work, but I got a lot of the assignments done by copying from some of my classmates. Nobody cares if you copy work they already got a grade for. My grades were still considerably low, but at least I knew I had a shot at passing.

As I sat at my desk, I looked out the small window at the people who were walking by. A flash of a bright blue sweater snapped me out of my dreary trance. My heart began to beat faster, and it was like someone had dumped a bucket of water on me. I was finally awake, and I finally felt a surge of energy. I knew who wore the bright blue sweater, and I knew where'd she be going. I had to see her, and I had to talk to her.

The truth was that I kept running from the urge to walk with her, but at that moment, I couldn't think of a logical reason not to talk to her. I was nervous, of course, since we hadn't spoken in weeks, and I wasn't entirely sure how I was going to explain that to her. I knew I had to do it. I needed something to brighten my day, and no one could do that better than Sophia.

I quickly raised my hand and asked if I could use the bathroom. My teacher was skeptical due to the time, but I insisted it was an emergency. Once she let me go, I rushed out of the classroom, making my emergency story a bit more believable. Once I was in the hallway, I started heading toward the school library. Sophia would always return her books at the end of the day and spend the last few minutes of school reading a new book she had checked out. I remembered because I would always hang out around the library when the final bell rang, hoping I'd catch her walking out. I didn't know what I was going to say or how I was going to say it. I wished I dressed nicer that day, but I had to do the best with what I had.

When I got to the library, I looked through the window to see if she was in there. I saw with her nose in a book. I started to pace around the hallway and tried to work up the courage to go talk to her. I started to sweat a little, and my hands started to shiver. I didn't want to walk in there and make a fool of myself again. I almost didn't walk in, but the librarian saw me and gave me a curious look. I quickly walked in and pretended to look for a book. I didn't know if Sophia saw me enter since I was doing my best to keep my eyes on the ground. I looked through a few books and decided to check one out. I wasn't going to read it, but at least I didn't look like I had gone to the library for nothing. When I went to the checkout table, I noticed that someone else had sat down in front of Sophia. I didn't know who he was, but he was talking to Sophia, and by the looks of it, Sophia was only half listening. The librarian checked out my book, and I tried to wait for the guy to leave, but he kept talking. When I realized I was looking stupid standing in front of the desk, I made my way for the door and started to walk back to class. I stopped in front of a water fountain, hit the button, and let the water hit my face. I wiped my face with my hand and used the inside of my shirt to dry it.

I stopped myself from moving any closer to my class even though I knew I had been out for a while. I quickly rushed back into the library, not giving it any thought and not stopping for anything. I had to talk to her. Luckily, by the time I walked into the library, the guy was gone. She was staring into her book and looking more beautiful than I had ever imagined. I sat in the chair in front of her.

It was nerve-racking few seconds that felt like an eternity, but I didn't have to wait long for her to notice me. She looked up the second the chair moved, but I didn't meet her gaze until I was completely settled in. Looking at her, I realized how much comfort I took in her company. I didn't want to be anywhere else. I wasn't worried about anything else. I was just so taken by her.

"Hi, Sophia," I said when I was finally comfortable enough to speak.

She had a smile that reached from ear to ear. Looking at her smile at me the way she did that day made me glad I had decided to run back into the library. It made me glad I had gotten over myself and decided to say hello. "Hi, Timmy," she replied.

"What you been up to?" I asked, feeling my nervousness slowly leaving my body. I was a bit embarrassed that I had to conjure up that much courage just to talk to Sophia. I almost always forgot that, despite me being so in love with her, we were still friends. Sophia wasn't going to bite my head off for talking to her or look disgusted by my presence. Thinking about it now, I realize she was pretty down-to-earth.

"Oh, you know, just school, nothing." She kept that expression on her face that she was happy to see me and happy to talk to me, and I couldn't have asked for anything more. Sophia reminded me that there was beauty in simplicity. Sophia was perfectly herself, and she didn't have to make a lot of noise to be noticed. She wasn't someone who begged or tried to force herself into the spotlight, and she wasn't trying to impress anyone. Sophia was something God gave that the world took for granted—like the trees or the sky. They're all so beautiful, but they go unnoticed, and they don't wait for someone them to notice to be beautiful. They just always are. You'd have to almost die or be blind for all your life to appreciate them. Sophia was just that. She was that spring day; she was that oak tree that no one notices until it's cut down. Sophia was simply amazing. She was someone to be appreciated.

"So, what are you reading?" I asked.

"Something girly ... I probably won't even finish reading it," she replied.

"You don't like girly books?"

"Not really ... they're too predictable." She started to play with the pages of her book.

"What kind of books do you like?" I asked.

She thought for a moment and said, "I like adventure books."

"Adventure books?" I repeated.

"Yeah, they're exciting, and they don't get boring after you finish reading them."

"You look nice today." My words caught me by surprise. They slipped out of my thoughts and made themselves real.

She smiled warmly and replied, "Thank you."

I stared at her for a moment without saying a word. I was dumbfounded and completely and utterly in love.

"What?" she said, breaking the silence between us.

With a sigh and a giggle, I replied, "Nothing. I'm sorry."

"You're weird, Timmy," she said as the final bell rang.

As everyone stood up to leave, I quietly replied, "You have no idea."

Sophia stood up and started to pack her things in her book bag.

I stood up and realized I had spent the last fifteen minutes of school supposedly in the bathroom, but I was returning with a book.

"Are you walking today?" she asked as she threw her book bag over her shoulder.

Before I could respond, I was interrupted by Gina. She had been standing behind me the whole time. "Timmy, can I talk to you?" she looked sad and depressed. Her peppy, happy face was worn and weary.

"Maybe tomorrow then," Sophia said as she headed for the door.

I nodded and waved.

Sophia waved bye and walked out of the library.

"Is that your girlfriend?" Gina asked once I turned around.

"No … I wish. How's Abel?"

"He's okay, I guess, not really, but you know. Did you tell him about me and Charlie?" She was looking straight in my eye and doing her best to intimidate me.

"What?" I asked.

"Did you tell Abel about me and Charlie?" she repeated.

"Fuck no. I didn't tell him. I didn't tell anyone anything, but everybody wants to tell me everything. I'm sick of it—so I'm not having this conversation." I headed for the door.

Gina nearly shouted, "He tried to kill himself!"

"What are you talking about?"

"That night, the crash, Abel was trying to kill himself. When he came to, he told us what he tried to do. They had to put him on a suicide watch at the hospital. He kept talking about me and Charlie and how he was going to kill him and himself—and he was talking about me and these other people. I don't know where he was getting these stories. Did you tell him about me and Charlie?" she demanded.

"No, I didn't," I stated firmly.

"You were the only other person who knew!" Tears began to form in her eyes.

"I didn't tell him anything. When we hung out, we smoked—that was it."

"He kept saying that he hated me … that I was the reason he was going to die. Somebody told him, and he tried to kill himself. Who told him?" The tears started to roll down her cheeks as she begged for an answer.

"I did not say a word to him … I swear. I never said anything."

"Somebody did!" She started to sob, and the librarian began to look suspicious.

I sat Gina down at the closest table. "Look, just calm down," I whispered.

"That night at Josh's house was never supposed to happen." She was sniffling and trying to regain her composure. "I wanted him to like me. I wanted to be noticed. I thought we were just going to drink and hang out, but then he took me into the room. I didn't know what we were going to do. You know, I hate the way people look at me now. I hate the way they talk to me; everyone always wants to talk to me. They won't leave me alone. Abel was the only one who was nice to me. He was the only person who didn't want anything from me. Abel was so nice, but then Charlie came. I missed him so much, and they didn't know. They didn't know." Her speech was broken up by her sobs.

I sat and listened.

"You know, I had to stay home some days just to avoid looking at them. We never talked again, but they told everyone I was their groupie. For a while, it hurt, but when I met Abel, it didn't matter because he didn't know. Now he and Charlie both know, and they hate me for it. It serves me right though. I don't know why I even decided to like anybody … to trust anybody. Everyone will abandon you the second you're not their idea of perfect. They hear something about you that they don't like, and they just leave. They leave you to suffer alone because you're no longer their problem. Abel used to tell me he loved me—they both did—but now I'm just a whore." She finally stopped crying and stared at the wooden table. She looked empty, like she had died on the inside. "That's all I am, you know. Maybe I should just accept it. Maybe that's what I deserve."

"Gina—"

"You once told me I look like I should live in a castle. Do you remember that?"

"Huh?" I answered.

"We were at a party at Charlie's house, and you said that I was so pretty I should live in a castle."

"Yeah, I remember that," I said.

"What about now?" she asked.

"What do you mean?"

"You said I deserved to live in a castle and I'm asking what about now?"

I didn't know how to answer her question. At that point, I didn't even know how anything I said could be the right answer. No was the answer she was reluctantly expecting, and yes was the answer she knew was a lie.

Before I said anything, she stood up and asked, "Do you still think I'm a princess?"

Before I could answer, she turned and left.

My teacher scolded me for returning twenty minutes after school to retrieve my bookbag. I told her I had stomach problems, but she didn't believe me. I had to walk home alone, really alone. There were no kids left on the sidewalks. There was nothing ahead of me except the path home. I didn't want to go home. I felt anxious. I felt an urge to go fix something or go talk to someone, but there was nothing to fix and no one to talk to. There was nothing. I felt guilty, and I had every reason to. I wasn't anything like them. I wasn't like Dale or Andre. I wasn't someone who relentlessly slept with whomever I wanted without any regard for the other person. I still felt guilty because I wanted to be someone without a conscience, someone who lives only for himself, not caring about anybody else. Maybe I would have fewer problems if I was as selfish as everyone else was and if I didn't care so much.

No matter what, Dale was the lucky one. He didn't have to deal with the aftermath, and he didn't feel the repercussions of his actions. Gina did. It was all on her, and she had shared the weight of her sorrow with me. I would never truly know what she was feeling, but my capacity for empathy had started to become a handicap.

For a moment, I didn't care who told Able or why. I was starting to question why I cared about their situation in the first place. I regretted making someone else's business my business. The second I did, their problems and their pain became my own, and I had to deal with it when it had nothing to do with me. It wasn't fair really because I was sharing their pain, but no one was sharing my pain. I was hurting, and to be completely honest, I didn't know where the pain was coming from. It was a burden to be as depressed as I was, knowing very well I had no reason to be. My sister didn't die. I wasn't publicly painted as a whore. I had no drug-dealing brothers or wife-beating fathers who eventually went to jail. I didn't have a cousin who went spiraling down to her death after one horrible night at a party, but it was like I did. With every tale they told, every story, every rumor, they revealed to me the true wickedness of humanity.

The worst part about it was that we weren't even grown yet. I was fifteen years old. None of us had even lived two decades of our lives yet, but they were as cruel and unforgiving as any adult on the other side. That wasn't how I thought growing up was going to feel. When I was younger, I couldn't wait to be a teenager. I'd have a car and a girlfriend, I'd go to parties, and I would have a group of friends to go on wild adventures with. I had none of those things. The parties I imagined when I was younger were nothing like the parties I attended now. I was nothing like the person I imagined as a kid. I was the exact opposite.

Is anyone who they thought they were going to be? Do we all dream of who we're going to be just to watch that person not exist? Do we all become the monsters under our beds? Are we in control of who we are—or are we the sum of our regrets, mistakes, and insecurities? Maybe life is just a sob story.

23
CHAPTER

I hadn't smoked in a week, but I didn't know whether to think of that as an accomplishment or a burden. Either way, it was the worst week of my life. I had already planned on going to Charlie's apartment for no reason other than I wanted to smoke. I didn't want to hear about Gina, Abel, or anybody. I didn't want to go home either; it was almost like sitting in a very comfortable jail cell. Going home, watching the same old TV shows, eating the same food, staring at the same homework assignments I was not going to do, and staring at the same old ceiling with nothing but my imagination to entertain me would have been agonizing. I wanted at least a few hours to just relax.

All I wanted to do was smoke, but even thinking the wrong thing at the wrong moment could ruin a night. I saw Josh smoking on the steps, and I suddenly had a thought. I was starting to think that thinking was a bad thing. I saw Josh sitting there high and mighty with his know-it-all arrogance, which got under my skin for some reason, and something clicked in my head.

Gina told me that someone had told Abel about her exploits. Abel tried to commit suicide, which forced us to run him to the hospital and crash into a tree. I realized I could have been killed because someone decided it was a good idea to tell Abel, the guy still mourning the death of his little sister, that his girlfriend been cheating on him and had been with four other guys—but she wasn't with four other guys. She said that she had only been with Dale. What was Josh talking about? I didn't want to think about it anymore, but Josh was lying or Gina was lying. I didn't know who to believe, but the stories didn't add up—until they did.

It was Josh. Josh was there, and he was the only one there. He said that he was practically in love with Gina. Was this his way of getting back at her? She wasn't with four guys; she was with one, and Josh couldn't take it. I was furious. I rushed over to speak to Josh. I needed to know what I was used for.

"What did you tell Abel?" I asked.

"Whatever happened to hello?" he replied, intentionally blowing smoke in my face.

"What did you say to Abel?" I demanded.

"What makes you think I told Abel anything?"

"By how reluctant you are to answer the question," I quickly retorted.

"The fuck does that mean?"

"You lied about that night at your house, didn't you?" I yelled.

"Calm the hell down, all right? What are you talking about?"

"Can you ever just answer a fucking question honestly?" I was furious and tried to stare a hole through his eyeballs. I wanted an explanation, but I knew Josh was going to be difficult, which pissed me off even more.

"Okay, what's the question?" Josh asked.

"Did you lie about how many guys were with Gina that night?"

He grinned that evil grin of his and intentionally flexed his muscles as he rubbed his arms through his thin white T-shirt. "What does it even matter anyway?" Josh stared at his slowly burning blunt.

"He tried to kill himself."

That caught Josh's attention. His eyes widened a bit, and I could sense a speck of guilt, but it vanished as quickly as it appeared. "What are you talking about?"

"That night at the party, Abel was intentionally trying to overdose, and it was only after you told him lies."

"I didn't lie about anything. Who the fuck do you think you are accusing me of shit?"

"What did Gina think I told him then? He ran off after hearing something. You told him something. Did you tell him about Gina and your teammates?"

Josh's face went blank. The fury that was starting to build turned into a dumbfounded look, and for once, Josh was speechless.

"You told him about that, didn't you? You told everyone. You did it to spite her, didn't you? She wasn't with four guys. She was with one—and you hated that it wasn't you."

"What? Fuck you. I don't give a shit about Gina."

"Except you do. If you couldn't have her, no one could, right? You manipulative fuck! Everything was all right, and you decided to turn the girl Charlie was in love with into a ho!"

"She was already a ho," Josh countered.

"Why? Because she didn't fuck you?"

Josh stood up, still smoking the blunt, and his bloodshot eyes were filled with rage.

I realized how much bigger he was than me. He towered over me, I might as well have stood in front of a giant; even the way he dressed made him look more robust. He wore a plain white T-shirt and some old ripped blue jeans; it was almost cliché.

"You think I walked up to Abel and just decided it was time to tell him about that night? You think I knew he was suicidal? Do you honestly think I'm out to get Gina or Charlie or anyone? I have a girlfriend. I get laid. I have a life. I don't have to entertain myself by spreading lies. Okay, Abel came to me and asked me some questions, and I told him what I saw. I told him the truth, which is more than anyone else has done for him."

"Oh, bullshit. You lied about what you saw that night and then told everybody about it. So, don't pretend that you're his friend," I replied.

"Why not?" Josh said, "Isn't that what you were doing? I told him the truth. I told him what I saw, Timmy, which is what he asked for, and you're giving me shit about it. Are you any better? They used you to watch him while they fucked around behind his back. You did it willingly. Why? Because they were in love? If they were so in love, why didn't she break up with Abel?"

"You don't think that maybe when you walked in the room you were seeing double because you were hammered? You're the one who told me Charlie and Gina were in love. You told me their Romeo and Juliet story and said they were only not together because her parents didn't like Charlie.

"Of course they didn't like Charlie. Would you let Charlie date your daughter? You're standing there defending who? Gina? That ho was fucking two different guys she claimed to love. And you told Abel lies about her because she didn't claim to love you.

"You watch way too much fucking TV. Okay, Abel came to me, and I told him what I saw and what you were doing, and that was that. I am not responsible for what he does with the information I gave him." Josh spit when he spoke, and the veins in his neck were about to explode. It was almost frightening, but I couldn't be scared. I was too angry.

"You sure? You gave him the wrong information, and it doesn't bother you that he tried to commit suicide?" I asked.

"Oh, please. If he wanted to die, he would have jumped in front of a fucking train. Instead, he tried to drink himself to death."

"It's your fault we nearly died."

"What?" Josh growled and stepped a bit too close.

"Abel tried to kill himself because you couldn't keep quiet, because you never keep quiet, because you walk around like everyone around you is stupid and lying and talking shit when—really—it's all you. You look down on everyone, and you do it to feed your ego. It's like you lift weights just to make sure everyone else is smaller than you. You're pathetic."

It happened in a flash. It only took a second. It didn't hurt at all at first—it was mainly shock—but the surprise of being punched in the jaw got to me. It was quick, and it was powerful. Before I knew it, I was knocked off my feet. I was angrier than I was hurt.

Josh just stood over me with a smug look on his face.

It made me furious, and I got up as quickly as I could.

"Oh, there he is." Josh grinned.

As soon as I saw the whites of his teeth, I hit them as hard as I could. I cut my knuckles on his two front teeth and managed to knock his head back. I also knocked the blunt out of his hand, which was the first thing he reached for once he got his balance back.

He smiled at me again with blood on his teeth.

I didn't care. I wanted to knock that smile off of his face.

"I don't know what your problem is with me, Timmy. You and I are a lot alike."

"My problem is that you didn't consider how cruel it was to tell someone mourning the death of their little sister something like that. Even if it is true, you had no right. It wasn't your story to tell. Maybe you did tell the truth, but what makes you think he should have heard it from you? And I am nothing like you." I grinded my teeth and felt the pain from his blow.

"Of course, you are. I think that's why you don't like me. You might be right. I might consider myself better than the people I hang around, but so do you. If it's not with brawn, then it's with brain, and if it's not with the brain, then it's with heart. You think you're better because you feel bad about the wrong things you do, but they don't. I know how you feel. You ponder the idea that they might not know any better, but that fact doesn't apply to you. You do wrong things despite how good you think you are, but you're not good. No one is good. And you're wrong. If Abel had died, if the car crash had killed any of you, I would have felt guilty—but not as guilty as you would have felt. I told him what I thought I saw, what I knew I saw, and I also told him what you were doing—but you're still the ones who did it to him. It would have haunted me, but it would have killed you inside. Abel wasn't a bad guy, but you did it to him anyway because you knew he wasn't good. Is Charlie any better? Now you're not good, and it kills you, doesn't it? It kills you finding out that not everyone is as pure or as innocent as your precious Sophia. Not even her. So, before you accuse anyone of ruining your life, you might want to consider the operator." He clenched his jaw and used his tongue to wipe the blood off of his teeth.

"I didn't come to you claiming I was innocent. I wanted to hear you say you were guilty. You say you don't care about anyone, yet you seem to know everything about everyone. You just sit there and watch everyone telling their lies, spreading their bullshit, and you just watch, comment, and speculate like an indifferent asshole. I don't understand why? I didn't mean for any of this to happen, but I'm the only one feeling any remorse. I'm the only one taking the blame. I want to hear you say that you lied."

Josh sighed and took a long drag from his blunt. "I can't do that for you, Timmy. I didn't lie. I never lie, and that's sort of the problem. I was hammered that night, but I knew what I saw—even if you don't believe me. Either way, none of that shit is my problem. Abel made his own decisions; if he died, it'd be his fault and not mine."

I wasn't even angry anymore. I was in a state of disbelief. My eyes were wide in shock, and my mouth hung open. I was unable to spew out any words. He didn't care at all. None of our potential deaths bore any weight on his conscience. I didn't honestly believe he could be that ruthless, but a part of me knew he was just someone who would never admit he was wrong.

"How could you be so cold?" I asked. Josh would go so far to avoid responsibility.

"Welcome to the world, Timothy." He started to head upstairs, and then he stopped in his tracks and turned around. "You still got that bowl?"

It was almost like an instinct. My muscles remembered where I kept it. I pulled it out of my pocket and stared at it for a moment. I didn't know that I was carrying it around everywhere I went. That small blue dolphin bowl had become an accessory, like a cell phone, or an iPod. I carried it everywhere I went; it was a witness to everything I'd done.

Josh held out his hand and said, "Let me see it. I'm out of wraps—plus we don't have that much weed anyway."

I handed him the bowl.

He said, "That was a good hit, by the way, but next time, I'll break your jaw."

It felt like he already did. I glared at him, undeterred by his threats and his stature. I hated him, and I hated myself. If Josh had truly spread lies just to ruin her life, he had failed. He had ruined Abel's life. Josh was right. I shared the blame. We were both almost accessories to suicide.

"You coming up?" he asked, changing his tone.

I nodded and started to follow him. I still wanted to smoke; all I had to do was put up with Josh until the weed hit. Then I wouldn't care. I turned around, and I noticed Allison waiting for me to notice her.

Josh turned to look at her and then at me, and then he continued up the stairs.

I walked down to meet her. She was wearing a light green sweater, faded blue jeans, a white shirt, and pink Converse sneakers. I still took notice of her figure despite her casual clothing. Her eyes were emerald stones that shined like they were competing with the sun.

"Did you guys just fight?" she asked as I approached her.

"Yeah, I think so," I answered.

"I never thought of you as a fighter, Timmy." She nervously half-smiled when she spoke, which wasn't reassuring.

I was getting sick of the sob stories. "Neither did I," I replied.

She played with the tips of her hair and looked directly at the floor. I honestly hadn't thought about that night. I didn't want to hear apologies, explanations, or the true story after having heard thirty false ones.

"I tried texting you, but you never answered," she said.

"Yeah, I meant to. It's just ..." I stopped before I could explain more.

It was not that I didn't think Allison would understand what I was dealing with, but I didn't want to deal with it anymore—and talking about it would force me to do so. "I was dealing with stuff."

"I know. I'm sorry. I heard about the crash, and I wanted to talk to you."

"The crash?" I gave her a confused look.

"That wreck with the drunk driver. I wanted to see if you were okay."

"The crash happened almost a week ago. How did you hear about it?"

"A lot of people were talking about it. I wanted to make sure you were okay."

"People knew I was in the car?" A that point, I was just thinking out loud.

"That's just what I heard. You were in the car, right?"

I ignored her. I could barely hear her. I was trapped in my brain, but I was thinking out loud. "That happened a week ago."

"I know." She sighed. "I'm sorry. I know it took a long time, but I guess I was dealing with a lot too."

It didn't bother me that Allison waited for a week after the crash to check on my well-being because she was the only one who did. It also dawned on me that the only people who could have known I was in the car didn't seem too concerned. For a week, I assumed that no one knew I was in the car. That was the only thing that could explain why no one asked me about it. I thought I was lucky because I was spared from the judgment of my classmates, but I wasn't. I was just oblivious to them. I'd never felt more alone. It was heartbreaking to know that a week after nearly dying, only one person had asked if I was all right. How many people knew? Did Sophia know? Andrew? Josh knew. I wasn't the most popular kid in school, but a lot of people knew me. No one asked me anything. I was grateful that I wasn't berated with questions or bombarded with accusations. It still cut me deep that no one wanted to know or cared enough to want to know; apparently, they knew enough. I didn't like knowing I was someone people talked about because no one talked to me.

"Timmy?" Allison said.

I shook my head. "I'm sorry. I have a lot on my mind."

She stared at me, and her eyes begged for forgiveness. Her hair fell perfectly on her shoulders, and seeing her like that made me want to weep.

"I'm sorry," she said. "For the other night ... I know I led you on, and I—"

"Allison, stop. It's okay. I haven't thought about it," I answered honestly.

"I wanted you to understand I never meant to hurt you—"

"Allison, it's fine. You were sad. You needed a friend. It's okay. I can't do this."

"Do what?" Allison asked.

I tried to avoid her gaze. "You're going to tell me something about Andrew. It's going to be sad or fucked up, and then I will have to feel bad when it has nothing to do with me." I realized what I said only after I said it. I didn't mean to sound so cruel. I was disgusted by my response. I was starting to sound like Josh.

"Fuck you, Timmy." Her voice cracked, her eyes watered, and she stormed toward her car.

"Wait, Allison. Just wait. I'm sorry." I beat her to her door and blocked her from opening it. The tears were already rolling down her face, and I wanted Josh to hit me again for being such a dick.

She hid her face from me, looked away, and pushed her hair in front of her face. She covered her mouth with her hand.

"What's going on, Allison?" I felt terrible for snapping at her.

She sniffled, took in deep breaths, and tried to calm down.

We were standing pretty close, and I knew I should have held her or tried to comfort her, but every time I moved my hand to touch her, she would flinch.

After a long, deep breath, she said, "Timmy, I'm sorry. I have to say this to you. You're the only person who ever listens to me."

"Okay. Allison, just tell me what's wrong," I replied.

"What did Andrew tell you." She finally showed me her face. Her tears were dry, but her cheeks were still red.

"I don't know what you mean."

"Andrew told you I cheated on him, didn't he?" She wiped her tears with her sleeves and then put her hands in the pockets of her sweater.

I nodded my head even though the question sounded rhetorical. Then she unveiled it to me. It was the final dart to my chest. I'd been on the edge for weeks, and it was like Allison had just shoved me into oblivion.

"What was the story he told you?" She was no longer crying, but I could still see the hurt in her eyes. I couldn't understand why.

"I don't know. He said that night you went to that party, that you didn't have just one beer, you got drunk and had sex with some guy." I was careful in my tone of voice. I didn't want her to think I was on his side because I wasn't. I wasn't on anybody's side anymore. I was on my own. I wasn't even completely my own anymore; I was bits and pieces of myself. I was picked apart by all the lies everyone told me—and all the lies I told myself.

"Did you believe him?" She crossed her arms and turned to me without actually looking at me.

"I honestly don't know what to believe anymore, Allison," I replied.

"Would you believe me if I told you the story?" She finally looked me in the eye.

I didn't like hurting Allison, but after everything that had happened, I lost the ability to sugarcoat how I felt. The friendly white lies around the edges of the ugly truth were scraped away until there was nothing but the brutal facts. "I don't know that I could," I stated bluntly.

"Timmy, I'm sorry," Allison said. "I'm sorry for ever getting you into this. That night, I was really mad at Andrew. He broke up with me, and I hated him for it. I wanted—"

"I don't understand what that has to do with me," I lied through my teeth. I lied because I did know my part in it. I hated how my mind worked and how it waited until the end of a situation to start piecing things together. I hated how it was always presented to me as a simple question with an obvious answer, but I decided that life was far too complex for the answers to be so easy. My mind rummaged through various networks and searched for an answer I could be satisfied with, but the simple answers— the real ones that are as clear as day—were never satisfying. They were agonizing.

"You were using me to get back at him?" I asked. My sympathy for her was beginning to fade.

She didn't speak, but the silence between us was answer enough.

How could I be so stupid and so naïve to think that a girl like Allison would be interested in someone like me? I surprised both myself and Allison by laughing. It was short and quiet. It wasn't that I wasn't hurt or angry; I was. I honestly don't know why I laughed. I should have been screaming, cursing, crying, or doing something other than laughing. After everything that had happened, I knew the joke was still on me.

"I think if I told you the truth, maybe you'd understand why I did it," she said.

Wow—she wasn't even denying it. I was right. I was a sucker. I got played, and it was funny. I laughed again and said, "I think the truth will be the death of me."

"That night wasn't supposed to happen, and I don't mean that night with you. I went to that party because my friend invited me. I wanted to have fun, you know. It was just me and a few people from the volleyball team. I didn't know they were going to be drinking, but all my friends were. I don't know … I wanted to have fun, you know. I drank and tried to have fun, but there was this guy.

"I barely remember his name, but he kept talking to me and drinking with me. He was actually kind of sweet. I never drank that much before, and everything was just happening so fast. It was so loud, and I couldn't find my friends. They left me alone with him." She paused to try to fight the tears.

My silly little brain started to connect the dots.

"I didn't know what was happening. The room was spinning, I drank way too much, and he kept touching me. I don't even remember how we got into that room together. He just kept feeling on me, and I tried to fight him off—I did—but I was just so wasted and weak. I couldn't even talk. I didn't even know what happened until after. I didn't know what we did—what he did—until the morning … when it hurt." Tears fell down her cheeks, but her speech wasn't broken. Allison fought to keep from sobbing, but she couldn't fight the tears.

I was stupefied. My anger toward her and all my self-pity vanished in the wake of an even darker truth. I may have been played, used, and lied to, but the grim look on Allison's face couldn't lie. Allison reeked of the truth, and it made my stomach hurt.

"Did you tell anyone?" I said.

"I told Andrew," Allison replied after taking a deep breath and wiping her tears away. "I told him like a week after it happened. For a while, he said he believed me. I cried on his shoulder when I told him. He kept saying that it was okay, that he wasn't mad, and that we'd stay together, and that it'd be all right. I believed him when he said it, and for a minute, I thought everything was going to just go back to normal—and I could forget it. Then, one night when we were alone, we were kissing and stuff, and he kept trying to do more. I told him no, that I didn't want to, I told him I wasn't ready.

"He got mad at me. He pushed me off of him and said, 'You fuck some guy at a party, but you can't do it with your boyfriend?' He called me names. He said I was a slut, a ho, and a bitch. Then he broke up with me. You know, I can almost forgive the guy who did that to me because I don't even think he knew he did anything wrong. The guy texted me later and said, 'I had a really fun time with you, you're really sweet, and I want to see you again.' I could almost forgive him—if I didn't hate him much—but I will never hate him as much as I hate Andrew for not believing me and for saying that he did when he didn't. I should have told you the truth, but I was just so mad at him." Allison clutched at her sleeves.

I still couldn't find the words to speak. I wanted to kick myself in the face for having even one selfish thought. I wanted to strangle Andrew, and with my newfound aggression, I felt like I could. I wanted to hurt whoever did that to Allison. *Who could do something like that to someone like her?* "You don't remember his name?" I asked.

"It started with an A or something. I think you know him; he was in the van with you when it crashed. I saw his picture on Facebook."

"Andre?" I asked—only to be pierced through the heart with the facts.

"No, the other one … Amale … or something like that."

"Amiel?" I whispered in disbelief.

"Yeah, him," Allison said.

At that point, I really couldn't speak. I could hardly breathe. My heart wasn't broken; it had been ripped out of my chest and vaporized. I knew why Allison tried to use winning my affection as revenge, I could forgive her for it, and I did.

"Can you do me a favor?" Allison walked past me toward the driver's seat of her car. "Can you not tell anyone? Please. I want to forget about it and just focus on school and volleyball. Please promise me you won't tell anyone. You have to promise me."

I nodded, feeling like the wind had been knocked out me.

Allison got in her car and started it, but before she left, she rolled down the window and said, "I'm so sorry, Timmy."

I looked her straight in the eye and replied, "Don't be. You shouldn't be."

24
CHAPTER

Thinking back, there were a lot of times when I should have just gone home. That could have been the answer to most of my problems. Doing nothing could have also been the answer, but according to my school grades, attendance, and my nagging mother, I had been doing nothing for the past few weeks. If I was as careless as Andre or Charlie, I wouldn't feel so bad about my problems. I thought the absence of emotions could solve my problems. In other words, if I didn't care, it wouldn't matter—but that also wasn't true.

That day, I finally decided to just go home instead of smoking more. I couldn't feel anything. I didn't even know that was possible. The world kept moving, but it was like my heart stopped. I couldn't cry over Abel or Allison. I couldn't be angry with Andrew or Josh. The only thing I could feel was confusion. It didn't make sense. Nothing made sense, and it was almost alarming how normal everything else looked when I finally hit my lowest point. The only thing that kept playing in my head was Amiel's name. The only person I thought about at that point was Amiel.

Allison couldn't have been lying. She had no reason to. I believed her, but I couldn't believe it was Amiel. It couldn't be Amiel. He was my friend, an actual friend. He was someone I could hang out with, who didn't ask me to deceive anyone, who didn't judge me for smoking weed, who cared enough to try to make me look good for a party, and who could remain levelheaded even when he was drunk. I wouldn't have been surprised if it were anyone else, and I wouldn't have been as hurt. Amiel was the only real friend I had. He couldn't have done something like that; he wasn't like that. He wasn't innocent, but he was good.

I started to see that innocence was merely an aspect of time. Innocence is simply something people grow out of. Innocence is for children, and

I was stuck in limbo. I was stuck between not wanting to be a little kid anymore and not wanting the suffering that comes with being an adult. *Part of growing up is the ability to recognize that no one is ever truly innocent.*

Despite all that, I still viewed Amiel as the best of them. The best of us. Josh was wrong; I didn't see myself any better than Charlie or Andre. I was just as damaged and misguided as they were, but Amiel was stronger than us. Wiser than us. There were never rumors about him. He never dealt with things he didn't have to deal with. He didn't treat people badly. He was always ready for a fight, and he knew how to be a friend. He knew how to empathize without becoming too emotionally attached, which was a quality I desperately needed. I think it was my idea of people that troubled me. I believed that if a person seemed decent, they were—and they'd always be decent—but people aren't constant. People as a species and as individuals are always changing for better or for worse. *This is my worse.*

When I arrived home, my mother was in the living room with her Bible and a notebook. I silently walked past her and entered my room, leaving the door open in case she needed to say something to me. Even though I knew she saw me going into my room, she kept quiet. My room was a mess, my clothes were all dirty, and I felt as bad as I looked. I decided to shower, found the cleanest towel and shirt, and walked over to my dresser to find pants.

The drawer was stuck, and after a few strong pulls, it still resisted me. I was frustrated, I was angry, and I was tired. Even something as simple as opening a drawer was difficult. How I felt about everything finally reached its climax. It was an emotion that couldn't be dealt with internally. In an explosion of mixed emotions, I shouted out of rage, ripped the drawer out of my dresser, and tossed it to the other side of my room.

I was breathing heavily, my hands were trembling, and I had an almost irresistible urge to hit something. All their faces, all their words, and all their lies ran through my head. I hated them all for making me a part of their drama. *God, I hate that word.* I was also mad at myself, knowing damn well that my own choices had led me down that path. I hated that I had almost no control over my own decisions. It was like I decided to do things I knew I shouldn't do, and I would never understand why. I made my own choices, but my choices made me. They turned me into this mess of a person. *So, who is in control?*

"Timmy?" My mother burst into my room. She looked concerned and confused.

I looked at her and saw the same pair of loving eyes I had seen my entire life. I saw a look that was so common to me. That's when it hit me the same way it always did. I wasted all this time running around, caring for the wrong people, and doing all the wrong things, but none of it was real. Nothing was real. My friends and the love they claimed to have for each other were not real. Josh was right. My life was no Hollywood movie. In the movies, the endings were always happy, love always found away, and the hero would overcome any obstacles. I was no hero, but I was the main character in my life. I was the hero of my own story, but I was being crushed by the weight of everyone else's stories. I was hurt by everyone else's lives and desires, which were more important than anyone else's.

My mother was the only exception. I realized it as I stared into her eyes and saw the same person I had always seen. She was the only person who valued my life, my wants, and my needs more than her own. She was the only person who would ever sacrifice her happiness for mine. Her eyes begged for an explanation, but I could never give her one. I could never tell her what her little boy had been doing. The innocent boy I once was would eventually be nothing more than a distant memory to me. That little boy would soon vanish from my being, but he would never disappear from my mother's eyes. My tragedies, pain, and suffering were hers too because I was her little boy.

"I'm sorry," I whispered as I felt my anger melting into tears. I didn't notice the first one drop. The first tear snuck its way through the wall I had built to prevent them.

"What's going on with you, Timmy?" She walked up to me and touched the side of my face, which was still aching from Josh's blow. I didn't flinch and hoped there wasn't a bruise that she would notice.

"I'm sorry," I said.

As my mother drew nearer, I felt like I couldn't bear the weight of the world anymore. I couldn't bear the weight of my problems. The worst part was that I didn't know what to do next. I had no protection, no escape from reality, and nothing to ease the pain from all the daggers I felt jabbing my heart.

"I'm sorry." I had nothing else to say. The tears were flowing like a river, but I did my best not to sob or crack completely. I thought about the night of the crash. I watched my mother cry over me, and I walked away. It wasn't fair that she wouldn't do the same thing to me. She wouldn't let me cry on my own, and she wouldn't let me bang on her door and scream for an explanation. My mother would never shut me out the way I had shut her out. She was completely open to me, and I let myself go.

"I'm sorry." I fell into her arms and soaked her shoulder with tears.

She held me tight in the same way she always had, the way she always would. She didn't ask more questions, probe me, or force me to tell her what was wrong. She held me as I cried like a five-year-old who had discovered that the world wasn't a pretty place. I had never imagined people could be so ugly or so selfish.

My mother was my shield that day. My mother was my shelter. She held me as I struggled to regain my composure. My mother had always been my first defense against a cruel and unforgiving reality. She had always fought against the wicked truth of a terrible world with faith alone. She didn't use drugs or alcohol, and I found myself wishing I could be as strong as she was. I took my wise, loving mother for granted.

That night, she put me to bed. She held me until the tears ran out, and then she tucked me in without another word. We prayed together in the same way we did when I was a little boy. That night, I was five years old again, finding comfort and reassurance from my mother alone. It was terrible to think I would lose her someday. She was my lifeline. How could I survive?

"Good night," she said before leaving my room.

I fell asleep more quickly than I had in the past few weeks. It wasn't the deep sleep from smoking weed, but it was peaceful. My tears had dried, and my nerves were calm. I slept comfortably and felt so much relief. The last few seconds before I fell asleep where bittersweet because I knew the world had not gone anywhere. In a few short hours, I would have to wake up in it. At that moment, the only thing I had to worry about was sleeping. I don't think I had ever slept better.

After school the next day, I sat at the steps of the rec center and waited for something to pique my interest. For a change, the day went by quickly. I didn't completely dread going to school when I woke up, even with the jarring pain in my jaw. My mom had already left for work. School was uneventful, as usual, which I couldn't have been happier about it. Luckily, my grades had improved. They were all near the low Ds, which wasn't very sexy, but anything was better than failing.

I entertained myself mainly with small talk with classmates I hardly talked to. Those half-hearted conversations were my way of keeping my mind off of things. It was all fine and good until school ended—a time when no conversation was more important than going home. I sat there and watched as everyone who passed me by unapologetically lived their own lives. What was to become of mine?

I sat there and pretended to wait for a ride because I didn't feel like making the trip home. It wasn't because I wasn't looking forward to going home and doing nothing; it wasn't even because I wanted to avoid my mom after what had happened the night before. It was simply because I did not have the energy to walk that much. I wished I had a car. I wished my mother would give me her van. As shallow as it sounds, I wished Andrew was still my friend for ten minutes so he could drive me home. I didn't want to think of him or see him, but I was not used to getting what I wanted.

Andrew had parked his car at the rec center. He noticed me sitting on the steps and said, "Hey, man." He looked happy to see me. He had a big grin on his face, and he was wearing his orange Polo shirt, a green jacket, and khakis.

"What's up?" I replied coldly.

"Haven't talked in a while, man. What's up?" He was beginning to look more nervous, probably sensing that I didn't want to talk to him.

"Same shit," I answered as I looked away.

"Are you mad at me?" he asked as he fidgeted with his jacket.

"I don't remember saying that," I answered.

"You just seem pretty angry with me. I mean, we haven't talked since I dropped you off that day."

"Well, I've been busy," I responded sarcastically.

"Doing what? Smoking weed?" Andrew shot back with sarcasm of his own.

"What else would I be doing?" I asked.

Andrew scoffed and started to pace in a circle in front of me. "You know, you're going to get yourself killed. After what I told you about my cousin, you do it anyway? I know you were at Allison's the day I picked you up."

"And if I was? She's my friend," I answered.

"I thought *I* was your friend."

"Likewise." I started to walk away.

"What the hell do you want from me?"

I spun around as fast as I could and said, "Not a damn thing, Andrew!"

We glared at each other for a while and tried to figure out how we got to that point. We used to be best friends, and now we couldn't stand each other for completely different reasons. There was nothing more to do; we had nothing more to say to each other.

Andrew walked over to his car, but before he opened the door, he looked at me and said, "She died in a car crash. My cousin Alice died in a car crash, and you almost made me go through that twice. I hope you know that."

"Wouldn't that have sucked for you if I died. You seemed so concerned."

Andrew chuckled, but his smile only lasted a few seconds. He quickly entered his car and drove away without another word.

"Hey." Jackie snuck up behind me and stopped my brain before it overanalyzed the situation.

"Where have you been?" I asked.

"Where have *I* been? Where have *you* been? And what's going on with you and Andrew?"

I always thought it was weird how it always sounded like she was shouting even when she wasn't. I hadn't realized how much I missed that annoying little blonde girl. I hadn't seen her since the day we all went to the movies, which felt like a lifetime ago. Jackie was still stunning, and her bright blue eyes cut through the air and the sunlight. She wore a sundress with pink flowers, and her curly hair seemed to have grown since the last time I saw her.

"Did your hair get longer?" I asked curiously.

"They're extensions. You didn't answer my question." Jackie reached up, grabbed my chin, and roughly turned my head to see the big purple bruise Josh had left on the side of my face. "Did you get in a fight?" She had a motherly look on her face. It looked like a weird combination of anger and concern. "What's going on with you? Andre isn't talking to me, and you, like, disappeared. And when I do see you, you're all beat up?"

"Nothing is going on." I tried to storm off.

Jackie grabbed my sleeve and said, "You're going to tell me." She let go of my arm, stood in front of me with her arms crossed, and waited for me to respond.

We waited in silence for a little while, and I paced around as I tried to figure out how I could explain things to her.

"I don't know, Jackie. It's just hard, okay? I feel like I'm losing my mind. I try to be a friend to people and help them out, but it's like they don't even care that they have problems. They live in their problems. Plus, you think you know people, right—or at least your friends? You think you have them figured out, but you don't—and they turn out to be such assholes. It's like everybody is lying to everybody, everybody is out to get everybody, and all the stories and all the things everybody knows for a fact turn out to be rumors.

"Not only that, but with all the lies, the rumors, and all the bullshit, it's almost depressing how much of it doesn't apply to me. Like, none of it was my business or my problems, but somehow, I'm in the thick of it. It's like I'm just there to witness how petty and low people can get. I don't understand. I try to be a nice guy, and I try to do the right thing, but for what? And for who? I could have died in a car wreck, and the only person who asked if I was okay waited a week only so she could tell me that she used me as a way of getting back at her ex. It's like I don't even count. I could've died, and it wouldn't have made any difference. I wish I meant something to someone—maybe then I wouldn't feel so … useless."

Jackie waited for a moment to respond.

I hardly knew I was ranting. I didn't even realize I was speaking. It seemed almost impossible before that moment to verbalize anything I felt. It came as a surprise to me that I could make sense of it all.

"I didn't know you were in a wreck," Jackie said in a hushed voice. "What happened?" She took a step closer to me.

"I'm sorry, Jackie," I whispered. "You don't want to know."

She nodded her head as if she understood, took a deep breath, and smiled warmly. "You know, my mom used to drink a lot. She stopped after she had me, but she was still broke. We moved around a lot until my mom had enough money to rent an apartment. It was really small and only had one bedroom, but it had a walk-in closet. When I was nine, I didn't know that closets even got that big. When I saw it, my mom just told me it was my room. I remember being so excited to finally have my room. I put posters on the walls, and I used the old mattress from my crib as a bed. It was cozy, but my mom eventually had to put her clothes in there. By then, I knew it was a closet, but I still liked to think of it as my room. It was like my own little world."

I had never met anyone who could hold a smile through an entire conversation the way Jackie could. It looked almost like a reflex or like her mouth just naturally curved that way. "What does that mean?" I asked.

"Well, maybe it just means you don't have to be miserable if you don't want to be." She quietly grabbed the tips of her hair. "And for the record, it would have made a difference to me if you died. You're not as alone as you think."

A white sedan parked a couple feet away from us and honked.

"I have to go," she said in the softest voice I'd ever heard, especially coming from Jackie.

I nodded my head, but before I could talk, she ambushed me with a hug. It didn't last very long, but I was quickly reminded of how much I loved receiving hugs from Jackie. After she pulled away, I stood there frozen. I did not know what to do with myself. I watched as Jackie left, and even though the windows were tinted, I could see her waving at me from inside the car. I looked around and noticed that the sidewalk was clear. I was the last one left.

I wanted to wait some more. I wanted to sit down and wait for things to get better and wait for people to make sense. *Maybe if I sit here and wait, I'll eventually morph into someone else.* I would have given anything for life to work that way. Hearing Jackie's story made me hate myself more than everyone else. Everyone had sob stories, terrible tales that turned them into terrible people. All of their stories had an antagonist, and they all had a villain. For Charlie, it was his father. For Gina, it was Josh. For Andrew, it was drugs. For Allison, it was Andrew. I was the exception. *I did this to myself—and my mom. Everyone else can justify their actions by saying the world was terrible to them, but I can't.* Jackie made me feel blessed, but she also made me feel small. She could go through life without breaking, but I couldn't.

As I made my way home, I forced myself not to think about anything. I kept reminding myself that everything was all right—that the world wasn't ending—but it sounded like an empty promise. Sophia didn't flood my thoughts the way she used to. As I walked home, I tried to only think about her, but it wasn't the same. I had to make an effort to think about her; seeing Sophia might have been the only thing that could rekindle whatever crush I had left for her. I was still taken by her, but it was different. It was like being in love with a character from a book or a movie. You don't like them; you like the idea of them. You replay whatever fantasy you can think of in your head, but it's always half-hearted because you know it will never come true. I was coming to terms with the reality that Sophia might never like me, and I didn't know if that was a good thing or not. I was starting to come to terms with reality in general. *My reality sucks.*

When I got home, it was empty. I collapsed on the couch and stared at the blank TV screen. If I turned it on, it would be no different than leaving it off. I'd be just as bored. My mother not being home allowed me to leave the apartment. I didn't want to go to Charlie's place—I couldn't stomach it—even though I knew I'd eventually end up there. I wasn't in my living for five minutes before I decided to leave. I didn't know where I was walking to; all I knew was that I didn't want to be home.

As I watched the cars speeding by, I figured out where I was heading. I walked far past Charlie's apartment complex, and I was much closer to Andre's house. If I knew one thing, it was that I didn't have to worry about Andre getting personal. With him, I knew I could just smoke and not think about anything important.

The sky darkened as I walked, and when I stepped out of my apartment, the sky was full of clouds. The clouds swallowed the sky and made everything look gray. I was speed-walking the entire time, anticipating the possibility of rain.

Andre was in his garage when I got there. He stood in front of a table with his purple cup in his hand and was using his other hand to throw ping-pong balls into red plastic cups that were half full of beer.

"Timmy!" Andre shouted. "Just in time."

Josh emerged from his house with a bottle of vodka. He nodded at me when he saw me, but I kept my attention on Andre. "Yo, I got some girls coming over, dawg. My mom won't be home the whole weekend; it just can't be like last time, man. Only good vibes here, man."

Andre set down his drink on the table and pulled out the blue dolphin bowl he had given me. "We're going to smoke up because, in a week, I won't be able to smoke any more."

"Why not?" I asked as he placed the bowl in my hand.

"I got court in a week, actually like in a few days. They're probably going to put me on probation, but I don't know. All I know is I'm probably not going be able to smoke weed anymore." He packed the bowl with weed, and I held it in my hand. He handed me a lighter.

I hit the bowl immediately, suddenly feeling like a virgin to the effects of marijuana. I coughed and choked and didn't consider that it had been a while since I smoked.

Andre grabbed the bowl from me while I was coughing and then hurried into his house, leaving Josh and me alone in the garage.

Josh did his best to avoid looking at me.

I tried to pretend that he wasn't even there, and I focused on how great the first hit made me feel. The first hit was like the last deep breath you take just before you go to sleep. It was like a signal indicating that all I had to worry about for the next few hours was relaxing.

Josh drank his liquor like it was water. He kept a straight face and took large sips from his bottle.

I took the seat far away from him and waited for Andre to return.

Josh kept drinking by himself, sitting in his chair, and mumbling to himself. "You know, all the coaches like to talk about, they like to talk about integrity, being decent, you know all that bullshit. When they talk about how we need to act right on and off the field, I always wondered if they told us that only because they didn't want us to embarrass the team— or if they care about decency." Josh used his hands a lot when he talked. It looked like he was trying to paint a picture in the air.

"I didn't know that me sitting this far away from you looked like an invitation for conversation," I answered casually.

"Ha!" Josh stood up and stumbled toward me. "You're a funny guy, Timmy. You're smart too. So, answer me this—why do you think they care about what kind of people we are?"

"I have no clue, and I honestly don't care, Josh." I stood up and walked toward Andre's house.

"They don't," Josh said as he stepped in front of me.

"As talented as people say you are, I don't understand how you can still manage to be a piece of shit."

"You think people would even know me if I couldn't play?" Josh asked calmly.

"Probably not."

"I'd be just like you, Timmy. All alone in this great big world. I wouldn't get a second thought. The second I fuck up, all these friends would vanish. I hate that my worth is measured by how hard I can hit somebody. I don't think I'm better than anyone, Timmy. I actually might be worse, but we get what we deserve, Timmy. No matter how shitty life can be, we always only get what we deserve."

"Allison deserved better," I mumbled to myself a little too loudly.

"Who's Allison?" Josh asked.

"Can I ask you something now, Josh? Since you're so smart, what happens when the best person you know does the ugliest thing possible? How do you live with that? How can you restore your faith in people?"

"That's a tricky question, my friend. People will always fuck up in the worst ways—good, bad, doesn't matter. You know, you don't get to choose the mistakes your friends make."

"So, what do you get to choose?"

"How you react to them."

Andre emerged from his house with more red plastic cups and a six-pack of beer. He set them down on the floor next to the table, opened a beer, and started chugging it.

Josh was already drunk and collapsed in his seat.

I gravitated toward Andre and started to drink and smoke whatever he handed to me.

By the time people started arriving at Andre's house, I was already drunk.

Andre kept the beer coming, and even Josh shared some of the liquor he kept clutched in his arm like a football. Luckily for me, we started to smoke before the alcohol started to make me feel sick. I saw the same kind of faces as I saw the night of the crash, but I couldn't tell if they were there or not. I didn't know any of them. I couldn't remember seeing them before, but for some reason, they all looked so familiar.

After a while, I started to care less and less about the people I was partying with. They were all blank faces in my blurred vision. The rest of the night was just noise and movement. It was fun, and it was nauseating. I couldn't tell the difference between the two anymore. For the rest of the night, I was nothing more than a witness to my terrible deeds. Those deeds would be completely erased from my memory by the morning. My brain had lost its ability to record anything important—or perhaps none of it was important. The last thing I remembered was watching Josh leave. He was driving a dark green Kia Rio. I didn't even think about how drunk he was; the only thing I noticed was his car.

After Josh left, all I could remember was bumping into people. Everyone was shouting, constantly reminding one another how drunk they were. I think I was shouting too. I think I saw Amiel. I think I kissed a girl. I couldn't remember any of it. The best part was that I forgot what I went there to forget. I smoked away all my troubles, drank away all my pain, and that was when I woke up in a garage with a bunch of sleeping nobodies. I was one of them.

I woke up wondering if I could stoop any lower. I wondered if I already had. I was still too high to be hungover and way too hungover to feel high. *Disorientated, nauseous,* and *sick* were all words that had become redundant. There was smoke still in the air, my clothes were a mess, and nothing was new. The only bright side I could think of was the weed in the center of the garage. I could steal it and wake up in a few hours feeling the same way. I'd just be waking up on a different floor.

I didn't know what the white lines by the bathroom sink were. Andre was sleeping in his tub. The obvious guess raised too many questions, and if I had learned anything in the past few weeks, it was how dangerous curiosity could be. I couldn't help but wonder, but I let it remain a mystery. It was better that way. Maybe that's why the Riley brothers looked so happy all the time; they had mastered the art of not knowing.

I walked to Charlie's place, and woke up their bum asses. The three of us were overwhelmed by the things we couldn't control and ashamed that we couldn't control the things we used to control. Truth be told, sitting there and smoking with Charlie and Josh felt right. I knew skipping school was wrong and doing drugs was stupid, but I couldn't help but cherish that moment. We were all just a bunch of kids given the task of figuring our lives out. In the meantime, we could just relax, play video games, listen to rap music, and be our natural selves. With all the smoke in the air, there were no smokescreens.

Josh tapped me on the shoulder and handed me the blunt.

I accepted it and smoked, and they reminisced about their first time smoking. Charlie started at eleven, Josh started at thirteen, and I was the lucky number: fifteen.

"Aye, yo, Timmy whatever happened to Amiel, man?" Charlie asked with his eyes glued to the screen.

"Yeah, I haven't seen him in a minute," Josh added.

I smiled at them and said, "I don't remember."

Printed in the United States
By Bookmasters